JAIME QUESTELL

Entangled Publishing, LLC
2614 South Timberline Road
Suite 109
Fort Collins, CO 80525

Entangled Teen is an imprint of Entangled Publishing, LLC.

Visit our website at www.entangledpublishing.com.

Edited by Stacy Abrams
Cover design by Anna Croswell
Interior design by Toni Kerr

ISBN 978-1-63375-900-8
Ebook ISBN 978-1-63375-901-5

Manufactured in the United States of America

First Edition February 2018

10 9 8 7 6 5 4 3 2 1

entangled teen
an imprint of Entangled Publishing LLC

For Dane, who is my constant.

CHAPTER ONE

Emma

Apologies to the people who love it here, but Claremore, Oklahoma, might actually be a circle of hell. Not one of the horrible ones, for the people who do unspeakable things to cats, but definitely one of the places where people who cheat on their taxes go to live out their monotonous afterlives. The thing that sucks is Claremore is exactly where my mom has ditched my brothers and me for a year, leaving us to live with our dad while she's off in Guatemala, investigating this teeny tiny isolated village for a grant.

The only good thing about our abandonment is that Mom dropped us off just as Le Grand's Carnival Fantastic was ending its engagement on the outskirts of the city.

"Have you ever experienced the life-altering joygasm of the deep-fried Snickers bar?" Juliet bounds along beside me, same as she did when we were younger, her golden curls springing in time to her steps as we cross the dusty parking lot toward the carnival entrance.

It's a struggle to keep up, her long legs and general giddiness propelling her forward far better than any jet fuel could. The carnival sits in the middle of a field next to an abandoned mall. Graffiti cartoon animals run laps around the dilapidated building. Someone had written EAT ME in four-foot-tall letters near one of the entrances, only to have someone add an *M* at the beginning later. In another color, someone else had scrawled MEAT IS MURDER, to which another artiste contributed, AND IT'S DELICIOUS U DIRTY HIPPY. Charming.

"Jules, I can say with some certainty that never have I ever experienced a candy-induced joygasm."

"Then I can say with some certainty that *you* aren't living your best life."

Shame that once Le Grande's Carnival Fantastic blows town, there will pretty much be absolutely zero to do here that doesn't involve late-night visits to Walmart or football.

We follow the gathering crowds toward the ticket booth, funneling into the entrance beneath pennants made of sun-bleached calico, the patterns mere ghosts of their old selves. We're not even through the ticket gate and already I can smell sawdust and burned sugar. Shrieks of terror and joy stutter through the wind, mixing with the excited chatter of those waiting in line. Hand-painted boards taller than I am lead up to the ticket booth, each one featuring a different performer. A knife thrower done in stark black, white, and orange. Two golden girls standing atop a spotted horse, no saddle or reins to hold them. A boy and girl, near mirror reflections of the other, hovering over a crystal ball, dark shadows creeping in around them. The biggest belongs to a trio of tumblers who tangle their limbs together until they're one muscled mass of human impossibility. The sign is a boast, a dare, a promise—*come and see these men and be amazed*.

And I want to be amazed.

"Look!" I grab Jules by the wrist and tug her out of line to get a better look at the murals. I haven't painted since the move, and, more than that, nothing here has made me *want* to paint. "These are *fantastic*."

"They're all right, I guess," Jules says, taking her fingers from mine, her eyes already tracking toward the carnival entrance. "Do you think they'll have those giant turkey legs? I had one at the state fair and thought I was going to die. On. The. Spot."

Somewhere in the middle of her litany of praising poultry, I'm distracted by a flash of glitter and the soft clopping of hooves on concrete. A girl—slim and slight and decked out in what looks like a sequined bathing suit and fluffy bustle—pulls with all her might on the reins of the obstinate palomino before her. The thing is so huge and she is so tiny, it's like watching Tinkerbell trying to tow the *Jolly Roger*.

She lets out a holler somewhere between a yelp and a grunt of unending frustration. "Benjamin!"

A blond boy—Benjamin, I assume—sets the battered red tool kit he had been carrying down on the ground and wipes his palms on his jeans. His glasses slip down his nose when he straightens, the lights of the carnival reflecting across the lenses. He gently takes the reins from the girl, and it's impossible to ignore the way the tendons in his arms flex as he takes the giant horse under his control. He slowly strokes the animal's cheeks and I wonder if the words he says to the horse are as soft. But just then the horse's ears prick forward, and its feet dance in the dust.

"Hey, Whiskey," says an olive-skinned boy, approaching from the row of tents nearby. "You need help?" As he looks at Benjamin, his mouth twists into a mockery of a smile. "Looks like the gaucho can't handle a horse."

"*Benjamin* was handling this horse just fine until you showed up," the girl says with a snarl. I half expect to see fangs glinting in the fading light. As if to prove her point, the horse tries to rear, but Benjamin's grip is firm, and the horse doesn't break free. "Why don't you go find some old lady to charm out of her pension?"

The boy scowls, but as the horse snorts and tries to rear up once more, he walks away. As he leaves, he knocks into Benjamin's shoulder, muttering that word again, the one reeking of disdain even though it seems harmless enough to me. "Gaucho."

Benjamin doesn't respond, his fist still firmly wrapped around the horse's reins, but the girl is slowly turning a violent shade of pink. But before she can say a word, King Jerkwad turns, gifting a million-watt smile to the line of soon-to-be patrons as he approaches. He runs the last few feet, and as he's about to crash into a family with two chubby-cheeked toddlers, he launches into a backflip and lands kneeling before Jules and me. His chest puffs out and his arms spread wide. "The Fabulous Moretti Brothers are here to astound you! Come and find us inside!"

What an ass.

Juliet cocks her hip and rolls her lip between her teeth. Some predators roar to intimidate their prey. Juliet does this. "So, uh, if we were to want to find you later…"

I glance back toward Benjamin and Whiskey, stifling a laugh when I see the glare the tiny redhead is shooting at the tumbler. Benjamin is still, somber. He catches me looking and gives me the tiniest shake of his head. A warning.

I don't question it. This Moretti brother might be fabulous, but I think we'll pass. I hook my arm around Juliet's and tug, leading her in the general direction of the ticket booth.

"Ugh, Emmaline!" Juliet says, her feet finally getting with the program. "That boy had serious make-out potential."

"Correction, that was a walking, talking douchebag wrapped up in a pretty package, and friends don't let friends make out with douchebags."

Juliet stretches to graze the tip of the bunting swaying above us with her fingers. "It's not like I wanted to bring him home to my dads and have a nondenominational commitment ceremony, I just wanted to kiss his brains out."

God, this girl. Laughter bubbles out of my chest, and it feels good, *I* feel good for the first time in weeks. I nudge Juliet toward the ticket booth.

When we reach the front of the line, a woman with coppery red hair in a messy topknot sells us our tickets. "Be sure to check out the equestrian stunt show," she says, her smile broad and bright. "The riders are my daughters."

We take our tickets and almost immediately give them up again, to an older man who tips his tattered newsboy as we enter the carnival. The moment we cross the perimeter, we're awash in golden light and popcorn-scented air. Shrieks of delight fill the night, mingling with Juliet's mile-a-minute chatter about where she might find a deep-fried *anything.*

Red flashes before me, and it takes my eyes a second to realize it's a rose. A boy holds the flower so close its petals tickle my chin. His face is painted white, with rosy circles dotting his pale cheeks and dark powder shaping his eyebrows into wry arches. His glossy black hair has been styled into a plastic-y, slick wave that makes me think of a twenties soda jerk. When he grins, his teeth are all perfect and white. "Pretty flower for a pretty lady."

A flush colors my cheeks. "Oh! I couldn't." The rose is lush and perfect, so big it looks artificial, but there's no way to fake the heavenly scent coming off it.

But the boy's grin widens, and then he's pressing the stem into my hand. "I insist. You can pay me back by bringing your family to visit my booth later."

"Oh," I say, "it's just us."

The boy's grin turns wolfish. "Us?"

I whirl, my brain finally realizing that if Juliet *had* been behind me, there's no way she'd have let the boy's words from before go without comment. The crowd swirls around me—families and some people I vaguely recognize from school—but no Jules. "My friend is here… somewhere."

The boy's bright white teeth flash in the rapidly diminishing light. "Of course she is. When you find her"— he presses something small and cold into my palm— "come and see me."

I glance at my hand. It's just a quarter, shiny enough to reflect the dancing lights from a nearby booth off its surface. Why on earth would he give me a quarter? I shove the coin into my jeans pocket and am about to ask him that very question, but he's already gone.

CHAPTER TWO

Benjamin

The roll of cash in my pocket thumps against my leg as I jog across the yard. I counted it three times to be sure, and if I'm right, then Marcel and I finally have enough money to leave this carnival for good.

The evening is crisp and cool and the kind of bleak that makes the world seem like everything is washed over with gray. But the backyard crackles with life. Trailers creak as other roustabouts—those like me who work in the background, making it easier for the performers to seamlessly weave their magic—wearily climb into them, eager to catch a quick meal and a little rest before going back out to help clean up the grounds after the patrons are gone. Happy shouts of greeting echo up and down the rows of trailers as the performers make their way toward the grounds, ready for the first shows of the night, and the yips and grunts of Mrs. Potter's dogs make a strange layer of sound hanging in the air.

It's home for all of them, but not the kind of home I

ever wanted for myself.

Even though we've only been here two weeks, the pathways on the grounds have been made flat by dozens and dozens of feet. As I wind my way through the yard, I tick a few items off my to-do list—checking the wiring on the neon ice cream sign affixed to one of the outermost booths, fixing the awning on Lars's trailer. I'm about to call it quits when I see Lorenzo, the youngest Moretti tumbler, horsing around a trash can fire with a new carnival recruit whose name is Mikey, I think. If I run into the last Moretti brother, Antonio, after this, then I'll have concrete proof that bad things come in threes.

"Do you trust me or not?" Lorenzo asks. The new guy's cheeks are flushed pink from the fire, and the bright flames flicker in his wide, wet eyes as he holds one hand over the trash can. "Come on. We've all done it. It's like a rite of passage!"

Damn it.

I dart toward them and yank the new guy's hand back. "What the hell do you think you're doing?" The heat from the fire wafts over me, making my skin feel as though it's being stretched too tight.

"But the charm would have protected me." The new guy points a wavering finger toward Lorenzo. "He said so."

Anger threatens to sharpen the edges of all my words, so when I speak, I try my damnedest to be calm. "That is *not* how it works. The charm keeps you safe as you work, makes sure you don't trip when you perform, and keeps us healthy, keeps us young. It does *not* miraculously keep your skin from burning to a crisp when you purposefully *shove your hand into a fire.*"

"Maybe," Lorenzo says, the word drawn out all long

and lazy, "the charm worked by having you come along." The grin he gives me makes it perfectly clear he doesn't believe a word he's saying.

My teeth grind. Did this really just happen? Did I just stop a guy from putting his *hand* into a fire? I have no idea why Leslie welcomed some stupid kid naive enough to be fooled into almost burning off his own hand into the fold, but she must have seen *something* special in him. "That isn't how it works. Don't purposefully try to hurt yourself." The trash can lid lays on the ground at our feet, and I slam it down, smothering the flames. "And *don't* listen to anyone with the last name Moretti. Now go."

The new guy shoots a nervous glance at both of us but walks away quickly. Smartest decision he's made all day. "Leave the new people alone," I say.

"What do you care? You're not really one of us."

Anger flares, hot and bright in my gut. *Just* because I haven't been with the carnival all my life and *just* because my family doesn't have a mile-long list of carnivals or circuses we've worked for, *I* don't belong. "Been here a lot longer than you have."

Lorenzo smiles, and he has to know he's hit a nerve. "Still doesn't mean you belong here. You or your bitch of a mother."

My fingers twitch into fists, but before I do anything stupid, he's gone. As he makes his way down the aisle, chatting easily with passersby, the anger inside me continues to simmer. It's not my fault the Morettis couldn't get their father a job with the carnival because my mom already holds the master carpenter position. And it's not my fault they're arrogant pricks who think the world should be handed to them on a platter because they bring in tons of paying customers. But soon, *very* soon, I won't have to put up with shit like this.

A shriek of laughter pierces through my anger. I peer between two trailers and catch a glimpse of a pair of girls—a blonde doubled over in laughter and her dark-haired friend, who looks on with some mix of pride at having made someone else laugh so hard and disbelief that anyone actually *could* laugh that hard. As she tugs on the other girl's arm, trying to get her to move along, I realize this is the girl I'd seen earlier, the one whose blush lit up her pale skin like sunlight through a flower petal. The blond girl straightens, and as she does, she gives her friend a swift smack on the ass, which sets the both of them giggling. The anger I'd held in my chest doesn't completely dissolve, but it does loosen its hold as I watch the girls walk away.

Well. I guess the carnival isn't all bad.

Gin Connelly perches delicately on a crate next to the rusting Gran Torino Marcel and I bought, already in the glittering costume she'll wear for her shows this evening. Beside her is an origami configuration of jutting elbows and long torso as my best friend, Marcel, strains to reach a hidden part of the engine block of our piece-of-junk clunker.

I kick at a raggedy length of rubber on the ground, and as it tumbles to a stop at her bare feet, Gin snaps to attention. "Oh hell," she says, grabbing Marcel's wrist to look at his watch. At her touch, he startles, nearly knocking his head into the propped-open hood of the car. "I'm late for my first show. I'll get up with you early in the morning to practice our new routine, okay?"

She's up and off in a flurry of sparkles, jogging down

the pathway between trailers, the crowd parting to let her through. Marcel absently rubs at the smears of grease marring his dark skin with an equally greasy rag, oblivious to the fact that all he's doing is spreading the gunk around.

"Hey, man," he says, only managing to draw his gaze to me once she's out of sight. He's got it so bad for Gin that I can't even be mad at him for ignoring me till now. "Hop in and turn her on. Let's see if I got rid of that squealing sound."

The ever-present smell of gasoline hits me as I slide into the driver's seat. At first, starting the car was a gentle and precise dance of pumping the gas, turning the key, listening, knowing when to back off and when to push harder to get the damned thing to turn over without flooding, but now all it takes is a simple turn of my wrist.

Our parents had questioned the need to buy the thing in the first place. What traveling did we do, outside of the carnival? The car was a gas-guzzler, couldn't we see that? But neither Marcel's parents nor my mother thought to ask the real reason behind our purchase—*are you planning to leave us?*

The car roars to life, the rumbling of the engine vibrating the chassis so much it's like I'm sitting inside the belly of a bellowing dragon. The thick, cloying scent of gasoline gathers in my throat, and I throw the car door open so I don't wind up vomiting all over the restored leather. But happily, the high-pitched whine that used to accompany the car's start-up is gone.

Marcel slams the hood down and takes a bow—the same theatrical bend of the waist and flourish of the arm that punctuates the end of every knife-throwing show. He empties his pockets of tools, tossing them into the toolbox on the ground with his usual precision. "And that," he says, a socket wrench crashing into the box, "is how"—his pocket flashlight lands with another clatter—"shit gets done."

While Marcel checks out the RPMs, I walk around the car to see what I need to work on next. The ancient weather stripping around the passenger window crumbles beneath my fingertips; I'll need to see about replacing it when I go into town. And I'll need to finish patching up the gaping wound of rust over the left rear tire.

I run my fingers along the body filler covering the spots where rust had eaten through the metal, searching for any imperfections in my patchwork. I have a scrap of sandpaper in my pocket, and as I reach in, my fingers bump against the other reason why I'd stopped by this evening.

"Hey." I toss a roll of cash Marcel's way. "Half of this month's wages." I kneel and begin to buff away the small ridge that had caught under my fingertips, hopefully hiding the giddy tremble in my fingers. "That should do it, right? If I didn't screw up my math, that gives us plenty to live off of for three months."

Marcel riffles the corners of the bills with his thumb, staring at them like he's trying to memorize the serial numbers, before tucking the roll of cash alongside its brothers in a hidden compartment of his toolbox. Rows and rows of money, most of our wages and tips from the last several months, line the tray. I've never seen that much cash before. It's our future. Our ticket out. And the sight of it makes me feel lighter than I have in months.

"So when do you want to leave?" I glance at Marcel over my glasses, sure I'm going to see a roil of excitement playing over his features, but he's busying himself with tightening the clamps on some tubing coming off the engine. And that's when I know that after months of meticulous planning, Marcel and I are no longer on the same page.

Putting the only thing I have that resembles a home in my rearview mirror will be hard, but we both have our GEDs, a good store of cash, and, though the car isn't much to look at, she'll get us where we need to go. We won't have the charm's protection, but I don't want to depend on it forever.

I stop sanding and rock back on my heels. "What's up, man?"

Marcel stands, shaking out his long arms and cracking his knuckles. "I need more time." A nervous sort of energy that's not like him at all limns his edges, makes him jumpy. Like he expects me to lash out in anger.

Instead, I drop to the ground with a little flurry of dirt and lean against the car. "It's Gin, isn't it?"

Marcel plops down beside me, yanks the scrap of sandpaper from my hands, and begins to shred it into tiny pieces. "I gotta try, right? I mean, if we ditch this place and I never tried to see if there's something between us, I'd always wonder. And that's no way to live. Or so Mom's self-help books tell me."

Marcel has never understood why I don't want to be dependent on the carnival. Maybe it's because his family has been circus performers for generations, or maybe it's because what I want seems contradictory. And I *get* that. But to me, there's no contradiction at all. I want to choose a place and for once in my life put down roots. Let them sprawl and grow until I know where I belong.

The longer I stay with the carnival, the more the charm feels less like an oddity and more like a necessity. Less like a safety net and more like a net to pull me along, forever in the wake of something bigger than myself.

"Okay," I say, plotting my words out carefully. "My birthday is in three months. That's plenty of time for you to get off your ass and ask her out." Marcel opens his mouth as though to argue, but I cut him off before he can get started. "It's *plenty of time.* We'll stick a pin in this until then, but…we *will* make a decision about leaving on my birthday and we *will* stick to it. Deal?"

I hold out my hand, and I need him to take it. Even though we move around the country every few weeks, even though there are dozens upon dozens of people who would love to take my place, I'm done. Each day that has the potential to run into a Moretti is one too many. And Marcel might have Gin, and that's great, but there's no one here for me. Briefly my thoughts flicker to the dark-haired girl, to the wry quirk of her lips as her friend laughed her head off, to the pretty flush in her cheeks as the blond girl gave her a friendly smack. But by the end of the night, she'll be gone, too, and in a week, so many other faces will have passed before me that I won't even be able to remember hers.

Slowly, with none of the surety that typically flows through his movements during one of his shows, Marcel reaches out and takes my hand. "Deal," he says. His grip is loose, and even though we've come to an agreement, it doesn't seem like we have, and I feel no closer to leaving this place than I did yesterday.

CHAPTER THREE

Emma

Jules can't sing for shit. Unsurprisingly, it hasn't stopped her from scream-singing her lungs out for God, Jesus, and the rest of Oklahoma to hear.

"Jules!" I have to yell to be heard over screaming children and the rush of the nearby roller coaster running on decades-old tracks. I tighten my coat, a small measure in a losing battle against the cold. "Leave the guy alone, he's just doing his job."

After I'd found Jules cradling a bacon-wrapped turkey leg like it was the world's most precious cargo, we'd made our way through the carnival, working in ever-tightening spirals until we wound up here. The carnival has set up a booth to look like one of those old automated fortune-tellers. The bottom half is ornately carved wood painted a red so fiery it almost glows, and the panels of glass making up the top half are covered in swirling gold paint proclaiming *FUTURES SEEN! FORTUNES TOLD!* Small bulbous lights line the ceiling of the booth, filling it with a warm light, but it doesn't hide the fact that the paint is chipping and the glass is covered in sticky, child-size fingerprints.

Inside, the poor schmuck in question stands at attention, arms held out in awkward angles like he's going to start doing the robot at any minute. A bowler hat tilts a rakish angle over his brow, and when I take a closer look I see it's him—the boy from earlier, the one who gave me the rose.

Jules insisted we find the booth after Tracy from our politics class told us there was a contest to see who could get the guy to break character. But five minutes and one butchered song later, the only things Jules has to show for her efforts are cheeks pinked from exertion and some angry glares from passersby.

"Em," she pleads, giving my nickname more syllables than it deserves, "I'm just having fun."

The wind, heavy with the sugary scent of kettle corn and some kind of meat most likely served on a stick, ruffles my short black hair until I'm sure it's a mess. "Right," I say, "at the expense of his poor ears. At *least* give him a quarter so we didn't completely waste his time."

The Boy in the Box's lips twitch up, but, unable to see his eyes from beneath the brim of his hat, the effect is more sinister than he probably intends.

"*Fine,*" she says, again displaying her unrivaled talent at lengthening one-syllable words. She digs around her gigantic bag, and I don't know which is more miraculous— the fact that she has a quarter or that she managed to find it in there. It's a Broadway production as she puts the coin into the slot and throws her arms to the night sky. "Soothsayer! What does my future hold?"

The Boy in the Box springs to life as the quarter rolls

down a chute and into an almost empty bowl beside him. A long finger taps the corner of his rouged mouth as though contemplating, while his other hand twitches over the small cards lining the shelf in front of him.

Finally, he pulls a card and holds it up to his temple. His dark hazel eyes close, he gives a crisp nod, and then drops it into the tray that we can access on our side of the booth. Jules squeals as she pushes her hand past the brass flap to retrieve the card. As she reads, her eyebrows furrow. She scans her fortune again. All I can see is the back of the card, printed with the delicate red swirls and loops framing a stamp of a marionette boy. At this angle, it's impossible to tell if the puppet is dancing or falling, but the expression is gruesome, which is impressive given how few lines make up his little face.

"What's wrong?" I ask.

Jules slaps the offending fortune against the booth. "This"—her finger taps the card, her breath condensing in an angry puff on the glass—"is *bullshit*." She rips it in two and the scraps flutter to the ground. The pieces read *Pretty feathers do not a songbird make* and I have to cover up my snort of laughter with a cough. Jules glares at me. "Come on, Emma, let's get out of here."

I swear the boy behind the glass is grinning, but his face is turned down and all I can see are his rounded cheekbones.

Jules whirls on her heel, her gaze landing on some boys we know from school playing a game at a nearby booth, the kind where you have to fill up a balloon with a water gun to win a prize.

"Come with," she says. "Let's see if we can get you a date with Chris."

"I don't *want* a date with Chris," I say. "He smells like onions and he thinks Shanghai is a country, not a city."

"Yeah, sorry, he's kind of a doofus," she says, gnawing at her lip. "Do you know he once tried to convince me that sneezing with your eyes open will make them blast out of your skull? But what about Jeremy? Or Sam? I…I want you to like it here."

I nod and gather a deep breath, rallying. I know this is her way of trying to help me fit in, to transfer me into the carefully tended group of friends she's spent her life cultivating. And part of me wants it, but part of me wishes it wasn't even necessary. "I get it, I do. This is all weird and new and it's a lot, you know? Just…give me five minutes, okay? Let me get my fortune, and I'll catch up."

The smile Juliet gives me is small but firm. The desire to slot me right back into her life is practically rolling over her head like the ticker constantly running at the bottom of a twenty-four-hour news station screen. But she reaches out to squeeze my arm, then turns to face the cluster of her friends nearby. Soon enough, she's in the middle of them, and strains of their laughter drift my way.

The Boy in the Box has his hands folded neatly in front of him and is staring right at me, a quirky smile on his face. All the tension welling up inside after that weird conversation with Juliet melts away at the sight of him, and my belly gives a twist.

He springs to life, his fingers jerking and flexing over the cards. He waffles over two fortunes for the longest time before settling on the one in the bottom right corner. His fingertips graze the paper and then he freezes. I wait, staring at his long, white fingers, willing him to pick up the card. Then I look at him.

The smirk is back, and when my eyes meet his, his gaze slips down to the bowl of coins.

Oh!

I check my bag, searching for change. Nothing. Who the hell even carries around coins anymore? My fingers falter over a lump in my pocket—the coin this boy gave me earlier. I slip it into the machine and like magic my Boy in the Box starts moving again, like he'd never stopped in the first place. He picks up the tiny white card, touches it to his lips instead of his temple, and drops it into the tray.

My fortune is six words, surrounded by hand drawn, curling hearts. Hearts that were not on Jules's card. Did he draw them when I was looking for that quarter? A faint line of red that mimics the shape of a kiss runs over the words. *You will soon take a fall.*

My gaze snaps up, but the curtains that run the perimeter of the booth have been drawn. A knot of disappointment sits heavily in my stomach, followed immediately by a wave of embarrassment. *Stupid, Emma, you're being stupid. You weren't the first girl to get tricked out of a quarter tonight and you won't be the last.*

I turn away, only to bump into someone. A hand grips onto my arm to keep me from slipping.

The Boy in the Box stands in front of me. The black bowler hat covering his slicked-back hair makes him seem taller, and though a dark jacket covers his old-fashioned shirt and suspenders, below the waist he has on a very modern pair of jeans and scuffed black boots.

"I'm sorry! I'm sorry!"

"No, I'm sorry," he says. His voice is warm and sweet, like the caramels they're selling two booths over. "I was

standing too close, and I shouldn't have been. Anyway...
I'm due for a break," he says. "Entertain me?"

I am close enough to see the line where his white face
paint meets his true skin color, not that there's much of a
difference between the two. The red circles on his cheeks
are garish under the flashing carnival lights, but his green-
gold eyes seem brighter, more alive.

And even though every warning about strangers my
parents ever gave me blares through my head, there's
something about the look he's giving me—the pure,
focused attention to the me in the here and now, not the
me that could be—that makes it impossible to say no.

He shoves his hands into his pockets and starts to
walk. The crowds are thinning, and vaguely I wonder
what time it is and when Jules is supposed to be home
and then whether or not *my* dad would notice what time
I came home. I glance up at him and find that he's already
looking at me.

"Want to talk about that fight with your friend?" he
asks, gently nudging my arm with his elbow.

I shrug, hoping that he chalks up my pink cheeks to
the cold. "It wasn't a fight. I just moved back to town and
I'm having a hard time fitting back in. My friend has a life
that doesn't include me and it's been...weird."

"You've been gone awhile, how could it *not* be weird?"
He peers down at me, and I feel my stomach squirm in
a weird, happy sort of way. He *gets* it, really understands.

I want nothing more than for him to take my hand,
but his are firmly tucked away in his pockets. I move
closer, hoping that he'll get the hint. He smells like pine
and dust and wool, probably from being cooped up in
that box all day.

"You don't have a problem with heights, do you?" I ask. I nod toward the Ferris wheel that looms before us. I want more time with him, and all I can think of is sitting next to him in one of those little cars.

The boy follows my gaze to the ride and smiles at me, soft and inviting. "That would be perfect."

Without warning he veers toward a tent. One of the flaps at the corner isn't secured very well, and he reaches in. His hands are pale and elegant, and almost as white as the paint on his face. After a moment of fishing, he triumphantly withdraws a bottle of wine.

I vow to not let him know that I've only ever had beer that one time at my friend Andrew's birthday party. Or that I hated it. Or that I threw up. Hell, or maybe I will. I'm practically buzzing just from having someone listen, *actually listen*, to me like he has.

We wend our way through the thinning crowd toward the ride. A broad and burly man operates the Ferris wheel. He's covered in ginger curls, from the unruly mop on his head to the tiny springs of hair that poke over the V-neck of his black-and-white striped sweater. It matches his ruddy skin, making him look like a huge angry carrot. A giant mustache covers most of his mouth and it shifts, though I don't know if it's a smile or a frown.

"If it isn't my favorite boy wonder," he says. His voice is gruff and curt.

"Hello, Lars," the boy says. Hearing him say someone else's name makes me realize that I don't know his. "May we go up?"

Lars glances at the wheel. There's no one on the ride, and, as we're nearing closing time, it seems unlikely that there will be. Lars sighs as he opens the tiny door to the car and gestures for me to get in. My Boy in the Box follows, and shortly after that, we're off. The wheel swoops upward, leaving my stomach back on the ground, and when I glance at the boy to see him looking down at me, I realize the funny feeling in my belly won't be going away anytime soon.

Lars lets us spin around twice before my companion yells over the side. "Mind letting us enjoy the view for a while?"

The only answer we get is the ride stopping at its apex, with the lights twinkling below us and the moon shining above. The wind is cleaner up here, free from the scents of the carnival, and stronger. The car rocks violently in a sudden gust, and I grip the sides. My self-preservation instincts kick in, and I realize that I am up here, alone, with a boy I don't know.

"Oh, don't worry," he says, sensing my distress. He leans over the side, the car jerking as he shifts his weight over, and yells, "Lars! Tell the lady that your intentions are honorable, and you'll let us down the moment she asks."

Lars's big, booming voice is half swallowed by the night. "It's not my intentions you need to worry about, missy."

A nervous giggle escapes me, partly from hearing Lars call me "missy" and partly from the look the boy in the car is giving me, all smoldering eyes from beneath thick lashes. He pulls the bottle of wine from his coat, and with a quick flick of his wrist, produces a pocket corkscrew from out of nowhere, releasing the cork with a satisfying *pop*.

He wavers, like he's rethought giving me booze, and

something about the arch of his brows and the twist of his lips sends a rush of flirting courage through my veins.

"Here," I say, "let me make the decision easier for you." I snatch the bottle before he can argue with me—my fingers graze his cold ones; maybe I can use that as an excuse to get a little closer—and take a swig. It's sweet and oddly dry, as if once it leaves my tongue it takes some of me with it. A hot trail sears down my throat, and a flowery taste fills my mouth. This is so the opposite of beer. I take another drink before I pass it back to him. "So, what's your name? In my head, I've been calling you 'the Boy in the Box.'"

"Have you now?" He smiles, and my insides go all melt-y. He takes a quick sip, then passes it back to me. He watches as I drink more of this wonder wine. "It's Sidney."

"You don't look like a Sidney," I say. "Sidney is an old man's name."

"Oh really?" He tips his hat back so he can get a better look at me. "You don't look much like an 'Em.' Like Auntie Em? Like *The Wizard of Oz*?"

I roll my eyes. "It's Emmaline, but only my grand-mother calls me that. Emmaline King." More liquor takes the embarrassment away. The flowery taste grows with every sip until I can almost feel heavy, velvety petals lining my mouth. "But you can call me Emma."

"Emmaline," Sidney says. My name is warm and plush on his lips. "It's very pretty."

"Oh really?" I ask, throwing his words back at him. *Oh God, I'm flirting!* I never flirt. My cheeks burn in the frigid air.

"It is. Like you." I can't believe he's looking at me like that. More booze now. Booze for bravery. I pass the bottle back to him after that.

"Emma!"

It's Jules. I peek over the side of the car and see her blond curls flying out behind her as she runs past the machinery at the base of the wheel. I open my mouth to yell, but what will I say? Wait right there while I flirt a minute? Before I can decide what to do, she's gone, twisting her way among the shuttering booths and tents.

"Do I need to get you back to your friend?" Sidney asks.

"No," I say, either the liquor or his crooked smile making me bold. Suddenly all my problems with Jules feel stupid. As soon as I'm off this ride I'll find her, and we can get on the same orbit again. "I can catch up with her in the parking lot."

Sidney nods and gives the bottle back. An inch or so of liquid sloshes around the bottle. "That's all you."

I down it. I feel pretty, and this boy wants to talk to *me*, so I move closer to him in the car. There is no way I am still Emmaline King. Some other girl sits here with this strange boy. Not-Emmaline takes his bowler hat and places it firmly on her head.

"It suits you," Sidney says with a small grin.

So lightly that I can barely feel it, he traces the line of my lower lip with the tip of his finger. My breath catches, and his gaze flickers from my mouth to my eyes and back again. His hand slides along my jaw—*he's so cold*—until he cradles the back of my neck, his thumb stroking my cheek in a twitchy way that makes me think he's nervous.

It's like the carnival has died below us, and all I can hear is my ragged breathing and thumping heart. Sidney's grip is firm, and he's so close that again I pick up the scent of dust and dryness and quiet, lonely hours trapped in the box.

He's going to kiss me. My brain has gone electric with the thought that this is going to be my first kiss.

I lick my lips a second before it happens. His mouth presses to mine, unyielding, and the metal edge of the car cuts into my back as I'm pushed into it with the force of his kiss.

Something is wrong.

My brain is furiously trying to figure it out but can't. All I want to think about is this boy, and the way his mouth works against mine, except…except it's my mouth that molds to his, and he has no breath, no taste. I can't even find a hint of the sweet wine on his lips. My tongue darts into his dry mouth and his teeth are too smooth, and the edges sharp. I cut my tongue.

As my mouth fills with the coppery, salty tang of my blood, I try to push him away, but his chest is firm under my hand. Too firm. I ball my hand into a fist and slam it into him. I hear a heavy, solid *thunk*.

Finally Sidney draws back, his eyes wounded, haunted, his hands shaking violently.

He's as hard as marble underneath my hand and just as cold. I touch the spot over his heart and feel…nothing. No pulse, no heartbeat.

"What are you?" All my bravado has left me, and my voice is reduced to a thin whisper. Tears—of betrayal, of the knowledge that I have made a terrible mistake—well up in the corners of my eyes.

"I am"—he averts his eyes—"so, so sorry."

His fists hit my chest like an oncoming train. My hands flail out, straining to grab onto the edge of the car, the seat, anything. I open my mouth to scream, but only a strangled sob gets out. Sidney's fingers push hard enough to make it difficult to breathe, hard enough that my bones scream out. The slippery grasp I have on the cold metal won't last long. I lose my grip, and the low wall of the car can't keep me within it.

I'm falling.

Falling both fast and slow and the night air is cold but my blood is on *fire* and there's nothing but a roaring in my ears and the wide, wide sky and wildly tilting lights.

Then I shatter.

Something hot trickles down the back of my throat and pools underneath me. Every time I try to breathe I hear a strange bubbling noise, and there's a stabbing somewhere in my chest like my bones are attacking my insides. Red, red like the box, red like Sidney's mouth, red fills my vision and threatens to burn me to ash.

The lights of the Ferris wheel are spinning, then slowing. Next thing I know, Lars and Sidney are standing over me. Lars's pity is a terrible thing to see. I start to cry, and, thankfully, my tears muddle the sight of their faces.

A woman's voice cuts through the night. "Did she drink it all?"

My breath comes in sharp, hiccup-y gasps, not enough to fill my lungs let alone answer or ask what's going on.

Sidney's voice is grim but calm. "She drank it all."

Of course I did. That's why I didn't taste it on his lips. He fooled me, just another carnival sleight of hand.

The woman comes into my view at the same time I start to lose feeling in the tips of my fingers and toes, and I will forever associate her beauty with panic. She's all loose platinum curls and big blue eyes. I am suddenly, painfully reminded of Jules, and a sob escapes me.

"Finally got one, huh? You picked a pretty little thing for your replacement, Sidney," the woman drawls, and there's a thread of disapproval in her voice. "They always miss the pretty ones."

Her mockery is one more hurt to add to the pile.

"She and her friend had a fight," Sidney says. "Should be easy to pass off as a runaway."

I want to argue, to tell him that I didn't fight with Jules, we just don't remember how to be friends yet, not like we used to. But I can't move my tongue. I can't feel my arms or my legs. The fire in my arms dulls down to nothing as I lose control of my limbs, but I'd rather be in pain ten times worse than this if it meant that I'd be able to wiggle my fingers. *What the hell is happening to me?*

"Why's it got to be like this?" Lars asks. The realization that he must have known Sidney's intent all along makes my stomach churn.

"It is what it is," the woman answers. The tips of her boots knock into my side as the creeping sensation crawls up my neck, and I barely feel it. "What's her name?"

I want to scream at her, to beg her to make it stop, but my tongue won't work, I can't even make my eyes blink. Tears roll down my cheeks unhindered, and they burn against my skin.

"Emmaline," Sidney says, resignation clear in his voice.

"That's her true name?" she asks. Sidney answers with a tiny nod.

She crouches down beside me, and my vision is filled with her and her curls. "Emmaline," she croons. "The transition is hard, but it's almost over. Right now, I need you to give Sidney a kiss before we can set him free. You can do that, can't you, Emmaline?"

I couldn't argue even if I wanted to. Sidney kneels down in the dirt beside me. Sweat beads on his forehead, and a line of it trickles down the side of his face, taking a trace of the black powder from his brow with it. Feverishly hot fingers cradle the back of my neck as he leans in, and as his lips mold around mine, my fingers begin to twitch.

CHAPTER FOUR

Benjamin

I am plotting my way toward freedom across a weathered old map when I hear the screaming.

I roll off the couches that make up my bed, ready to see what's going on, ready to help. The icy linoleum shocks my bare feet as I grab for the jacket I wore earlier. The accordion door at the other end of the Airstream camper trailer rattles, and my mother swears, so I know that she's heard the yelling, too. Just to be safe, I cram my map into the crack between the benches and the wall; if my mother had any idea I was thinking of leaving, she'd have a meltdown.

We reach the narrow door at the same time, and she doesn't seem fazed at all, as if there's a disturbance like this every night.

We step into the crisp air, ready to do something. Our carnival is so small, so self-sufficient, that the urge to help is hardwired into all of us. The source of the yelling—a pale girl between the more familiar figures of Leslie and

Lars—comes into view. A dozen or so others rush in from between the parked campers, likely drawn from cleaning up the day's detritus and shuttering the booths.

Whiskey sidles up next to me. She must have grabbed her dad's boots as she ran out because the ones she has on are so big that they almost hit her knees. She's pulled a pair of jeans on over her glittering riding costume, the frilly ruffles tufting over the waistband, and her hair is pulled into a messy knot on top of her head. She's small and slight for fourteen, but she's a stunner on a horse, and she has an exceptionally foul mouth.

"Now that—" Whiskey pauses as we watch them get closer, and I don't know if it's for drama or to make a better assessment—"is fucked up."

Lars and Leslie are helping a girl who can't seem to walk on her own down the alley. It's like the packed dirt beneath her feet is ice, and her legs twist and jerk out from under her. Without warning, her arm convulses in Lars's grip, and it seems as though her shoulder should be jerked out of the socket, but it isn't. Her black hair falls into her eyes, and she tries to shake it out of the way, but this only elicits an angry shriek and another stream of curses.

"I had to do it," Sidney says, following after them in the trailers' slanting shadows. "*Had* to. You'll see. Not now, but you'll see." As he steps into a square of light from an open trailer door, I see a flush to his cheeks that's not artificial, a fluidity to his movements suggesting something close to grace, something the girl is severely lacking.

Her head whips up, eyes glassy and feverish as she stares at those of us who came to help but are stunned into immobility. Her gaze darts from face to face, and something like worry or embarrassment arches her eyebrows high. Then she sees me. I can't quite get a read on the frustrated twist of her lips or the furrow grooved deep between her eyes as we stare at each other.

And then her leg jerks from beneath her. The girl collides into Leslie, her arm slipping from Lars's grip, and the two women crash into the side of Mrs. Potter's trailer, setting off a chorus of muffled barking. The red glass lantern hanging from a hook beside the door sways wildly. The crash is as sharp as the ruby shards sparkling among the weeds and grass. It's been years since I've heard the sound, and it reverberates in my ears.

With a jolt that buzzes up my spine, I realize this is the girl I saw earlier this evening. Without thinking, I dart across the alleyway, ready to help Lars lift her up. I wrap my hands around her upper arm, and at first, it doesn't register. Then I feel it. She's cold. It's not the kind of surface chill that comes from being outside too long on a cool night. No, even though I'm only holding her arm, I can tell she's cold down to the bone, so much so that my fingers are beginning to ache with it.

My hand lingers a little too long, and suddenly I feel the girl's gaze boring into me. Her full lips are twisted into a frown, and her glare could probably incinerate me if I let it. If she were a painting, she'd be an avenging angel, the kind whose fury could level cities.

"Thanks, Ben," Leslie says, tapping me on the shoulder. "I'll take it from here." Before I can offer to help them to, well, wherever it is they're going, Leslie slips the girl's arm around her shoulders and they shamble on down the alley.

I watch them as they walk away, and when I finally

tear my gaze from them my mother is giving me a stare that could wither lesser men. Luckily, I've been on the receiving end too often for it to have much of an impact. Her words, on the other hand, can always sting. "She's none of our concern," Mom says.

My brows furrow up. Why did we rush out here, if not to help? "I kind of think she is."

Everyone working the carnival knows the story. The person in the box is at the center of the charm and the curse that holds us together. This person is the reason all of us living and working for the carnival are charmed with an unnaturally lucky existence and long lives. We don't fall. We don't get hurt. Sometime after twenty, we stop aging—at least outwardly. And our performers can pull off stunts and tricks other carnies only wish they could do.

But now there's someone new.

What will happen to Sidney? Sidney has been in the box so long that some of us thought it would always be that way. The fact that there will be a new face in the box is as unsettling as someone telling me that the carnival is disbanding tomorrow.

And to know the girl bearing the curse is the same one I saw earlier, the one who didn't just glance at my paintings in passing but had really *seen* them...

"I am telling you, *she is not our concern*."

I can feel a fight brewing between us, and I take this moment and file it away. This, *this* is part of why I need to leave. Even though I'm a few months shy of eighteen, my mom isn't just my mom, she's my boss, giving her jurisdiction over my every waking moment. But before I can respond, we're interrupted by a soft sigh.

"Poor thing." Gin, Whiskey's older sister, had ghosted

up beside us as we watched the sad little parade go by. Strands of silvery hair float around her face, and the night has leeched the blue from her eyes to make them gray. I sometimes feel like a giant cosmic joke was played on their parents. First they got Gin—quiet and graceful and thoughtful—and, perhaps expecting their next offspring to be similar, three years later they got Whiskey—loud and brash and impulsive.

"I know," Whiskey says. She tears her eyes off the girl long enough to glance backward at us. "Did you see her haircut? First thing tomorrow, you're going to help her."

"Me?" I ask, surprised.

"Yes, Benjamin," Whiskey says. "Take your tool kit and your power sander and give her a makeover." I get an eye roll and a snort of laughter. "I was talking to Gin."

"Whitney," my mother says sharply, upset enough to call Whiskey by her real name, "now is not the time. I'm sure you need to groom the horses before you stable them for the night."

"Audrey!" Whiskey whines.

"I'll help Gin make sure Whiskey doesn't try to go spy on the new girl," I say, jabbing Whiskey's side with my elbow.

My mother nods, one half curl slipping from her braid. "And straight back."

The second we're out of earshot, Whiskey mutters, "We're going to go spy on the new girl, aren't we?" Moonlight glints off the sequins of her costume and the wry, knowing look in her eyes.

"Of course we are."

We duck between two campers and cut across the dirt path toward a trailer that most definitely does not belong to Gin and Whiskey's parents. Leslie's glossy white travel trailer is parked at the very edge of our encampment. It's huge, the length of two pickup trucks, and the windows sit a good two feet over my head. A tangle of shadowy forms move across the golden squares of light above us, and I imagine Leslie and Lars must be helping to make the black-haired girl more comfortable. Finally, the shadows are still, and there's nothing more for us to see.

"I bet I could get on the roof if you give me a boost," Whiskey says. "Pretty sure there's a sunroof I can listen at."

"You always want to do things the hard way," Gin says, nudging me toward the trailer. "Take a knee, Ben."

I kneel onto the cold ground just under one of the small windows. The grass is slick with dew, and in seconds my jeans are soaked through. Gin slips out of her shoes and leaps onto my back. She doesn't waver, but then, she's used to performing stunts on the back of a moving horse, so I'm sure I'm no problem. Whiskey steps up close, the scratchy netting of her costume practically in my face.

"What do you see?" I ask.

Gin's toes dig into my shoulders as she moves around. "Hard to say," she whispers. "The blinds are down."

Whiskey scuffs up a clod of dirt with her oversize boot. "Well, what do you hear?"

"My kid sister nagging me."

The tire nearest to me sinks just a bit.

"We have to go," I say, right before the door to the trailer slams open.

Lars is so big he fills the doorframe, and the light from behind him lines his hair in such a way it seems to glow. "I expect this of you, Whiskey, but not the other two. Go.

All of you, before I tell Leslie to dock your wages." He plants one foot onto the stairs, ready to chase us off if necessary, but we're already headed down the dirt alley before he has to make good on his threat.

"I wonder what she's like," Whiskey says the moment Lars heads back inside Leslie's trailer.

"I saw her. *Earlier,*" I add, before Whiskey can make a smart-ass remark about the impossibility of my seeing the new girl from where I knelt on the ground.

"When you were helping her?"

"Well, yeah," I say. "But before that, too, when I was helping you with—" I get a rock-hard elbow to the kidney before I can accidentally mention that Whiskey was riding Gin's horse. Rubbing at the dull throb in my side, I continue, "She seemed…" I struggle to come up with a word to convey what I saw earlier, the gleam in her eyes as she studied my paintings and the way the setting sun made her brown eyes blaze like stained glass. Or a way to describe the deep chill that seeped up from the heart of her or the way her anger seemed as though her body could barely contain it. "Interesting."

"'Interesting,' Benjamin?" Whiskey asks. One eyebrow arches toward her hairline, a sarcasm-o-meter stretching toward its maximum reading. "You saw the new Girl in the Box up close and personal but all you can give me is 'interesting'?"

I stop in the middle of the dirt path, sending small eddies of moonlight-bleached dust whirling about our feet. "Well maybe I could have had more time to observe her the first time I saw her if I hadn't been busy helping this girl I know wrangle her sister's horse back into its stall."

"Benjamin Singer, you son of a bitch," Whiskey says.

"You took Tristam out for a ride without asking?" Gin's voice goes from zero to banshee in two seconds flat, and I wave to Whiskey as her older sister chases her into the night.

When I can no longer hear them yelling at each other—which just means they're now screaming inside their makeshift stable, not that they stopped fighting—I start to walk along the dirt path back to our Airstream, thinking about the new girl.

Having a body in the box is important. I don't know the specifics of the curse, but I at least know *that*. The new girl's going to have a tough time of things, adjusting to life with the curse; maybe there's something I can do to help. But worrying over what to do and how to help are problems for tomorrow.

The world is done up in shades of gray again, and I want nothing more than to be back in my bed, where I can pity the black-haired girl in peace. But Mom is waiting for me on the steps of the trailer.

"From here on out, you are to stay away from her."

I am far too drained to argue with her, but finishing the conversation is the only way I'll ever see my bed again. "You mean the new girl?"

"Yes, Benjamin."

As a boss, Mom is a hard-ass, but she's never been one to set personal restrictions on me, not even after the night my friends and I helped Gin and Whiskey earn their nicknames by breaking into Happy the Clown's trailer and stealing his liquor. I'd gotten sick enough the next day that a repeat was all but guaranteed to never happen, never mind the fact that she put me to work on the most obnoxious tasks possible. Hammers and power saws are not your friends when fending off a hangover. So this demand is ridiculous.

"Why? You never told me to stay away from Sidney."

There's a furrow growing between her brows and I'm pretty sure that my questioning—I never go against what she asks of me—is bothering her. The wind whips her hair across her face, and her lips press together in a firm line. "Sidney was never a pretty girl."

CHAPTER FIVE

Emma

I can't stop shaking. Twitching. Jerking.

A chill has seeped into my bones, into my skin, and it refuses to go away. Leslie—the blond woman who seems to be in charge—cranked up the heater in her double-wide, but it's not doing a damn thing. Every now and then, my arm or my leg will snap out—one time I hit Lars squarely in the chin, and punching him felt like a teeny tiny bit of retribution for his part in tonight's hellish events—but I can't stop it.

My skin still looks like skin, but it's gone hard, like I've been petrified. No one ever thinks about bending their arms or their knees, but now I have to, I have to really *want* it, and even then, my joints are stiff and everything aches when I move. Somewhere, really deep down, I can feel the sluggish beat of my heart. But there's only one beat for every two, and all the other signs of life—breath, pulse, tears, sweat—are long gone.

Everything I touch is dull and far away. I know I'm

sitting on a slick vinyl booth in the kitchen area of the camper, but I can't feel the plastic-y seat under my palm or the sharp angles of the wooden frame pressing against my legs. I can't tell if the table's surface is cold, or if the vinyl is trying to bond permanently with the skin exposed by the hole in my jeans. Everything feels uniformly the same. Everything feels like nothing. The only thing I can feel is the cold deep in my bones.

I should be panicking. I think if I could breathe, I'd be hyperventilating. Instead, I sit across from Leslie, unable to feel anything but the relentless cold. And the only thought running through my head is that I should have taken up Jules on finding and devouring as many fried candy bars as possible.

Oh God. *Jules.* Is she going to think I abandoned her? That she said something or did something to make me run off into the night? What will she do when her dad comes to pick us up? Will she lie, say that I went home on my own? Or will she tell the truth, that I've gone missing? And if it's the latter, how many times will she have to tell her story, to her dad, to the cops, to my family?

My family.

Shit, shit, *shit.* They're going to think I've run away. I never bothered to hide my dislike of this tiny town, of the cramped house, of the water stain on the ceiling of my room that kind of looked like James Brown. Will my dad think I don't care about the life he's put together for us in Claremore? Thomas, my older brother, is going to be pissed, and Jonah, only seven, isn't going to have anyone to go to when he has a nightmare and needs to cuddle before falling back to sleep. And my mom. She might have to come back from Guatemala. She might lose the research funding she worked so hard to get.

All because of my stupid decisions.

Leslie cradles a cup of something warm and steaming in her hands, and all I want is to shove my fingers into the hot liquid to see if I'll feel it. Sidney and Lars nurse their own mugs, though Lars slipped something from a flask into his.

"Can I have one?" I ask, pointing to the kettle on the little two-burner stove.

I might drown under the waves of their pity.

"It won't do you any good," Sidney says. His head jerks to the side when Lars bumps into him accidentally on purpose.

I glare at Sidney, at his cheeks with their flush of pink and his crooked teeth. "You need to shut the hell up."

"I am *trying* to help." Each word is sharp edges and overpronounced consonants.

"You want to help?" I yell. "Tell me what the hell you did to me and how to fix it!"

There's nothing but Leslie's unblinking silence, and Sidney chugging his coffee, and Lars standing uncomfortably in the corner.

Leslie spins her mug but keeps her blue, blue eyes on me. When she talks, it's with the slow, measured speech of someone trying to soothe a cornered animal. "First of all, you should know that we don't want to hurt you any more than you've already been hurt. We're here to help you and take care of you, okay?"

I don't know if I believe that, but Leslie takes my silence for agreement and continues. "A long time ago, before you or I were born—and I was born quite a long time ago—a curse was placed on our carnival."

"Do you have any oranges?" Sidney asks as he slams down his mug. "I would kill for an orange right now."

"If you're going to be an insensitive jackass," Lars growls, "then you should leave now." He looms over Sidney, like a storybook giant threatening some puny villager.

"No," Leslie says in the kind of voice that gets shit done, "I need him here. He's part of the story." She points to one of the cupboards by the sink and sure enough, after a few moments of digging, Sidney pulls out a fat orange. His fingers tear at it, like there's no way he'll ever get the peel off quickly enough. A thin mist of juice sprays out from the opened fruit.

I should be able to smell the bright citrusy scent, but I can't.

My legs are as hard to move as a porch door swollen from rain, but I manage to stand and nearly take the tabletop with me. "Someone tell me how to fix this! I shouldn't be here. All I did was kiss a boy—" I turn and point an accusing finger at Sidney, though what I really want to do is hit him. "My first kiss, by the way, asshole, and now I am *this*. I shouldn't! Be here! I should be at home…" My next words die on my tongue. Home is Mom, and right now, Mom is thousands of miles away. Home is a family who, if they don't already, will soon think I've abandoned them.

I'm even more alone than I thought possible.

I stare at my fingers and try to keep the wobble out of my voice. "Just take me to my dad, or call Jules, or if you can't be bothered, at least call 911 and I'll wait for the ambulance by myself!"

The three exchange a glance, and the chill in my bones deepens.

"Bad idea, Em," Sidney says. "So there was this one time, outside of what, Tempe? Somewhere. Point is, I was feeling rebellious. So rebellious that I let everyone believe I was with the caravan, when in actuality, I had stayed behind. I think they got maybe a mile or two away when it happened. Everything seized up on me, and I collapsed. I couldn't move, couldn't talk. The only thing I could do was stare at the passing clouds. I had to watch as the sun moved across the sky and the moon came up. I had no idea what I was going to do. Even if someone found me, what could I do? Stare into their soul until they figured out what happened to me? Pray that I had an 'If Lost, Return to Le Grande's Carnival' printed across my back that I didn't know about? Sit in an antique shop for all of eternity? Finally, someone figured out I was missing, and Leslie came back for me. The closer we got to the carnival, the more I could move. It wasn't until I was back among the trailers and the machines and the people that I was myself again. Well, as much as you can be yourself while cursed."

I stare at Sidney, at the way his skin looks so flushed against the white face paint and the way his eyes glint and sparkle. How could I have possibly thought he was alive before? How could I have been so stupid? "So you're telling me I'm trapped?"

"Not trapped, not quite," Leslie says, at the exact same time Sidney says, "Pretty much."

Leslie glares at Sidney but says, "We can't let you leave."

"Watch me." My chest heaves, like there's something in my lungs clawing up my throat to escape, and I realize this is what sobbing feels like in my new, alien body.

Sidney and Lars melt out of the way as I clumsily escape the trailer. The door slams behind me, a loud *bang* in the still night. It's colder out here under the silver stars. Slowly, so slowly I might not have noticed if it wasn't for the fact that I can barely feel anything at all, and what I can feel is amplified, the twitching worsens. I'm in the middle of a row of trailers, campers, two tents that have seen better days, and one old but brightly painted wagon.

Remembering how hard the simple task of walking had been earlier, I put each foot forward slowly, making sure my stiff legs are solidly planted beneath me before I take a step. Between two trailers I find a huge tin bucket; I flip it over with clumsy hands and sit with a dull *thunk*.

I splay my fingers over my knees. Under the glow of the moon, they're white like bone, like shell, like things that have had all the life leeched out of them. A shudder trembles at the base of my spine, but a quiet animal snuffling keeps me from giving in to my breakdown. Peeking out from beneath the shiny trailer is a little black nose bracketed by tufts of dirty white fur.

The rest of the dog emerges from the shadows, a wriggling mass of terrier-shaped happiness. I'm not sure if this dog is particularly friendly or maybe I just smell appealing (though what on earth do I smell like anymore?), but the dog immediately props its front paws onto my leg, leaving little muddy paw prints.

And oh, but he's warm.

Even that little bit of contact feels heavenly, warmth radiating out from where he's touching me. I heft him onto my lap, and it's more like I'm holding a small fire on my legs instead of a dog. Though a fire wouldn't nuzzle at my hands, slyly positioning them in the perfect place for a scratch behind the ears. Happy to keep this relationship beneficial for the both of us, I oblige, and scritch at the spot that makes his back leg go berserk.

I'm not sure how long the dog and I sit there—me happy to soak up all the warmth he has to offer, him ecstatic for the unending scratches and pets—but eventually I hear footsteps. Lars rounds the corner, and he sags against one of the trailers, an olive-green monstrosity that groans beneath his weight.

"Is this where you tell me that everything is going to be okay?" I ask, searching for the glitter of his dark eyes in the shadows that surround him.

"No," he says solemnly. The honesty hurts, but not as much as a lie would, I think. "There's a lot more about this curse that you'll need to know and that I can't tell you. And before you ask, I know I played a part in this, and I am sorry. And I'd do it again, because I've been here helping Leslie run this show for longer than you can imagine. But—" He pauses here, and the word is heavy, loaded. Something inside me clenches tight, like my rock-hard lungs are compressing into diamonds. "Leslie will tell you the technical bits. But here's what she isn't going to tell you."

My hands go still, mid-scratch. The dog in my lap gives a long, high-pitched whine.

"The curse changes you. It changes everyone it touches, really, because I hate having a part in it, but damn if I don't love the perks that come with it. Did you learn about the Korean War in school, Emma?"

He shifts over into a beam of moonlight, like he wants me to get a better look at him. Every detail is crisp. Laugh lines arc out from his eyes, but there aren't many and they aren't deep. Two furrows sit between his eyebrows, like they're permanently pinched together in mild frustration. His mustache covers most of his mouth, so I can't see if any lines have made their mark there. In this light, his orangey hair has been bleached to some sort of indiscriminate gray, but I don't remember seeing any silver in his hair earlier. He doesn't look to be any older than forty-five, though I know that if he's talking about the Korean War he must be older. "Are you trying to tell me that you'd be old as balls without the curse?" I ask, finding it hard to be excited for his relatively youthful appearance.

"I *am* old as balls, but only because of this place. Before I got here, I was dying from lung cancer. Docs said it was thanks to exposure to chemical agents in the war."

"Don't bullshit me." The anger I felt before, the stuff bubbling just under the surface, threatens to roil again, and my arms tighten around the dog, though I'm not sure if I mean to protect him or if I want him to protect me. My grandfather had lung cancer, died of it, and Lars could probably model for some sort of mountain man, outdoor living magazine.

"You want to see my old x-rays, kiddo? I was dyin', and now I'm not. Leslie found me doing chemo with her dad, thought I still had some life in me, and brought me here. I can breathe, and I don't even think I've coughed in decades. And I'm not the only one reaping the benefits of the charm. We like it, Emmaline. We want nothing more than for things to continue as they are.

"But that's just it. There are no perks in it for you. You won't age, but you won't *live*, either. Every day you'll need to be in that booth, waiting to trap the next sucker.

And the longer it takes for you to charm some boy—or girl, that's a thing now, right?—into taking your place, the more stunted and dark your heart becomes. You'll sacrifice bits of your soul all under the umbrella of *the curse*. You'll tell yourself it's okay when the lies tumble out of your mouth to steal someone's life away from them. Because that's the bottom line: if you want to leave, you'll have to screw someone over."

The breath blows out of him like the troubled rumble of a slumbering lion. "But this…this is the first time I've really been directly involved. Gotten my hands dirty, so to speak. And I don't like it much. I know we need someone in that booth, but it doesn't have to be someone I helped put there. So I want you to get up. Get in there. And let Leslie and that jackass tell you how to pass this curse along."

He places a big hand on my shoulder, just for a second, so quick that his warmth doesn't get the chance to seep into my skin. Then he's gone just as quickly as he came, surprisingly quiet for someone so big, leaving me to find solace in the black and gray and white world lit by the moon.

One by one, the sounds come back into the night. Crickets chirp back and forth at one another, and if I listen really hard, I can hear some people talking farther down the alley. But, louder than any of those things are the dull clacks of the dog's nails as he resituates himself on the hard, unyielding surface of my legs.

I want to go home. I want to tell Jules I'm sorry. Catch her before she tells my dad and brothers, to spare them any pain or anxiety that might result from my disappearance. I want to fix this.

I *have* to fix this.

Gripping him gently, I lift the dog from my lap and

place him on the ground. Slowly, so as not to set off another round of uncontrollable twitching, I stand. The little dog looks as if he doesn't understand why we had to get up, and, if we did have to get up, then why is he not in my arms, but I shoo him along, and he trots down the aisle, looking for trouble to cause or another lap to sit in. I take a careful step, and when my legs don't give out beneath me, I make my way to the trailer. The muffled conversation within is cut short as I clunk up the stairs. Stealth, something I never particularly excelled at before, is completely impossible in this graceless body. My fingers slip once against the door handle—just one smooth surface skipping along another—but I get it on the second try and go in.

Lars and Leslie watch me as though I'm a bomb about to go off; Sidney, occupied with a bowl of cereal and another cup of coffee, couldn't care less. I stumble back into my seat opposite Leslie and put my hands on the table, pressing one down hard into the other in hopes it'll calm the twitching.

"Tell me about the curse," I say.

Leslie shifts in her seat and sighs. "These are the basics as we understand them. The cursed one chooses someone to take his or her place. They get the—"

She pauses, her mouth tightening into a grimace, and I jump in. "Just say victim, because that's what I am."

"Hey," Sidney says around a mouth full of food, "I was that victim once, too."

"Are you asking me to pity you?" I feel colder than cold, more still than I have all night. I am an iced-over lake, a glacier. At that moment, I would have gladly accepted the consequences of the curse if it came with the ability to freeze him like an icicle I could shatter against the floor.

Leslie leaps back into the conversation before Sidney can make things worse. "There is a series of events that have to be done in a certain order. The *victim* must give up their true name. He or she must drink all the wine, brewed and charmed by our psychics, and if even a little of it remains in the bottle, the curse won't transfer. And then the victim must be broken, so the curse can put them back together again."

"Are you telling me that this asshole didn't have to kiss me?" I ask.

Leslie shakes her head. "The kiss seals the pact between you. It must be those things all together—name, wine, a kiss to enter the deal, and a kiss to seal it. Just one or two of those things doesn't mean anything."

"But I didn't agree to anything!" I'm close to running out again; my legs itch to get away from this trailer and keep going. To find my father and let him help me figure this all out. To get help from anyone who isn't a member of this damned carnival.

Leslie's hands reach across the table again, though far more tentatively than before. When I don't yank my fingers out of the way, she rests hers on mine so gently that I'm only able to register the touch because of the heat that radiates from her hand into mine. "You might not have agreed, but you kissed him, and the curse isn't all that discriminating. I know this is not how you expected your evening to end. But we're here for you, and we'll do everything we can to make you as comfortable as we can while you're with us, however long that may be."

My stiff fingers curl into fists. "Then take it back."

Leslie draws in a sharp breath and Sidney carefully puts his spoon into his bowl.

"No," he says.

Sidney stands in one fluid motion, graceful, like a dancer. "I got rid of it. It's a hard thing to manage, but I did it. You can, too."

Lars clearly wants to say something to him, but Sidney is out the door before he can. The heaving, shuddering feeling hits me again, and I feel like I might shatter into a hundred pieces. But then Leslie's there, wrapping her arms around me and pulling me close. Nonsense words meant to soothe and comfort fill my ears, but I don't really hear them. All I hear are the shuddering screams that pour out of my mouth.

I want my *home*. I want my bed and the four walls I've made mine. And if I can't have that, then I want the room in my dad's house with its shitty garage-sale bed and the water stain on the ceiling. I want to hear Dad and Thomas argue about which college team does or doesn't deserve a spot in the playoffs. Hell, right now, I'd walk across a fire pit of Jonah's Legos and smile like a pageant queen when I got to the other side if it meant I could wake up from this nightmare tomorrow.

But I don't have that. None of it. All I've got is Leslie, who holds me so tight her heat feels like it belongs to me, and Lars, who glares daggers at the door as though he might be able to strike Sidney dead with a look.

I search for stillness. For calm. Slowly, the shuddering, shaking explosion of emotions calms to a slight twitch here and there. If I want to go home, I need to know how to do it. I need to learn about the curse.

As my trembling becomes less violent, Leslie releases

her grip and returns to the other side of the table. "If you want to talk about this tomorrow…"

"No!" My response is loud enough to startle Lars from his attempt to psychically throttle Sidney. "I mean, no. Let's get it out tonight."

Leslie's gaze darts to Lars, then back to me, and when she talks, her voice is gentle. "Okay. As I said, there's a curse, and right now, it's living in you. And there's a charm, one that protects the carnival so we, in turn, can take care of you."

I roll my eyes at that bit but don't argue. From what Lars said, it sounds like they benefit from the charm far more than I do.

"But what most people who work here don't know is that the charm and the curse are codependent. When Sidney was stuck in that field after we had driven away, we had a string of accidents. Small things at first. Sprained wrist, twisted ankle. Then our fire-eater got a nasty burn, covered half her body. Of course, we didn't realize what was going on right away, but afterward, when we had Sidney back safe and sound and the accidents stopped, Lars and I put it together."

She presses her mouth into a firm line, and right then, I can see how she, like Lars, must be far older than she appears. Every year of her life is in the small tight frown and the hard glint in her eyes. My fingers clench around the fabric of my shirt.

"From right now until the minute you pass on the curse, we are linked," Leslie says. "The carnival thrives when you thrive. It suffers when you suffer. We need you and you need us, and there is nothing that will change that fact."

CHAPTER SIX

Emma

I don't sleep. Even though it's way past midnight, my eyes never become heavy; my limbs aren't tired. So with nothing but time on my hands, I worry. Leslie told me Sidney was saddled with the curse for fifty years. Fifty years of not breathing, not tasting, not feeling your heart pound in your chest. Fifty years of the cold. Fifty years of not being able to feel things beneath your fingertips. My parents might be dead and my brothers old men by the time I'm free.

Guilt over subjecting someone else to the same horrors I'm trying to escape keeps rising within me, but I can't stay here. I have to get back home. *It is what it is*, I tell myself, even as a smaller part of my brain yells that no one should be subjected to this. But the need to let my family and Jules know that I'm all right is so great that it's easy to not think about the poor sap that I'm going to swap places with. All I can think of is shaking off this curse like it's a bad dream.

When I begin to hear people moving and chattering outside Leslie's trailer, I sneak out, and after poking around a bit, I find the costume trailer. I'm hunting for some outfit that will bring people to my booth. The booth, I've been told, holds some of the charm, gifting the carnival with its preternatural luck. And because of this, people are drawn to the fiery red box. I could try my luck walking around the carnival, but supposedly, if I'm in the booth, the people will come to me.

The trailer is full to bursting with costumes of years past, an explosion of feathers and sequins and glitter. Taffetas and velvets and satins press against one another in two neat rows that line the walls of the trailer. And that's to say nothing of the colors. Aquas, pinks, yellows, and oranges vie for my attention, punctuated here and there by a stark stripe of black or gold or silver.

The sleeve of a plush red velvet jacket calls to me. I want to feel the soft fibers crush between my thumb and forefinger, and though I can see my fingers pinch down, I can barely feel the two layers of cloth, much less tell anything about their actual texture. The fabric twists as my hand clenches into a fist, and…nothing. If I had breath in my body, I'd have just sighed.

I asked Leslie about that. How is it that I'm walking and, more specifically, talking, when my blood moves sluggishly through my veins and I don't have breath in my body. She said that she didn't know, that no one knew. The carnival doctor was a former army doc turned clown, and he couldn't figure it out, either. They hadn't dared to seek outside help for fear that the original victim would be taken away and tested without end. All they knew was that the cursed *was* able to think and talk and be a part of the world, while looking like the horrifying offspring of a ventriloquist and his or her dummy.

I'm riffling through a section of clothing that clearly belonged to someone confident enough to parade around in just a complicated set of straps when the springs on the trailer door creak open. A tall blond girl, long lines and sleek muscle, steps inside.

"Hello," she says, her voice both insubstantial and confident, like she's a wisp of cloud that refuses to be blown away.

Her hair is pale and slippery, and it hangs down to the middle of her back. Her eyes are dark gray, until she gets closer and then they seem more blue. The way she moves is grace in action, and even standing still I feel awkward and clumsy.

"I was just… Leslie said I could…" I'm not sure why, but I feel like I have to justify my being in the trailer. But the girl walks over and lays what I think is meant to be a comforting hand on my shoulder.

"You're the new Girl in the Box, aren't you? My sister and I saw you on your way through the yard last night. And we heard you. It was impossible to do one without the other. I take that back. We definitely heard you before we saw you."

If I were still capable of it, I would be blushing madly.

"My name is Gin, by the way."

"Jen? Like short for Jennifer?"

"Sure. Why not," she says, a small smile picking up the corners of her mouth. "You should hear what they call my sister."

"And what do they call your sister?"

"Well I call her Wee Tiny Loudmouth," a brash boy

calls from the door, "but *I* am not *they* and *they* call her Whiskey."

For a second I think of Sidney and his perfectly coifed hair and what had seemed like impeccable clothes, but this boy is not Sidney. His skin is the cool brown of a smoky quartz, not pale like cream. His eyes are wider, his smile smirkier. He's got on a newsboy cap that's patterned in a small brown check and a faded Ramones T-shirt under a ratty tweed blazer with corduroy patches at the elbows. He stalks toward us down the thin alley made by the rows of costumes, brushing up against them and sending the hangers swinging. He thrusts out his hand for me to shake.

"I'm Duncan," he says authoritatively, his hand firm around mine, steadying the twitching. "You are new." His eyes flutter closed, and though I try to pull my hand away, he holds on. "And if I were you, I'd be crying my eyes out right about now. How are you holding up, darling? I mean, if my first kiss had gone as poorly as yours, I'd be crying into my pillow nonstop. As it is, my first kiss was with some townie girl who didn't know what the hell she was doing, and, don't ever tell her I said this, she pretty much firmly cemented the fact that girls are not my bag."

"Settle down, Duncan," Gin says absently as she holds up to the light an icy-blue costume that drips with crystals and feathers. "First impressions. A little goes a long way and all that."

"If it weren't true, I'd be offended," Duncan says. He swats at Gin but she sways away at the last second. "I'm one of the carnival's fortune-tellers. My shtick is romance, which pisses off my twin, Pia, more than you can imagine. She's good at the numbers, which isn't nearly as sexy, let's be honest. Oh! Almost forgot. Leslie told me to keep you occupied for a bit. The cops think you're a runaway and are searching the grounds."

Of course they do. I'd asked Leslie why they weren't just picking up and running away now that they had me. She said it might cause more questions if the carnival left town a night before the end of their promoted engagement when there was an alert out for a missing girl. Better to stay around and be as upfront and helpful as possible in order to throw off suspicion.

I part the clothes hanging in front of the trailer's windows and peek between the blinds. Two officers in dark blue patrol the alley. Hope flickers in my chest, like a flame to be cupped in a hand. I could step outside and have them by my side in seconds. My fingers are on the door handle when it hits me.

If I go out there now, the cops will take me back home to my dad, and before I know it, I'll be in front of doctors who want to poke and prod me, though with my petrified skin, who knows how much they'll even be able to poke and prod. No, what's going on here isn't science. It's something else. Something I've never seen or heard about in the world outside. As much as I don't want to be here—well, here like this—home isn't going to do me any good right now. The answer to my problem lies somewhere in the perimeter of this little carnival. I know it. The tiny flame gutters and dies.

Duncan riffles through the rack of costumes closest to him. Every time a hanger swishes along the rack, little plumes of dust and fiber flutter into the air. "Lars took your phone and ditched it in the parking lot of a Walmart in town."

Lars took my phone? And ditched it at a Walmart of all places? Oh God. My parents really will think I've run away. Or got kidnapped. Either option is viable, since I made it abundantly clear I hate Claremore. Will Juliet and her dad get in trouble? Will my parents be upset? Will my mom fly back from Guatemala or just bury herself in her research, too busy to be bothered with a missing daughter?

Duncan holds a lemony-yellow dress to my cheek. "God, the curse just makes them so *pale*, you know what I mean, Gin?"

Gin snorts. "You know you're talking to someone who keeps an industrial-size bucket of sunblock in her trailer, right?"

"Yeah, but you're Irish or something. I've seen copy paper darker than you."

Gin extends her middle finger, long and elegant.

"So rude," Duncan says.

"Hey, how do you know all that? About the phone and the kiss and everything?" I ask.

Duncan taps a hanger to his temple. "Psychic, like, for realsies. And I'm nosy as shit." He heaps a red-colored velvet jacket, a silky blue dress, and a pastel pink-and-gold marching band coat into my arms, then corrals me to the back of the trailer where a full-length mirror stands next to a vanity, the kind with big golden lightbulbs framing the edges. Gin gently pushes me down onto the worn velvet bench in front of the mirror while Duncan starts to rummage through the drawers.

"Did you hear about Fabrizio Moretti and the bullshit he pulled last night?" Duncan asks as he begins to line up trays of blush and eye shadow.

Gin huffs as she picks up a hairbrush and sets to work on my tangles. "No. What now?"

"He and his brothers were showing off, right—basically, they were breaking about five laws of physics." Duncan leans in close, like he and I are going to share in a great big secret. "Well, not *really*, but they were doing that thing where Lorenzo balances on Antonio's palm while Fabrizio climbs over the both of them like a deranged spider monkey. Anyhoo. Some local decided they must use wires or mirrors or something, and he stayed after the performance to tell the Brothers Numbskull that they're full of it. Fabrizio, the cocky little shit, maintains the only thing the rube is full of is hot air. You can see where this is going. In the end, it took four of the roustabouts to separate them, and Leslie had to offer the townies free tickets for tonight so they wouldn't press charges."

Duncan says all of this in a voice so sour it could have turned milk.

"Every morning I wake up and hope this will be the day Leslie will leave the Morettis by the side of the road, but every night, they're still here." Gin grimaces at my scalp, though I'm fairly certain it's not my hairstyle offending her.

"They bring in a shit-ton of money," Duncan says. "Besides. The charm makes them lucky, the luck makes them ballsy, and being ballsy makes them better performers."

Now it's Gin's turn to sound pissy. "Don't remind me."

A *bang* rattles the flimsy trailer door. "Police. Open up."

I freeze. Oh shit. *Oh shit*. This is it. They're going to drag me away and then—

"Don't move," Duncan says as he pushes me into a

chair in the corner and piles a heap of costumes over me.

The door creaks open, and Gin says, "Can I help you?"

"Officer Sharpe, Claremore PD," a man says. "We're looking for this girl. Have you seen her?"

The clothes weigh down on my chest like sandbags dragging me to the ocean floor. I tug a tutu down a fraction, just enough to catch a glimpse of Gin.

"Never seen her," Gin says. She lifts one shoulder lazily to match her bored tone of voice.

"Anyone else in there?" the officer asks.

Gin turns, gesturing toward the rows of costumes. "Just me and Duncan," she says.

"Hel*lo*, officer," Duncan says. The officer's eyes go wide with shock, and though I can't see him, I have a feeling Duncan is giving the officer the flirtiest look he can manage.

"Well," Sharpe says. The trailer dips under his weight. "Still need to take a look." Heavy footsteps accompany the officer's slow perusal of the trailer. I go as still as possible, hoping the pile of clothes will keep me hidden. And then the officer's toe nudges mine.

The shirt covering my face whips away, and I get a good look at Officer Sharpe. He's dark-skinned and handsome, uniform crisp, badge gleaming, and eyes growing wider by the second. Behind him, Duncan's mouth flaps open and closed, as though he's flailing for words. Oh God. He's going to take me away.

He whips a paper out of his back pocket, and I catch the quickest glimpse of my face before he's holding the flyer next to me. "Holy hell," Sharpe says, eyes never leaving mine. "This mannequin looks *just* like the girl."

Duncan jumps up. "Are you sure?" He taps my forehead with his fingernail, hard enough that we all hear the faint *click, click, click.* "We've had this old thing as long as I can remember."

I grind my teeth, but no one seems to notice.

"Really." Suddenly Sharpe, though he doesn't seem old, is the jaded cop from every TV show. "Exactly what use does a carnival have for a mannequin?"

If Duncan is stumped by this very good question—because, seriously, what use *does* a carnival have for a mannequin—he doesn't show it. "I think she started as something for the knife throwers to use during practice, but then she just kept popping up all over the place. And then it became a contest, to see who could leave her in the weirdest place. But we had to stop when someone left her inside one of the porta potties. Scared the hell out of a little kid two towns back and made him wet himself."

I'm going to punch Duncan.

Officer Sharpe nods slowly. "I'll bet she did." I don't think Duncan or Gin catches it when he presses a finger to what should be the soft flesh of my forearm; it's only when he meets cold resistance that he straightens and turns toward the door. Gin gives him a thousand-watt smile as he hands her a flyer with my face on it. "Keep the flyer, and call us if you see her, all right?"

"Yes, sir!" Gin and Duncan say a little too brightly. The second Officer Sharpe is out of the trailer, Gin locks the door.

Duncan lifts the pile of clothing off me and heaps it onto the floor, and the instant he does, I begin to tremble.

"Hey," Duncan says, laying one of his big hands over mine. "You're okay, honey. You're okay."

I nod, though I feel like I might have emotional whip-lash.

I want to bask in their friendship, but after last night, it feels idiotic to not question their kindness. They're only nice to me because I am, essentially, their meal ticket to a life free of injuries, illnesses, and aging. Who wouldn't be nice to the girl who gave those kind of gifts? The golden bulbs give off a soft heat, as does Duncan's nearby body. I want to lean into both but manage to restrain myself when I realize how much of a creeper that would make me.

Neither Duncan nor Gin notices my momentary weirdness, the both of them returning to the tasks they'd started before Officer Sharpe interrupted them.

Duncan helps me stand only to immediately lower me onto the padded bench in front of the old-fashioned vanity. "I hope you don't mind, but I thought I'd give you a bit of a makeover," he says. A flat disc of powder, trays of eye shadow in a succession of browns, and a tube of lipstick are placed on the counter. "When you work in a carnival, everything has to be bigger. Brighter. Your everyday look isn't going to work here. Enter: me. And Gin's a peach, always helpful. She's going to pick out something for you to wear while you work in the booth."

"Thank you, Duncan," Gin says, in an airy sort of way that makes it seem like the costumes in front of her are far more interesting than what Duncan has to say. She reaches around to drape me in a little black flapper dress that has beads in swishy rows all over it.

"Plus, I'm selfish. It's been years, *years* since we've had fresh blood besides the Morettis in this place. And while my groin-al area would prefer you were a boy, the rest of me is glad to have anyone." He begins to apply makeup. The brushes sweeping across my face don't register as touch; I only know he's making progress because I can see it in the mirror.

When I look at my reflection I see that Duncan has already painted my lips a deep ruby red, and he's even put a fake beauty mark at the corner of my mouth. He shapes my long bangs into a swoop across my forehead.

I take hold of his wrist to stop him before he can apply a set of false eyelashes to my lids. "Why are you helping me, really? I mean, I get what you just said. But are you just doing this so I'll be happy and complacent? Keep the charm that benefits you in place?"

Part of me can't believe I just said that. The other part thinks I wasn't harsh enough. Above my reflection, Duncan and Gin exchange a loaded glance in the mirror.

When Duncan speaks, he's concentrating a little too hard on swirling a makeup brush around in the lid of an eye shadow pot. "Because this sucks. Because not all of us are epic douche canoes like the Morettis; some of us were just born into this place and don't really know any other way of life. Because I don't know you but I'm going to go out on a limb and say you're scared and lonely and don't deserve any of this. Take your pick, doll."

Flurries of golden dust motes dance in the air as he brings a powder brush to my cheeks and swirls some color on, and I feel a smile stretch my mouth. He seems to mean it. And so does Gin, judging from the encouraging smile she gives me in the mirror. They want to *help* me. Maybe I can do this after all.

CHAPTER SEVEN

Emma

If someone had told me a day ago that in a few short hours I would have a one-way ticket out of town, I'd have been ecstatic. But somehow, leaving as a cursed puppet-girl doesn't have the same excitement factor. More like a panicking-the-hell-out factor. I guess there's a perk to not being able to sob my eyes out—my makeup won't run.

Leslie assigned Sidney to watch me this first night and to give me pointers when applicable. His breath is a barely visible white plume in the night, and never in my life did I think I'd be jealous over a simple bodily function. Sidney leans against a silver trailer near the entrance to the carnival grounds, a quickly disappearing apple in his hand and two cores at his feet. I haven't eaten since yesterday, and I hate that the last thing I tasted was a corndog and some cotton candy.

"That's what you're wearing?" he asks as I approach.

If I could still blush, I would. I've got on the black flapper dress, the beads dangling off it softly clacking every time I move. At the last minute, Duncan threw on the red velvet marching jacket for a burst of color. More than a little pissed, I shoot back, "Is that what *you're* wearing?"

He looks permanently rumpled, like the clothes from the bottom of the dirty laundry bin, a far cry from the perfect brows and pressed shirt of just last night. His hair is actually curly now that it's not slicked into perfection, unruly waves falling across his forehead from underneath the bowler hat. His mouth isn't as red, but it's more mischievous, more knowing. He's wearing the same jeans, but the suspenders hang loosely from his hips, and he's replaced the stiff white dress shirt with a faded green T-shirt. He's wound a chunky hand-knit scarf around his neck a few times and tucked the ends under a heavy wool coat.

He's not the same boy I saw last night, but he is a more human version of the boy from last night. Though the knowledge of his assholery makes him decidedly less cute.

"That reminds me." He plucks the hat from his head and drops it onto mine. "This is yours now."

I stomp away as he reaches out to put the damned hat on my head, but he's fast and gets it on anyway. "I don't want it, jackass."

Sidney drops the third apple core onto the ground and follows me to the carnival. "I meant it when I said it suited you. Look, I'm sure my opinion doesn't count for shit with you right now, but I do want to help. Others might want to make you comfortable, but there's a difference—like it or not, I'm the only person who knows what it's like to be in that damned box, and I want you to get free one day."

I bark out a short, sharp laugh, but Sidney likes the sound of his own voice enough to continue.

"Always make sure that the booth is strategically set up. We're at a venue a day before we open to the public, so if they stick you somewhere that won't work, there's time to make them move it. And *do* make them move it. You won't win any friends, but they're not the ones stuck in a box and screwed five ways from Sunday, so they can deal with it."

We're walking into the carnival proper now. Booth employees are putting up awnings and rolling up screens. A woman drizzles some batter into a fryer and another is dipping frozen bananas into chocolate and I *wish* I could be hit by the scents that belong to the sights I'm seeing.

A man stands on the roof, checking that the giant black-and-purple spider with yellowed fangs is secure atop the haunted house ride, and another worker yells instructions from below. The rickety plywood building has cartoon skeletons dancing across a gloomy cemetery painted all along the side. Jules and I rode it last night, and the rickety roller coaster inside almost made her lose her fried Twinkies. The men can be heard arguing long after we pass them.

"What you want is to be on the edge of the midway," Sidney says. "Close to the food, close to the games. I was stuck in that box for a long time, and I got the most hits here." He steps up to the box and pats the wooden frame with some strange combination of familiarity and distaste, if that's even possible.

"Why…" I pause, almost chickening out before deciding I care more about getting out of here than hurting Sidney's feelings. "Why *did* it take you so long? You got me to fall for your shtick pretty easily last night."

His mouth twists into a grim smile before he lifts his hand to hover somewhere above my head. "You must be at least this tall to ask that question, and you fall woefully short."

I smack his hand away and take a little too much pleasure at his grimace when my rock-hard fingers strike his.

We walk around to the back of the box. There's a door but no handle. Sidney stretches up to depress the top right corner, and the door springs open. With no other handle in sight, it's a smart way to make sure that some jerk doesn't just barge into the booth. Sidney pulls back a faded curtain and gestures me inside.

The craftsmanship of the box is clever, thoughtful. Even though the outside needs some paint touch ups, everything inside is pristine. The shelf where the cards lie is lined with a heavy brocade patterned in black on black, and directly beneath it is a slim drawer. The chute that feeds coins into the gilded porcelain bowl is polished copper. Sidney points out a small pedal on the floor, and when I tap it with my foot, the perfect rows of golden bulbs lining the ceiling light up. It's a little like a jewelry box.

It's a lot like a prison.

"Smile. Flirt. Keep that jacket on and show as little skin as possible. Don't let them see what you really are. Smile. Exaggerate the robotic movements so the rubes can't tell that you can't stop the twitching. If you get a rube to talk to you, be charming. And *smile*." He gives me a big toothy grin at that last command, as if I need a reminder of what smiling looks like. "It's terrible being cursed, but you can't let them ever, *ever* know how terrible it is."

I want to ask him how he can sleep at night knowing he was working to condemn someone else to take his place in this "terrible" box, to ask how it feels looking at the person who has taken his place, but the words die on my dry tongue. Because I'm about to do the exact same thing. But the anger still simmers.

If Sidney has a conscience, it doesn't show. "Now, the cards." A small drawer runs underneath the waist-high shelf the bowl sits upon. Inside there's a stack of the cards with that awful marionette—who now looks more feminine than I remember—along with a lone pen. He pulls one loose from the stack. With a flourish he flips it over to show me a blank card.

I remember how perfectly tuned the cards Jules and I received were. "Am I supposed to write something on all the cards? How will I know what I need?"

"Hold your horses, Em," he says.

My fingers twitch into a fist. "*You* don't get to call me that."

"Fine. Take it, *Emmaline.*" He thrusts the card at me.

"I don't see how—"

"Take. It."

My plastic-y smooth molars attempt to grind together, but they're perfect little cubes and they simply glide over each other. I watch carefully to make sure that I've taken the little card, since I can't feel it in my grip, and hold it up to stare at the creepy doll on the front.

"Now give it to me," Sidney instructs. I clamp my mouth shut but fork it over, jamming it against his chest. As he's looking at it, he smirks, a movement that brings out a dimple and crinkles his eyes. "Tell me what you really think." When the card is flipped over, there's text in vibrant red ink where there had been none. *You are an asshole.*

Sidney jumps in before I get my wits together. "Don't ask me how it works. The freaky twins tried to explain it to me once, but all I heard was blah, blah, psychic intent, blah, blah, physical manifestation. If you want to know more, I'm sure that Pia would be happy to talk your ear off about it."

The night is quickly darkening around us, the golden glow of the lightbulbs burning brighter. I'm fairly certain some of the people walking down the alley are patrons and not carnival workers. What if someone from school comes by? What if they call the cops? Duncan did a good job with the makeup—he sculpted cheekbones out of nothing, and with my darkened brows and cat's eyes I could easily pass for twenty—but is that enough? A low thrum of disquiet falls over me, and my fingers twitch rapidly.

"Expect to screw up tonight. But I'm going to be right over there if you need me." He points to a nook between a cotton candy maker and someone selling kettle corn. Why is he doing this? Is it guilt? I mean, I know Leslie told him he had to watch over me, but that doesn't mean he has to actually *help* me. "Tomorrow you and I will ride with Leslie and go over my notes."

Wait, *notes?* So not only am I stuck in this poor excuse for a body, but I'm being critiqued, too? Before I can tell him what I think about his idea of "notes," the curtain swishes back in place and the booth shakes as the door slams shut. I'm still reeling when I see him walk around the side of the booth, waving a brief hello to the woman pulling cotton candy and settling in against the other booth. His gaze flicks down and up and down again before he pulls his hands out of his pockets and mimes laying the cards on the shelf.

Right. The cards.

The moment my clumsy fingers touch the neat stack, the cards scatter in the drawer. I don't dare look at Sidney to see what he thinks of my bumbling. Instead, I concentrate on laying out orderly rows of cards on the black-fabric shelf.

When they're all laid out and there's nothing inside the booth to worry over, I look around. People flood the aisle between booths. Their hands are full of deep-fried meats and unruly ribbons of prize tickets, soda cups, and neon-furred stuffed animals. Their gazes dart from booth to booth, pausing briefly on that which is bright, brighter, brightest. All too rarely do their glances stop on me.

How am I supposed to trick someone when no one ever gives me the time of day? All I want is to go home to sleep in my own bed tonight. But as the avenue pulses with people who are looking every which way but at me, I know that's not going to happen.

The night wears on, and I have a few lonely quarters in the bowl on the shelf and I've given out some senseless fortunes, one to a girl who couldn't have been more than ten, one to her brother who was even younger, and one to an old lady whose husband dropped the coin in the slot for her. All the while, Sidney has been watching, empty food wrappers and soda cups piling at his feet

The night grows darker, the patrons fewer and farther between, even in this crowded area of the carnival, and my feeble hopes of passing along this curse tonight are suffering a slow death. Sidney is chatting up the girl who works the cotton candy machine instead of watching me. The chill night air from outside is seeping into the box, making the twitching and jerking worse. I have failed.

That's when Jules walks by.

Her hair is a ratty mess, the curls crushed and twisted up into a messy knot. She has on the same clothes she wore last night—an oversize purple sweater slipping off one shoulder and jeans that used to be black but have faded to a smoky gray. Her eyes are puffy and red, and her shoulders slump. Shawn, the boy she left me to go flirt with, is by her side, looking as though he'd rather be anywhere but here.

Sidney didn't say what to do when the only person you could call a friend comes looking for you. What to do when this girl has been crying her eyes out for you. When a walking, talking reminder of what you've lost comes trudging past your booth.

If this body were any softer, it would crumple beneath the weight of the stupid mistake I've made.

"Come on, Juliet," Shawn says. The crowd muffles his voice, but the noise of the carnival patrons can't hide his boredom. "Do you really think you're going to find Emmaline when the cops couldn't?"

Jules stops suddenly, forcing Shawn to a halt, too. "*Yes*. Maybe." Tears streak down her cheeks, and it's easy to tell they're not the first of the night. "She came here with me. And I left her when I should have stayed, and now she's gone. I have to make it right. I *have* to."

"Yeah, but…" Shawn makes a circling motion with his hand, as though encouraging Juliet to put the pieces of some obvious puzzle together. "She was kind of a bitch, so I don't see why you're so worked up."

Juliet slaps him, fast enough he didn't see it coming and hard enough to leave a mark. My jaw drops. I want nothing more than to run out there and hug her, one of those bone-crushing hugs where neither of you can breathe but no one dares to let go. My chest feels tight, like it's clamped in a vise.

Shawn skulks off, rubbing his cheek and leaving Jules in the middle of the alley. Once the crowds swallow him up, Juliet tilts her head to the night sky. Her lids are swollen and pink from crying, and her whole body sags, like all the fight's gone out of her.

As she turns away, her gaze roves over the booth and our eyes meet.

I don't want her to see me like this. If she looks at me with an ounce of pity, I'll break. I'll let her convince me to leave, to go home where I can't be fixed. And I want to be fixed.

Jules runs to the booth, her palms slapping against the glass. "Em!" she screams, her words slightly dampened by the glass, "Em, thank God! Get out of there!"

Tears make her eyes jewel bright. My chest feels like bands of iron are constricting around me, but I can't give in, I can't.

"Where have you been? Your dad won't stop crying, Emma; we're all going crazy." She looks lost now, like I should have given up the ruse already. Her fist hits the wooden frame. "This isn't funny, Emma. Come out, please."

My dad hasn't stopped crying.

I almost break. Maybe it wouldn't hurt to tell her now, so she can let everyone know I'm okay. Well, okay-ish. But I can't. *I cannot.* My fingers twitch, and I pray Jules doesn't notice. I turn the movement into a slow sweep of my hand toward the coin slot.

Jules looks down to dig in her purse, and when she does, I remember how Sidney had worked the box, and I change my pose. Let her think that I've been doing this for years. Let her doubt. Just let her think that I'm not Emmaline.

Jules finds a quarter, and she slips it into the slot. The coin falls down the track and lands next to the others I've collected tonight. Fine. Again, I pretend that I'm Sidney, a coldhearted jerk who doesn't care, just another part of the show.

I turn and twist and pretend to think about just which fortune is the right one for Jules. I need her gone, as far away from here as possible. If the cops think I'm a runaway and Leslie is saying she never saw me, I need Jules to believe that for now. I force every thought of Jules and home away and play my part. The card in the corner seems as good as any, and I pick it up.

My chest hitches, spasms with tears I can't shed. *Just let the card go, Emmaline. Just drop it into the tray and get it over with.* The card falls into the tray.

Juliet chews her lip and I know that she's doubting now, unsure as to what she should do. The card I've given her has just four words on it, four words that I was mentally shouting as I plucked the card up from the shelf. She pulls the tray open, retrieves the card, and reads them now. Her eyes fill with new tears.

Know when to quit.

Jules drops the card. There's almost nothing to her voice, as though the very essence of it has been wrung out when she says, "It's not you. Emma would never be so mean to me."

Something inside me cracks, a fissure of stinging pain radiating out from my heart. I force myself to hold my pose as Juliet throws one more glance my way. It's only when she's melted into the crowd, when the squeezing around my chest subsides, that I pull the curtains of my booth closed. I am done for the night, *done*. I crash to the ground with enough force to rock the tiny box. A gust of wind swirls the curtains when the door opens, and Sidney looks down at me, his eyebrows arched in pity and panic.

And that is when I know that I am well and truly fucked.

CHAPTER EIGHT

Benjamin

The stripped carnival grounds echo with the sounds of car doors slamming and shouted instructions. The tents and booths and rides are loaded up, and this tiny town is about to become one more memory to fade as we put it in our rearview.

I sit behind the wheel of the Gran Torino, waiting for Marcel to finish checking the fluids. A few workers dart from truck to truck, making last-minute checks before we drive off. The windows are cranked down, and a breeze carrying a hint of rain rushes through the car.

"Ben!" In the rearview mirror, my mother storms toward the car.

Marcel peeks around the extended hood, and I can just barely hear him say, "Aw, shit."

My mother is a study in determination. She strides toward us with purpose, her long golden braid swinging in time behind her. In the last two days, she's been on a rampage. The to-do list she gave me yesterday was a mile long, and included some things I'd taken care of not even a week ago. When I'd asked her about it, she said I hadn't done it right the first time and needed to do it again. Which is bullshit. The day my mother lets me get away with doing a half-assed job at *anything* is the day she goes into the ground. As my mother draws closer to the car, she gives Marcel a quick nod before bending down to peer at me through the open window. "I want you to ride with me."

Around us, the other trucks and cars rumble to life, exhaust fumes wafting in the open car windows.

"Marcel and I are taking the car. Same as we have the last few months." As if to punctuate my point, Marcel chooses that moment to slam the hood down, but let it be a testament to the iron will of my mother—she doesn't flinch.

"I would prefer it if you were to ride with me," my mother says, slowly pronouncing each word. The only time Mom gets like this is when she is seriously pissed. Problem is I have no idea what she's so pissed about.

The big truck loaded with the dismantled roller coaster pulls away from the grassy lot, and never have I been so grateful to get on the road. Mom watches the line of vehicles lurch forward and we both know she needs to get to her truck and get moving before people start to get impatient. She sighs.

"We will discuss this later," Mom says, one finger stabbing the air between us. She turns on her heel with military precision, her braid swishing after her.

I slump into the driver's seat as Marcel climbs in, then fire up the car and slide into a gap between the Connellys' horse trailer and the big truck carrying Lars's

Ferris wheel. Neither of us says anything until we pull onto the freeway.

My grip tightens on the steering wheel, and by the time we've merged into traffic, my fingers are throbbing in time with my pulse. "I can't do this anymore, man, I can't." I take a deep breath and ask the question I know he doesn't want to hear. "Are you sure we can't just leave now?"

Marcel focuses on the road in front of us like he's the one driving. "I thought we said another couple of months?"

"You saw what I'm dealing with! Another couple of months and I'm going to go crazy."

"My mom would flip out!"

"*My* mom is *already* flipping out!"

"I *can't* go yet, Ben. I just can't."

I want to scream, to slam my fist on the steering wheel, but I don't. He's right. He's right and it's not fair to pressure him to leave now when we *just* came to the decision to stay a little bit longer. And it's not his fault my mom is on the warpath for reasons unknown.

Doesn't mean it isn't a suckfest.

So I let it go, for now, and watch the fields blurring past.

We're parked at a truck stop somewhere in Oklahoma, waiting for all the cars and trucks to fill up on gas. Marcel and I eye the meter as he pumps gas into the Gran Torino, watching the dollars and cents hurtle toward the amount we'd prepaid and while the gallons creep toward an amount that might fill our tank halfway. I love this car, but it burns through gas like there's no tomorrow.

There's a dull *thunk* as the fuel line shuts off and Marcel caps the tank. "You want anything from inside?" he asks, jerking his finger toward the minimart. I shake my head, and he nods and heads into the little shop, the bells hanging over the door jingling merrily as he swings the door wide.

Dirty gray water streams off the ratty squeegee attached to the pump, but it still works, so I use it to scrape the haze of dead bugs off our windshield. My thoughts flicker over the new Girl in the Box, of how painful it was to watch her stumble between the rows of trailers and how lost she must feel. The way she'd seemed so vibrantly alive when I'd seen her before, and how sadness seemed to ooze out of her every pore afterward. Her situation sucks, but it's not enough to keep me here. I don't even know her. Water from the bucket sloshes onto my jeans as I toss the squeegee back into it.

A streak of girl whips past in my peripheral vision. Heavier footsteps pound the concrete behind the car, and when Duncan pulls up beside me, he's soaked, his white T-shirt stained by dirty squeegee water.

"Help a brother out," he says, tossing a small pack of convenience store doughnuts in my direction before chasing after the girls again. I rip into the flimsy plastic wrapper on the doughnuts and take off, seconds behind him.

Duncan can't aim for shit, but you don't need good aim if your target's right in front of you. I tear across the parking lot, following Whiskey's exuberant shrieks. Once I'm close, I fling a doughnut at Whiskey and hit her square

on the back. It startles a squeal out of her loud enough
to turn heads, and she runs faster.

I follow, gaze locked on her back. Gasoline-scented
air fills my lungs and blows back my hair. I have a handful
of doughnuts at the ready when something soft hits my
chest and little plumes of white billow upward. The first
hit is followed by another, and then another. A cloud
of black curls peeks from between two of the carnival's
trucks, and I about-face to chase after Pia.

As I race toward one girl, the other attacks. I wheel
around to face Whiskey, and she grins with devilish glee.
My grin mimics hers, I know. Whiskey backtracks and
begins to run loops around Leslie's truck. When she turns
to see how close I am, there's a powdered sugar circle on
her cheek and one over her eye. A small white object flies
past my shoulder and hits Whiskey on the nose. "Duncan!"
Whiskey screams. "You motherfucking twat weasel!"

"You kiss your mother with that mouth, Whiskey?"
Duncan asks. He's put on an extra burst of speed to catch
up with us, and more doughnuts have appeared out of
nowhere.

Almost as if she can sense her impending doom,
Whiskey glances back at us over her shoulder. "I kiss
your mother with this mouth!" she shrieks. She tumbles
to the ground in front of the truck as Duncan throws
every sugary doughnut he has at her. Whiskey gasps for
air between bursts of laughter. Duncan's out of ammo,
and I reach down to help Whiskey up. The flecks of sugar
scattered across my glasses blur her face. Just as I'm about
to call truce, Whiskey stuffs a gravel-crusted doughnut
down the front of my shirt and takes off once again.

I'm doubled over laughing, both unable to believe the

balls on that girl and also completely aware that Whiskey probably has more balls than the Moretti brothers combined. I still have a few doughnuts left and am about to go chase after her, when I feel someone staring at me.

There, in the cab of Leslie's truck, sits the new Girl in the Box. She stares at me with wide, somber eyes. She was pretty before, and while she still looks like herself, she also looks ethereal, like she's not from this world. The paleness of her skin contrasts sharply with her dark hair, which swoops across her forehead to curl over one cheek and beneath her delicately pointed chin. Her gaze locks onto mine, dark honey-gold eyes piercing, and I realize how we must have looked to her. How exclusionary, cliquish. The urge to apologize is an ache in my chest. But before I can figure out what to say, the girl turns her head, focusing on Sidney, who sits beside her.

I'm halfway back to the Gran Torino when I see Gin leaning gracefully against the passenger door. Marcel has one hand propped up near her shoulder and seems to get closer to Gin with every word that comes out of his mouth. The message couldn't be clearer.

Part of me is ridiculously happy—if Marcel can come to a decision one way or another about Gin, that puts us one step closer to getting away from here. Or at least, it puts *me* one step closer. But while I know I should let Marcel drive Gin in the car, this means I'm stuck doing the very thing I didn't want to do earlier—riding with my mother.

But getting what I want in the long run is better than a potentially uncomfortable conversation with my mother. I mean, I've survived hundreds of those. How bad could one more be?

My mom's eyebrow twitches upward when I climb into the cab of the truck, but she doesn't say anything, not yet. The cars and trucks and vans file back onto the highway, those up front setting a slow pace so the caravan can stick together. It's not until we're all rumbling down the highway again that she speaks. "I don't appreciate what happened earlier."

I sigh. I love my mom, I really do, but it doesn't help that she's quite possibly one of the most combative people I've ever met in my entire life. Maybe it has something to do with excelling in a field typically dominated by men, always having to stand up for herself and prove that she can do anything a male carpenter can do, if not better. Or maybe she's still protective of me, always thinking of the car accident that killed my dad and nearly took me with it. Whatever it is, I'd be really glad if she would at least tone it down with me. "Sorry," I say, though there isn't much by way of apology in the tone of my voice. "I just needed some space."

She huffs out a small, sarcastic laugh. "Space" can be hard to come by in our cramped living quarters and the fact that we see the same people day in and day out. "Well, strange things are afoot. Time for us to really stick together."

The "we need to stick together" shtick isn't new. But her intensity is.

I dare a glance toward her, but she's concentrating on the road as if we were driving up a curving mountain in the snow, not the flat, barren plains of Oklahoma. "I don't really see how I'm not," I say, bracing myself for her to go into great detail as to how I'm wrong.

Her gaze darts over to meet mine. "You know who I'm talking about."

• • •

Ardmore, Oklahoma, is flat and brown and dull. At first glance, none of the buildings seem to be more than one story. The streets have fewer cars and more people walking around. The caravan stops on one of the smaller side streets. A select group of performers—Gin and Whiskey, the Moretti brothers, the fire-eaters—clamber out of trucks and vans, ready to perform as we make our molasses-slow trek through town.

Leslie once told me this was cheaper by far than an actual parade. The sight of the brothers tumbling and plumes of fire spilling from our fire-eaters' mouths piques the interest of the passersby. Gin and Whiskey, barefoot and wearing simple dancer's leotards and tights, balance on the naked backs of their horses as they clop alongside trailers laden with tarp-covered machinery. Even though our truck is toward the end of the procession, the effect our performers have on the townies is evident. Faces glow with wonderment, children twist around to watch even as their parents lead them away. One can't help but smile in return.

A loud, hollow *thump* breaks my concentration. Antonio Moretti has leaped onto the hood of our truck, the metal groaning in protest under his weight. But he nimbly jumps from the hood to the roof of the cab to the top of the Airstream, and even though our windows are rolled up, I can hear the gasps of the townies as they follow his movements.

"Show-offs," I mutter.

"They get butts in seats," Mom says, grinding out the words from between her teeth as she leans forward in her seat to check the hood for lasting damage.

After our makeshift parade, we set up in a field not five miles away from city hall. Even though I've helped make it happen hundreds of times, I'm always amazed at the way the carnival unfolds with clockwork precision. The trucks and trailers zip to their places, always the same, no matter where we land. Machinery and rides unfurl like the petals of big mechanical flowers. What had been nothing more than a pile of pipes and carriages turns into Lars's Ferris wheel. The massive tarp covering the haunted house ride comes down with the aid of a handful of workers and the giant spider and bat are hoisted to the roof.

Within two hours of our arrival, a little city has sprung up. The moment the Airstream is parked and Mom goes off to find the cook shack, I gather up my tools and head for the edge of the yard, where the small wooden wagon meant for the person in the box is usually set up.

The old wagon has always been on my maintenance list. Mom never had much to say about it, so I took that as my cue to do whatever I wanted. A few years ago I gave it an overhaul; the body of the wagon is painted a flaming scarlet and trimmed in an orange that is cheery and happy. Copper nails as bright as new pennies run along the slats over the rounded roof and gleam in the sunlight. The door is a cerulean circle, with a little window of dark glass set in the middle.

Sidney has lived in the wagon for as long as I can remember, but the wagon belongs to the person in the box. Before we broke camp, I saw Sidney, a weak cardboard box crammed full of his things in his arms, talking to Mrs. Potter. After a moment Sidney climbed the rickety steps leading to her trailer, and he didn't come back out.

When I try to open the wagon door, it swings outward with a creak. A narrow bed runs along one side of the wagon, buried beneath a heap of pillows in a myriad of colors. Patchwork quilts lie in a tangled heap on the floor, and the big leather trunk by the door skews toward the middle of the small space. There wasn't much to the place to begin with, but what there was, Sidney trashed.

I stack up the pillows and fold the blankets. The trunk goes back along the wall where it belongs. I sweep the cobwebs out of the skylight set into the ceiling and oil the hinges on the door and the little window sitting over the bed. A small glass lantern hangs near the entrance, and I pull it down to give it a quick polish. It's not much, but the place looks better now than it did when I walked in. I hope she likes it.

As I'm headed back toward the Airstream, I hear Leslie one row of trailers over. I stop and watch as they walk toward the little wagon.

The girl walks beside Leslie, her shoulders rolled in, her chin tucked to her chest. As though she can't bear the thought of anyone looking at her. There is a nearly overwhelming urge to rush over to where they stand and wrap my arms around her, as if I could be a shield for her. They stop a few feet away from the wagon, and if I hold my breath, I can hear what Leslie is saying.

Leslie smiles at the girl with a mixture of pride and tentative hope. "It took us a few days to get Sidney set up somewhere else, and I'm sorry about that. But this wagon belongs to the occupant of the box." Leslie strokes the side of the ladder that leads to the door. "What you're going through is terrible, we know it is, though we can never truly understand. It's a small comfort, but we want you to have a place that's just your own, a place that you can use to escape."

A weak, wobbly smile lifts the corners of the girl's mouth as her gaze roves over the outside of the wagon, a shadow of the smile I saw the other night, when she was with her friend. I wonder what it would take to get her to smile for real.

"What about Sidney?"

"Sidney can make do." Leslie's smile broadens into a grin. "Have you seen the way he's been eating? I wouldn't be surprised to see him waddle out of the cook shack one of these mornings like Templeton the Rat." She dangles a small copper key from the end of a length of faded red ribbon. "It's like I said—the carnival owes the person in the box. This is the least we can do for you in return."

The girl's hand shakes as she reaches for the key, and she wraps her slender fingers around it tightly, as though she's afraid of dropping it. I lose sight of her as she steps inside, and all I can do now is hope she likes the wagon.

I turn to head home and feel the sickening lurch as my foot lands in a slick patch of mud and whips out from beneath me. I throw out my arm. A flash of white-hot pain flares through my hand, but I manage to keep my footing. I step out of the mud that had nearly sent me sprawling on my ass, unsure as to how I even missed it in the first place. Then my hand begins to throb.

A gash runs diagonally across my palm. Blood wells from the wound, filling my cupped hand. The pain sets in, a deep pulsing starting in my palm and radiating up my arm. I glance over at the trailer and see a splash of red smeared along a sharp flap of metal. I must have sliced my hand on that as I tried to grab onto something to keep from slipping.

Falling on carnival grounds doesn't happen; the charm sees to that. But my bloodied hand begs to differ.

CHAPTER NINE

Benjamin

I spend the morning sanding away all the peeling paint on the haunted house and sketch in new bats and skeletons and spiders. I talk to Mrs. Potter, spending a good forty-five minutes with her as she gestures wildly and periodically shushes her little white terrier while she tells me what she'd like her new mural to look like. I make a few quick line drawings of the dog—I can never remember if his name is Toffrey or Joffrey or what—for reference and promise her I'll be back.

After lunch, I find Lars and give him a demo of the new remote control I've built for the Ferris wheel. Originally, he'd asked me to fix the control panel; the wood covering had become so weathered that rainwater had seeped inside, shorting out the wiring. Once I had a good look at the electrical system, I figured it would be pretty easy to build a remote, so he wouldn't be stuck hovering over the control panel all night.

"It's pretty easy," I say, my gaze locked on the smoothly

spinning wheel. "The green button sets the cars spinning; the red stops them." To illustrate my point, I depress the red button, and the wheel slows to a stop. I'm not as good as Lars is, and the car doesn't line up with the platform, but I manage to get it close enough.

Lars takes the controller from me. His giant hands make it look like it should control a toy car, not a carnival ride. "Nicely done, Ben," he says. I try not to preen. Praise from Lars is a rare thing.

"Afternoon, boys." Leslie stomps up the steps to stand beside us on the platform. "I hate to run you off, Ben, but I need to talk to Lars for a second."

"Sure," I say, tossing a few odds and ends back into my tool kit. But as I stand, my tools in hand, I can't make myself leave. "Actually, Leslie, I have something I've been meaning to talk to you about."

Her pale brows lift. "Oh? Do we need to speak in private?" She gestures toward the stairs, but I shake my head.

"No. I don't mind if Lars is here."

"Okay then," Leslie says, leaning her hip against the guardrail. "What's going on?"

"I don't think the Morettis should be here." Once that first statement is out, everything else follows in a rush. "I mean, I understand that they're talented and that they bring in crowds, but they're kind of jerks, you know? And the other day, I caught Lorenzo trying to convince one of the new kids that if he stuck his hand in a trash can fire, the charm would save him."

Leslie's eyes go wide, but she doesn't say anything, as though she knows I'm not quite done. And I'm not. I want to tell her that they're not the kind of people who belong here, that they don't appreciate what the charm does for them, but it's too hard to find the words to explain that don't also make me seem petty. So I shrug and say, "That's all. Thought you should know."

Leslie blows out a breath as she steps away from the guardrail, gaze trained on the well-worn wood we're standing on. When she looks at me, she's as serious as I've ever seen her. "Thank you for telling me, Benjamin, and thank you for stopping Lorenzo from hurting that employee. You see or hear anything else, let me know, and I'm going to keep an eye on them, okay?"

I nod, even though I want more than that. I want them gone, even if I myself don't plan to stay very much longer, because the brothers feel like a splotch, a tarnish on this place. "Thanks, Leslie," I say as I collect my tool kit and leave.

Suddenly I feel tired, as though confessing to Leslie has physically drained me. The cut on my hand throbs, but I still have work to do, especially if I don't want to catch heat from Mom. And in particular, I need to power through if I don't want her to keep me from working on the box.

The fortune-teller's box is the one task that has always fallen to me, ever since I was old enough to use the power saw unsupervised. When I was thirteen, I rebuilt the thing from scratch. I know it's silly, but I'd almost be offended if Mom decided to take that away from me, and given how weird she's been about the new girl, she just might. So I know that if she catches me slacking off even a little, she'll have a reason. I wrap the bandage on my hand a little more tightly and get back to work.

After lunch, I find the box set up along the outer

perimeter of attractions, near Lars's Ferris wheel. I don't know why the crew decides to change the setup every now and then—maybe just for the hell of it—but they do. I also know that some old superstition keeps most of the vendors from setting up close to the Ferris wheel, and in this spot, the little red booth sticks out like a blemish at the edge of the carnival.

They just dropped the box down, not caring about how it might look to passersby, so I wipe some dust from the base and pull the weeds poking from underneath. I check her out. She needs a good cleaning; fingerprints dot the glass, and dirt clings to the molding at the base. There are a couple of chips, and the gold paint has flaked off the glass in a few spots, but nothing too bad. I've just climbed in through the door at the back to test the bulbs when someone yells at me.

"Hey! What are you doing to my booth?"

My head crashes into the drawer under the shelf. As I rub the throbbing away, I take a look at the girl yelling at me.

It's the new girl. Her eyes widen in recognition when she sees me but narrow again in righteous suspicion. Full lips tug downward to an almost frown, and I wonder what they look like when she's smiling. She's been raiding Gin's closet; I'd always thought Gin was thin, but now that I see one of her sweaters swallowing this girl whole, I can tell Gin has muscles and strength to her. A twitch rattles her whole body to the left, and she hugs herself tightly.

"Just checking it," I say. "For maintenance."

"Oh," she says, her shoulders easing back to a more relaxed position. She looks around, taking in the Ferris wheel and the other booths standing a short distance away. "Do, um… Do you think you could move it? I need to be by the midway, where there's more people."

"Yeah." My mind is already in motion, trying to figure out the best place for the booth and where I last saw the dolly. Which is halfway across the yard. "I just have to get the dolly. But I swear I'll have it in place before we open tonight. Want to show me where you'd like it?"

She smiles so quickly that I barely catch it, like a star blazing across the night sky. But then she says, "That'd be great." Her gaze darts toward the ground, lingering on the random paintbrushes jutting out from my tool kit. "You aren't the one who painted those big murals out front, are you?"

"Of the performers?" I ask, even though I can't think of anything else she might be talking about.

"Yeah. You know, the fortune-tellers—I guess one is Duncan? And I'm pretty sure one is of Gin and another is of the tumbler brothers."

The grin spreads across my face quickly, fully formed before I'm even aware I'm doing it. She saw my paintings. And it sounds like she *liked* them. "Those are mine."

"They're *fabulous*," she says, eyes widening. "The way you used color in the one of the knife thrower was perfect, and you made Duncan and his sister seem so creepy. I tried to tell my friend Juliet how great they were, but she's not into art. Do you get to paint often?"

"Carpentry comes first, but Leslie likes my work, so whenever she needs something painted, she comes to me."

Her gaze goes soft, distant. "I miss painting. I hadn't done it before I moved back to Oklahoma, and well, now…" As her voice drifts off, she lifts a hand. There's a fine tremor in her fingers, interspersed with sharp jerks of her whole arm. She winces, and I don't know if it's because she's in pain or embarrassed, but before she can pull her hand away I take it in my own.

"My name's Ben, by the way," I say as I shake her hand. I'm so focused on trying to make her feel more comfortable that I don't notice right away. There's a chill to her skin that's off, and her fingers are unyielding, firm. It's like I'm not shaking a hand at all but rather a carving of one. Then she smiles, and the cold radiating off her doesn't even register anymore.

"Emma."

Emma. Okay, fine.

Maybe Mom was right to worry a little.

CHAPTER TEN

Emma

I don't care what Sidney said about the clothes I've chosen to wear—I like the dress and the jacket. But for some reason, I've kept his stupid hat. There's something about it that feels important, like it's a talisman or something.

Ben moved my booth earlier this afternoon, insisting I follow him as he did so to make sure I would be able to find it later. I'd offered to help, but let's be honest—walking in a straight line these days is hard. Besides, from my vantage point beside him, I could watch the stretch and pull of the muscles in his arms and catch a peek at his flat stomach as he dabbed the sweat from his brow with his T-shirt.

As I'm walking toward the spot where Ben moved my booth, I see Duncan waving at me frantically. He sits in the middle of a tent made of brightly paneled canvas on the outside, plush drapes and colored-glass lanterns on the inside. Only a few patrons are here this early, so I head inside.

It's everything that pop culture wants me to think a fortune-teller's tent should be. A small table covered in layers of scarves sits in the middle, but instead of a crystal ball, there are several chunks of quartz set upon it. A few teapots on electric burners sit in the corner, with a teetering stack of mismatched porcelain cups behind them. Loose teas in glass jars cover the surface the next table over. Thin plumes of smoke trail from cones of incense, and I miss the smell. Mom always, *always* had some burning in her office back home. And lined up neatly on a shelf at the back of a tent, near a loosely closed flap, are dark-green glass bottles that look way too familiar.

Duncan beckons me closer to the table. "Emma, meet my sister." He gestures to the girl at the back of the tent. A cloud of black curls frames a pretty, dark-brown face with perfect cheekbones. Both siblings have the same mischievous smile that probably did—and *does*—get them into trouble constantly. Curves strain at her vintage T-shirt, and she has stacks of mismatched bracelets on each arm.

"So," Duncan is saying, "this is Pia." As I get closer I realize she has a tiny silver stud at the curve of her nostril. When she grabs my hand, warmth fills it, and I don't want to let go.

"Sorry about the curse thing," Pia says as she plops down into the chair next to Duncan. She picks up a worn tarot deck, shuffling the cards between her hands as she talks, her plump fingers nimble and quick.

"Why would you be sorry?"

She shrugs and makes the cards jump from one hand to the other. "Family history says it was our great-aunt who started it." She points to the corner with the bottles of wine. "We make that. It takes a year to produce one bottle, and according to family legend, it's our penance. You can take a bottle to keep in the booth if you want, or just swing by here when you've got a rube."

"Is that why you helped me the other day?" I ask Duncan, thinking back on my makeover in the costume trailer.

He waves a hand at me. "Nah. That had more to do with my love of gossip than anything else."

"I wish I could do a reading for you," Pia says, grabbing my hand suddenly and running a finger over my unlined palm. "You'll have to come back when you transfer the curse."

"There are other ways to do readings," Duncan says, his eyes alight with interest. "But," he says with a sigh, glancing past me to the growing flux of customers outside, "it'll have to be another time."

I leave and make my way through the carnival, past a woman with impossibly purple hair and a pack of dogs—including the scruffy terrier who cuddled with me my first night here—jumping up and down ramps and through hoops, and past a pen where Gin is riding a horse bareback. There I have to stop for just a second to watch.

There's no saddle, just Gin and the horse. She runs him in an easy canter around the pen, and then rises to stand on his back in one fluid motion. She sees me watching from the perimeter and gives me a wave and a wild *whoop* before sitting back down. I continue my search.

After leaving Gin, it isn't long before I find the box, exactly where Ben promised me it would be, prominently in the center of the midway. The scarlet paint is a fiery glow in the lights of the other midway attractions. The glass glitters, the gold leaf swirls prettily on the sides. Inside, the curtain twitches just before Ben appears. He

ducks down, and a moment later the golden lights wash
the interior with their bright glow. He runs a cloth over
some smudge on the glass, drops a few quarters into the
bowl, and with one last look around, he exits the booth.

For whatever reason, it's easier to trust him, more so
than anyone else I've met so far. Maybe it's because he
oozes sincerity, like he can't even help himself but to be
honest. Maybe it's because try as I might, I can't seem to
find an agenda with him—no guilt to work off, no selfish
reasons for being here. Or maybe it's just because I'm
apparently a sucker for a boy with ridiculously adorable
Disney-prince hair and brilliant-blue eyes.

"Hey," he says, his voice as bright as the new bulbs he
just installed in the booth. His shirt has shifted, showing
off the line marking his golden tan and the lighter, actual
color of his skin. It takes me longer than I'm proud of
to drag my gaze away. "Made a few tweaks, cleaned the
thing up. The drawer on the inside was sticking, so I oiled
the tracks, but let me know if it gives you trouble, okay?"

I nod, racking my brain for something clever to say,
but it seems as though the curse has petrified the witty
part of my brain, too. I may spend a little more time than
is polite watching his slightly too-small T-shirt move over
the muscles in his back as he walks away.

When I get into the booth, I can see the small touches
he's put into place. The quarters make it seem like other
people have already found me interesting enough to take
a chance on a fortune. I think he's upped the wattage on
the lightbulbs, because the inside of the box is warmer
than before, and my twitching is just a little bit less than
it had been the other night. When your world is all about
being stuck in the cold, you notice things like that.

The crowds trickle in. I'm between a booth selling sodas and a row of Skee-Ball machines, so there are far more people around than last time. The quarters in my bowl multiply, but not a one of their donors seems like a good candidate to take over my position. I don't have the nerve to ask Sidney why he chose me—I know what he'll say and I don't think my delicate ego can take it. I was alone and I was gullible as hell. In a word—perfect. None of the patrons so far fit that description. There are too many bright and shining stars that would be missed if I forced them into this life.

Until the boy shows up.

He's alone, and that's a good start. His eyes are as dark as his hair, which seems like it might be curly if he grew it out. He wanders up with a vague curiosity, reading the swirling gold promises of futures told that decorate the glass. When he isn't looking, I put on the most charming smile I have in my arsenal.

A stab of guilt hits me in the gut when I think about taking this boy out of his life. But then a spasm knocks my leg into the side of the booth hard enough to make the boy look around, and I think about feeling warm again. About breathing and a breeze tickling my skin.

I can do this.

The boy digs into his pocket and finds a quarter, a bright and shiny thing in the dark, and he slips it into the slot. As it *plinks* on top of the others that fill the bowl, I start my act. I remember Sidney, and what he had done. The boy watches my every move, the way I gaze at him from under my lashes, how I tap my chin thoughtfully as I pretend to contemplate. There is a split second where I could change my mind, where I could offer him some banal fortune and send him on his way. But when I drop the card into the tray, I know what it will say.

You will soon take a fall.

His lips move as he reads the card, then pick up in a small grin. He rereads the words on his card, and I can see the flush climb up his cheeks, the pulse thumping in his neck. He is vibrantly alive. *I can't do it. I can't.* While his gaze flits over the words on the card yet again, I swish the curtain shut and dim the lights, dropping down to the floor of the booth.

As I sit there in the dark, my knees literally knocking, my chest vibrating with panic, the clumsy teenage boy steps circles around my booth, looking for me, or maybe a handle to get in to confront me. I am so, so glad for the hidden latch that opens the back door. The boy lets out a feeble, "What the hell?" before his steps recede into the sounds of other patrons, games, and rides.

I almost did it. I mean, I had no idea if the boy would have gone along with it or if he would have run off, but for a few seconds, I was going to trick that boy and steal him away from his family. To become a monster of the same brand as Sidney, callous and cold, willing to bring a kid to death's door for my own freedom.

A great hiccupping shudder runs through my body and I burrow my head into my arms, wishing for something more than the all-encompassing darkness surrounding me. Because maybe it's not even a matter of *becoming* a monster like Sidney. I had been willing to trick the boy, hadn't I? Ready to pass on this horrible curse even though he thought he was just out for a fun night at a regular old carnival.

Maybe I already am a monster.

CHAPTER ELEVEN

Benjamin

The night is crisp and cool, though not as cold as it had been in the last town. Mrs. Potter's dogs yap happily as she runs them through their paces. The Ferris wheel spins in a whirl of blue and orange lights against the navy sky; Lars stands at the base fiddling with the buttons on the new remote control I built. Nearby, someone has just rung the bell on the strongman game. I'm hit with the scent of turkey legs, followed quickly by butter and sugar as I near the kettle corn booth. The carnival food we sell to the townies usually gets real old, real quick, but tonight it smells delicious. That, or I'm starving.

I pass the red box again, but the bright rows of lights are off and Emma is nowhere to be seen. I stop in the middle of the busy aisle. What could have happened in the few hours since I last saw her? Is she already luring someone off, preparing him or her to take her place in the booth? I think that all she has to do is kiss him, or at least, that's what Whiskey told me once. It could be happening right now. Sidney is standing across the way, and I walk over.

"Hey," I say. I point to the box behind me. "What's going on?"

He swallows a huge chunk of caramel apple. "I could ask you the same. Haven't seen her tonight. I got here late, never saw her."

My brows furrow together, and I try to keep myself calm. If Sidney never saw Emma tonight, maybe she just didn't feel up to working. Either way, I'm sure she's fine. And even if she *was* kissing someone else, that's totally within her rights to do so. I shift my grip on my toolbox and walk on. If I drop off my things at the trailer now and run back from the yard, I might be able to catch Marcel before his next show. He's unveiling a new act tonight, a routine he's been working on with Gin, and it sounds like they've put together something spectacular.

But as I cross the alley, meaning to slip through the space between the box and the cotton candy booth it sits near, I hear a *thump*. And then another, this one followed by a soft whine.

Toffrey stands on his hind legs, tiny white paws scratching at the seam in the box. When I step around and he sees me, he lets out a long, trembling whine and paws at the door again. My fingers find the hidden latch and when the door swings gently open, my gaze drops to find Emma huddled on the floor. Pale arms hug her knees, elbows jutting out at stiff angles. I hear another one of those soft thumps as a great, rolling tremble starts at the base of her spine and rattles all the way up her shoulders, knocking them against the wooden wall. Toffrey scrambles into her lap, his nails clacking against her limbs, and her arms wind around him, hugging him tight.

"Hey," I say, hoping the panic I feel over seeing her like this isn't showing on my face. I crouch down to put us at eye level. "You okay? What happened?"

At the sound of my voice, her gaze drifts from my shoes to my face. Toffrey wriggles against her chest, tiny pink tongue darting out to lick the underside of her chin. "I should…" she says, glancing up at the darkened lights above, "I mean…"

"Girl in the Box!"

My shoulders tense. The Morettis crowd around us, their shadows covering the girl in darkness. Toffrey's low growl is barely audible, but the idea of the small terrier going up against any one of the brothers is as laughable as a kindergartner going up against a seasoned marine.

"Miss, is this roustabout bothering you?"

I turn and am practically nose to nose with Fabrizio, the oldest of the meatheads. His eyes, normally dark, seem even more so ringed with the thick eyeliner he wears as part of his costume. A costume that leaves no doubts as to how strong and muscled he is. And while hauling lumber around the yard means I can hold my own, I've got no doubts that Fabrizio is much faster than me, not to mention the fact he's flanked by a brother on each side.

I draw my shoulders back and don't budge. "I'm not bothering her. She clearly needs a break or a walk or something. And it's only her second time. I really doubt it'll matter if she takes a night off at this point."

Fabrizio glances down at the toolbox by my feet and the tiny dog barking madly from the girl's lap. "Look, roustabout, these matters don't involve you. She's a performer. You are not. Now get lost and let the girl do her job." He pushes me out of the way with one hand and flicks the other at his brothers. Each bends to grab one of the girl's arms and heft her up.

"Hey!" Emma shouts as Lorenzo and Antonio lift her. The black tips of her leather shoes hover inches over the ground. She wriggles in their grasp, but the Morettis don't falter.

"Let her go," I say.

Fabrizio pushes his way into my space, his chest bumping into me, his eyes inches from mine. "This does not concern you."

If that's how he wants to play this, then fine.

I break our stare down to bend toward my toolbox and grab my staple gun. I slam a strip of half-inch staples into the reservoir and click the covering back into place. The handle butts into the healing gash on my palm, the dull throb of it anchoring me to the here and now. "I think you need to leave her be."

Fabrizio's face twists into a scowl. "Get back to work, roustabout!"

My mouth tightens.

I lift the staple gun and let the lights dance across it, a medley of pink and blue and orange over a silver gleam, so that he can see. It's not going to seriously hurt him, but it'll sting like a bitch.

"Is that supposed to scare me?" he asks.

I shift my aim so that the gun is pointed lower and fire off three staples into the meat of his thigh.

"Asshole!" he yells.

I aim higher. "Next one goes in your face. Now go."

He weighs my words, trying to see if I'm serious.

I am so serious.

Out of the corners of my eyes I see his brothers move in to strike. I let my hand squeeze the trigger, and the spring inside makes an audible groan.

Fabrizio yelps and claws at his cheek. His stubby fingers can't get a good grip on the staple, and he gives up on trying to get it out himself. As he sidles past, never letting me out of his sight, he mutters, "I'm going, asshole, I'm going."

At a nod from their brother, Antonio and Lorenzo release Emma. She stumbles against the side of the booth, sliding along it until she's sitting on the ground. Toffrey jumps back into her lap, a growl that's too small to be intimidating rumbling from his throat. The brothers glare at me as they pass, but they both follow Fabrizio like good little foot soldiers. Even so, I don't drop the staple gun until he and his brothers are well and truly gone.

Toffrey chooses this moment to leap from Emma's lap, dashing a few feet ahead of me before planting his short legs in the gray dirt and yapping at the retreating figures. I can't believe I just did that. I'll have hell to pay now in one form or another, but at the moment, I don't care. Emma needed me.

Emma is still sitting on the ground beside the booth when I turn around, and Toffrey stations himself beside her. I drop the gun back into my tool kit and offer her a hand. The glazed look in her eyes slowly fades away as she returns to the here and now. She slides her hand into mine and lets me help her stand.

"You know them?" Bitterness tinges her words, sharp and cutting.

I let her go and back away, walking toward my tools. "Unfortunately. I work here. I know everyone."

"They always like that?"

The alleyway the Moretti brothers disappeared down is now filled with carnival patrons, but I still can't shake the notion that they're hiding just around the corner, listening to what I say. "Just with me. When Leslie brought them on, they tried to get their dad hired, too. As a carpenter. Leslie told them we already had two carpenters, and the best she could do for him was something in custodial. They've held it against my mom and me ever since."

She nods slowly as she digests what I've told her.

"Do you want to go back to work?" I feel stupid as soon as I ask her. Her face falls, a subtle dropping of her eyebrows, a small turn of the mouth. Of course she wouldn't. She would likely want to never see that box ever again. I am an idiot.

She doesn't answer me right away. Instead, she bends down and picks up Toffrey, scritching the darker fur behind his ears. One tiny leg twitches in midair.

When she talks again, her voice is smaller, all the anger leeched out. "No. No offense, but I kind of hate it in there."

She's paper white in the moonlight, and though she's dolled up in a pretty dress and fancy jacket and has her makeup done, she still looks lost, like she doesn't know what she should do next. I wish I knew what to tell her, but I sure as hell don't know what she should do. I barely know what *I* should do. The sliver of life showing between the two booths roils with passing people and flashing lights. "Why don't you come with me," I say. "I just need to drop off my tool kit and then I was going to see my friend's knife-throwing act, and we can return Toffrey to his owner on the way."

The smile I'd seen a glimpse of earlier grows, no longer a shooting star but now dawn creeping over the edge of the horizon.

"I'd like that," she says.

We slip into the crushing flow of people, letting them push us away from the box. Pia and Duncan's tent looms ahead, and when we pull even with it, I take Emma's hand and bring her along as I duck inside. I only want to drop off my tool kit there, but the tent is empty, and Pia is bouncing off the walls.

"Have you guys met Emma?" I ask as I tuck the tool kit behind a heavily embroidered length of drapery.

"Yeah, yeah," Pia says, wriggling her fingers in my direction. "Gimme your hand, Ben. It's been ridiculously slow tonight and I'm bored as hell."

Without thinking, I give her my right hand.

"Gross, Ben," Pia says when she sees the scabbed-over wound. "*This* is like giving me a book with pages torn out. What happened, anyway?"

A flush creeps up my neck as I think of how these two will make fun of me for hurting myself because I'd been distracted by thinking about Emma. That and hell would have to look like Wisconsin in December for me to admit that with Emma here next to me. "Just, you know, cut myself. While working."

Pia's brow furrows, each line a testament to her disbelief. "While you were working," she repeats. She frowns at my hand for a moment longer, as though trying to solve some complicated problem, before dropping it and picking up my left instead. My hand sits face up in hers, while one of her oval fingernails traces the slopes and dips of my palm. Her hazel eyes open wide, and in her best whispery, faraway voice she says, "You're going to have seven kids and live in a shack —"

"Damn, Ben," Duncan says with an appraising up and down glance. "Keep it in your pants."

"Wait, wait," I say, glancing over at Emma to see her reaction. "Did I build this shack? Is it a two-story shack? Because I'd totally build a giant shack to house my pack of feral children."

"Shut up, I'm in the zone," Pia says. "And nobody said they were feral."

"Yeah," Emma says, barely suppressing a giggle. "They're probably just dirty all the time."

Pia throws her head back and laughs, but as suddenly as it began, her laughter sputters and dies out, and she blinks a few times, hard.

"You okay?" I ask, ducking down to get a better look at her face. She's gone pale, and her eyes are glassy.

"Fine," she says, with a weak smile that's barely more than a twitch of the lips. She resituates my palm in her hand, twisting it this way and that. "You, um…you're going to want to build, but first you will destroy. You'll have no home, but you will have peace."

Duncan meets my gaze when I look his way, and he shrugs. This is not the silly fortune-telling from before, but if he's concerned, he doesn't show it. Pia continues in this strange, almost monotone voice.

"Things that are linked cannot be unbound. Things set in motion cannot be stopped. Your salvation will come in the form of an old woman in yoga pants."

"That," I say, unsure what to make of her predictions, "is the craziest fortune you've given me yet."

"Yeah," Duncan says, grabbing Pia's hand, which still holds mine. "Like, this older woman. Is she hot? Does she have a silver-fox brother or son or whatnot for me to ogle? More *info*, Pia!"

Pia drops my hand like it's a slimy fish and pivots on her heel to face her brother. "The portents tell me what they tell me. They're not your otherworldly dating service. Oh! But they did tell me to give you this." She reaches into her jeans pocket, and when she pulls her hand out, her middle finger is extended.

"Jerk," Duncan says, rolling his eyes.

"Tramp!" Pia counters.

"Prude!"

"Oh, I'll prude you!" Pia jumps up, hooking her arm around Duncan's neck and putting him in a headlock. But Duncan digs his fingers into her side, tickling her until she dissolves into a fit of giggles.

"Um, hello?" A man holding a dripping ice cream cone enters the tent, glancing around as if he's not sure he should be here. "Are you open?"

The twins straighten and immediately go serious. "Of course," Pia says, her voice about two octaves lower than normal. "Please take a seat."

I have to stifle a laugh at Pia's faux-serious voice before I ruin her chances of making any money, and take Emma's hand as we duck out of the tent. I lead Emma through the neat rows of the carnival. We see Leslie in her ringmaster's garb, looking like a completely different person when covered in sequins and makeup. Her blond curls glow in the spotlight, and heeled boots add a couple of inches to her diminutive frame. The tumblers—Fabrizio with a small square of bright white gauze taped to his cheek—form a pillar three people high, beckoning onlookers into their tent for the next show. A circle of patrons gathers around one of the fire-eaters, who sends plumes of flame into the black sky.

Emma is entranced, her gaze darting this way and that. She asks questions about *everything*, wanting any detail I can give her, no matter how big or small.

"It must have been so much fun growing up here," she says.

I shrug. "Well, I wasn't *always* here. Mom and I lived in Virginia for a while. Before Dad died."

Emma's cool fingers tighten around mine. "I'm sorry you lost your dad so early. Do you remember him?"

My gaze tracks upward, past the crowds and the rides until I find a patch of clear sky. I *do* remember my dad, but… "Sort of," I say finally. "I remember how loud his laugh was and how he liked to tell corny jokes. We had a little house at the end of a cul-de-sac, and the moment he got home from work, he filled the place up until it seemed twice as big. And Mom was always so much more…content when he was around. So I miss him, but I miss more than just *him*, you know?"

At some point as we've been walking along, Emma's pressed herself as close to me as possible, our arms touching from shoulder to wrist. And even though the cold from her skin seeps into mine, raising goose bumps, it's nice. Comforting.

"Oh, I think I know a little about missing someone."

Immediately I feel like an ass. "Shit! I'm so sorry, Emma, I—"

"No!" she says, laughing a little. "I mean, yes, I do miss my family. But I was only in Claremore because my mom is on a research trip, and she left my brothers and me with our dad. And I love them, but my mom was the one who understood me, who talked to me in what felt like our own language. She took me to museums and let me use her employee ID card at the library on campus to check out their books on art history. I want that back. I want her back."

I can hear the longing when she talks about her mom, the way knowing their separation isn't permanent doesn't make it hurt less.

And I get it.

Because it's about missing the person but also how that person made you *feel*. And I think I'm so desperate to leave the carnival so I can find a place to make my own, to make a home that feels like our little house did when my dad was there.

But in the meantime, I have this. I have sugar-scented air and wide-open skies. I have noises that blend together with the chatter of hundreds of people making a song like no other. I have the hand of a girl who fascinates me securely in my own. With Emma by my side, I can actually see the carnival for the thing of wonder that it is…

And it's beautiful.

For one brief moment, I doubt my need to get out of here.

But I know Mrs. Potter must be missing her dog, so I guide Emma through the alleyways among tents and booths until we're at Mrs. Potter's blue-and-gold striped tent. Mrs. Potter is between shows, calling for Toffrey from the entrance to her tent. When we hand him over,

I'm not sure who's happier—Mrs. Potter for the return of her favorite dog or Toffrey for the stream of treats.

Mrs. Potter insists that we stay for the show, so we find a seat in the front row. I'll just have to catch Marcel's new act another time.

The bright chatter in the tent dies out as a white-hot spotlight illuminates the small ring. Mrs. Potter, her purple hair electric, wears a vintage silk gown in a teal color that soaks up the light. Her *rat-tat-tat* patter fills the tent.

"Guys and dolls, boys and girls, ladies and germs!" Silk swishes in vibrant flashes as Mrs. Potter sweeps her arms open in greeting. "Welcome! I hope you are ready for this evening's delights!"

At the word "delights" Toffrey runs out from backstage, tent flaps whipping open as he passes through. He sprints up a ramp, snatches a treat from Mrs. Potter's hand, and darts backstage once again. Delighted giggles erupt from the children and more than a few adults, but Mrs. Potter continues without pause.

"My dogs will perform feats of wonder!" Three tan-colored dachshunds run from beneath the seats to the left of the ring, their stumpy legs pumping furiously as they speed up the ramps leading to the platform behind Mrs. Potter. One dog allows the second to climb up her back, and then the third clambers on top of them both. The dogs balance there patiently, staying in position even after they get their treats.

"My dogs will perform heart-stopping stunts!" The giant standard poodle runs into the ring, her slim body flowing between the lit torches circling the perimeter of the stage, not even sending one swaying.

"And by the end of the night," Mrs. Potter says, her lips curving into a sly smile, "you'll have quite a story to tell at work on Monday." The rest of the dogs scamper out, and for the next fifteen minutes, Mrs. Potter's dogs live up to every one of her promises.

Toffrey is clearly the star of the show, and there's a recurring gag where Mrs. Potter pretends to not notice Toffrey stealing treats out of the pouch at her hip. I've seen this act a hundred times, but it still makes me smile.

For the finale, Mrs. Potter brings out a hoop perched atop a six-foot pole. After it's placed in the gaps between ramps, Mrs. Potter flicks open her heavy silver Zippo and sets the hoop alight. Emma's hand finds mine. She's worried. But Mrs. Potter and her dogs have done this act nearly every night without so much as a singed whisker. So I grip her hard fingers tight, hoping she feels the comfort there.

Each of the dogs, from the poodle to the lethargic bulldog to the three dachshunds, leaps through the flaming hoop as Toffrey runs circles around the ring. When the last whippet gracefully lands on the other side, Mrs. Potter says, "Toffrey, baby, show the people how it's done!"

Toffrey runs up the ramp and sails through the hoop. But he doesn't stop there. The dog pivots at the end of the ramp and immediately does it again. His pink tongue lolls out of the side of his mouth, and I know it's impossible, but I swear the little dog is eating up the applause.

He turns again for what I know is his last jump. But just as he hits the crest of the ramp, he lets out a yelp, paws skittering out from beneath him.

And then he falls.

The tent goes silent, and I'm on my feet before the thought to go help fully forms. But Emma is quicker.

She's in the dirt kneeling beside Toffrey before even Mrs. Potter. Her pale hands flit about the small furry dog, and when she stands, something cold and solid lodges in my throat.

"That's all, folks!" Emma says with hollow enthusiasm. "We thank you for coming out and hope you get home safe."

She begins to usher those closest to the ring toward the exits, and one of the stagehands starts up some music. I carefully step around the other dogs, who sit at attention, small whines leaking from their strained mouths. Mrs. Potter hovers over the still dog on the ground.

Get up, I think. *You* always *get up.*

But he doesn't.

It's not until Mrs. Potter scoops the small body off the ground and I see his furry little head flop sickeningly to the side that I accept it.

Toffrey is dead.

CHAPTER TWELVE

Emma

The following morning, the yard is quiet and still. All
the hustle and bustle has completely disappeared. The
workers aren't working. The cooks in the cook shack
shuffle about with as few movements as necessary. Even
the wind has died, leaving the tall grasses surrounding
the backyard motionless.

Only one sound permeates the yard—the high,
mournful keening of Mrs. Potter's surviving dogs.

I ache to join them. To stand by Benjamin, to tell
Mrs. Potter I'm sorry, to do *something*. But a rock sits in
the pit of my stomach, anchoring me in place. So I hang
back, sticking to the edges of the crowd drifting toward
Mrs. Potter's trailer.

I find Sidney lounging against one of the nearby
trailers, watching the scene from beneath his dark hair. I
want to tell him what I saw. Or maybe let these hiccup-y
sobs trying to rattle their way out of me do just that. But
what right do I have to these emotions when I've barely

been with the carnival a week? So I pull my spine up straight and act as though it's a regular day and my heart isn't breaking for Ben, Mrs. Potter, and the little white dog who comforted me when I needed it the most.

Sidney gives me a grunt by way of greeting. It's before eight, so I nod toward the paper cup full of milky coffee and ask, "What cup are you on? Two? Three?"

"Two," he says, never taking his eyes from the trailer before us. "And please keep all questions that are harder than that one until after I get another cup in me. I'm useless until I'm on cup number three."

"So you must have been useless the whole time you were in the box, huh?"

That bit of smart-assery earns a mildly amused glare in return but that's it. When he doesn't say anything, I add, "You're up early for someone who doesn't have to be."

"Can't seem to sleep longer than four hours," Sidney says. "And I don't dream." He frowns, a sharp line settling in between his brows. "At least, I don't remember them if I do."

I don't know what to say to that, so I say nothing and turn back to the funeral and the churn of feelings in my belly.

After Leslie calms Mrs. Potter down, Lars picks up the small, cloth-wrapped body, and they bury the dog several feet away from the edge of the yard.

The reedy grasses brush up against my legs, the touch so soft I only register it's happening because I can hear the dry rasp it makes. Mrs. Potter, who had seemed as immutable as her blazing-purple hair, is shaking, her shoulders heaving with ragged breaths. I want to do something but I don't know what. It feels like anything

I might say would be insincere. I knew her terrier better than I knew her. But the dogs' howling has plucked at some cord deep inside me, and it reverberates with the ache of loss.

Ben had been shocked. Everyone had, but Ben had seemed particularly fond of the dog. The fuzzy white terrier had slipped off a ramp and didn't get up. The moment after the fall hung in the air like a bead of water about to drop from a leaf, fat and heavy with promise. Then everyone sprang into action.

The customers were quickly ushered into another tent by one of the clowns. Everyone else—Benjamin, Mrs. Potter, a grizzled-looking clown who had stayed back—all hovered over the dog, waiting. I don't think they were expecting a zombie dog resurrection, but it was more like they couldn't believe a dog could die in the first place.

Even now, a sense of disbelief pervades the carnival. It's in the way people slowly shake their heads and let their sentences trail off before completion. It's in the blank stares into nothingness, the startled faces when someone tries to catch another's attention. A few nervous glances are thrown my way, but I can't tell if it's because they think the accident was my fault or if they still hadn't gotten a good look at me. Common sense tells me it isn't the former. Self-doubt tried to convince me it is.

"I feel like I'm still missing something," I say, watching Sidney as he sips from his cup. Sometimes I think I miss food so much that I'll go crazy if I can't eat. But this body doesn't get hungry. And when I tried to sneak a bit of cotton candy, it stuck to my desert-dry tongue like cobwebs. Other times I feel so detached that it almost scares me that I've changed so much in such a short period of time.

Sidney looks in my direction but not *at* me, like he's occupied with something else. "You know those signs some places have that say something like 'Ten days since our last accident'?"

I nod.

"Okay. Well, imagine the carnival has one of those. Except instead of a number of days, try the word 'never.' All right, 'never' may be an exaggeration, but we've gone years and years and years without something like this happening." He stares off at Leslie leading Mrs. Potter away, with Lars and Ben herding the pack of howling dogs. "Years."

"Bullshit," I say, already sick of Sidney's hyperbole for the day.

Sidney gestures to the crowd, coffee spilling from his cup in a pale arc. Some of it spatters on the bare legs of one of the bright redheads who work the cotton candy booths, but Sidney ignores her glare. "Do you really think there'd be this much fuss otherwise?"

There *were* a lot of people gathered here. "Okay, fine. Let's say I believe you, and this *never* happens. Why did it happen now? And to that poor dog? Everyone keeps going on about the charm and how it protects everyone, but this doesn't seem very protected."

"That is an excellent question, Emma," Sidney says as he stares at me. I don't like it. It's not predatory, like the night he tricked me, but there is more to it than I can parse out at the moment. But like the showman he is, his expression switches, going from lost in thought to jovial carnival performer in a heartbeat. "But I thought I told you to hold all hard questions until I had more coffee."

We're silent as Mrs. Potter passes us, her gentle

sobbing the only sound. I reach out and grab her hand as she goes by, giving her fingers a quick squeeze. Her smile is watery, barely more than her hot-pink lips pressing together, but at least I offered *some* comfort for the poor woman.

"So," Sidney says as he pushes off the trailer. "I hear you and Benjamin had a run-in with the Fabulous Moretti Brothers."

Sidney walks deeper into the yard, and, since I don't have anything better to do, I follow. I wish it was warmer, and that my shudder didn't look like I did it out of fear from hearing their name. "Yeah. Assholes."

Sidney runs his hands over his face and through his hair. "I'm going about this all wrong. You need to take a few nights off from the box." I start to protest, but he holds up a hand to stop me. "Look, I know, okay? I know that all you want is to get out of there. But taking a couple of days to acclimate to the carnival isn't going to hurt you. If anything, it'll make you better, smarter. Seeming like you fit in is part of the illusion that makes it easier to trick someone. Trust me."

"'Trust me,' says the guy who pushed me from a Ferris wheel."

A half scowl twists up his mouth while he tries to find the right thing to say, though I don't know that there *is* a right thing to say in an instance like this. But ultimately, he just shrugs. "I'm only staying on to help. If you don't want me to help you, tell me, and I'll leave."

I stop walking and look at him. He jams his hands into his pockets and stops beside me. I can't tell if he means it or not. If he really stayed on because of me. Do real human feelings lurk beneath the shallow surface that only seems to be concerned with eating every meal he missed out on in the time he was trapped by the curse? But then his gaze is caught by something past my shoulder. It's Benjamin and a blond woman who looks incredibly like him, walking away from Mrs. Potter's trailer.

Oh.

Oh.

"Are you really staying for me, or does it have something to do with her?"

That snaps him out of it. "Huh? Wait, what? Ben's mom? Audrey? No. No, I'm staying to help. It's part of the deal. Even if you did pass on the curse tonight, you wouldn't get to leave. You have to help your successor. It's not a real rule, but it's more of an honor code kind of thing, so stop looking for a double meaning behind this"—he waves his arms emphatically around himself—"and just let me help you."

But there's something in his tone, in the way his eyes won't meet mine. He's lying. Again.

We leave the yard and near the carnival grounds. Mrs. Potter won't perform tonight, but the show must go on. As the performers and workers drift away from the little funeral, the carnival slowly comes back to life. Two women running games next to each other hose the grass and mud off the fronts of their booths. Leslie and Lars pass us on the path, the big man bent over nearly double in order to better hear the tiny ringmaster. We stop where Gin and Whiskey are stretching, getting ready to run through their paces. A man who must be their father leads a white horse with speckled-gray haunches around a circle.

"Listen," Sidney says, eyes firmly locked on the horse

making its way around the ring. "Some people think that the curse is just transferred with a kiss. Don't correct them."

I nearly stumble I stop so fast. "Why wouldn't I—"

"Because," Sidney says, his words sharper than I've ever heard them. "You can use it. To protect yourself." He drapes his arms over the metal tubing of the makeshift fence and watches the girls run through their act.

"Why would I need to protect myself by threatening people with the curse?"

"You never know, Em. Never know."

Sidney doesn't seem to have anything to add, and I don't feel like pressing him. The next time the girls' dad leads the horse around the circle, the girls run up a brightly painted ramp and jump onto the moving horse's back. They wobble for a second and I'm sure that one of them is going to fall. But then, with a smooth bend of her arm, Gin has Whiskey balanced while making it look like it was part of the act in the first place.

As the girls ride off to the far side of the ring, Audrey and Ben walk into view, and I take a better look at them. So Audrey is Benjamin's mother? The more I study them, the more apparent it seems. Ben has a narrower nose, a different line to his mouth. Their hair is the same, and so are their eyes, but then Ben has those charming glasses where Audrey seems fine without.

Sidney can't stop staring at Audrey, even though Whiskey is now balancing on one leg on the back of the trotting horse. Her balance never wavers, and neither does Sidney's gaze.

CHAPTER THIRTEEN

Emma

The carnival creeps across Texas, and I've spent the last month doing the only thing that makes the carnival bearable—watching Benjamin build and paint. The painting in particular is fascinating. On one gray November morning, I watch him from my perch on a nearby sawhorse.

"Do you want to paint?" he asks.

I shrug, and he looks from me to the spindly brush in his hand.

"You seem like you want to. Don't you?"

Neat dots of color sit on his plywood palette. They're fresh, barely muddled. His strokes are sure and steady. A smudge of bright sky blue mars the back of his hand, and now that it's dry, it cracks and peels as his skin moves beneath it. "I used to paint a little. Before. But these aren't exactly the hands of a painter."

I hold out one pale hand. My fingers flex and jerk, and there's a fine tremor that runs down the length of my arm.

Sometimes it scares me when I realize I'm almost used to it. If I tried to paint a straight line, I'd fail. If I tried to mix the colors, I'd drag the brush through three colors accidentally and mar the pristine circles.

These are the hands of a disaster.

He takes my extended hand and instead of just passing over the brush, he pulls me down to sit beside him. Curling one arm around me, his warm fingers flex over mine, helping me to hold the brush steady. "Try."

He's already sketched out the lettering for the sign—HAPPY BIRTHDAY, WHISKEY—so all we have to do is fill it in with her favorite colors—two different shades of bright blue on a field of pale orange. I want to sink into his warmth, to let it melt over me. The sun cracks through the downy clouds, warming our backs. I work slowly, not trusting my own hands, but, with Ben helping, the brushstrokes become more confident, and for short stretches of time the shaking actually stops.

I almost feel normal again.

I dare a glance at Ben, admiring the way his dark-gold lashes lie against his cheek, how his glasses are slipping down the bridge of his nose and he doesn't even notice that he's smearing orange paint across his face as he pushes them back into place. I could watch him for ages.

"Thank you," I say, though there's no way I could possibly voice everything I'm thankful for if he should ask. For his patience and his thoughtfulness, for the time he's given me and how he doesn't seem to fear me like the other carnies. Luckily, I don't have to say a word.

He turns toward me, so close that his breath ghosts over my cheek. "You're welcome."

But not everything is quiet afternoons spent painting.

Subtle changes are happening within the supposed perfect confines of the carnival. I don't quite know what the big deal is, but based on the reactions of my new friends, it is a *big deal*. A stubbed toe. A ride stuck on the tracks. A slight stumble during an otherwise flawless show. I'm told that these things do not happen in the carnival. They just don't.

But now they do.

Theories are whispered among the carnies. Most of them are bunk. But there's one that's growing traction. I think the Morettis are behind it, though I've never actually heard the accusations come out of their mouths. There are different variations, some more specific than others. But it all boils down to me.

One version of the rumor is that I'm not spending enough time in the box, though I put in a good four to five hours a night in there. Another version going around is that I *do* put my time in, but I don't care enough, and the charm can tell. Sidney tells me to ignore it, that our fellow carnies are suspicious by nature. It's hard to ignore the angry looks thrown my way by people who are not as subtle as they seem to think they are. Yet none of them approach me or try to tell me how to do my job to my face. Apparently having a mouth that can condemn someone with a kiss comes with benefits.

Tonight is our second to last night outside Austin, in a small town called Round Rock. It seems as though we've seen all four seasons in our one week here, but Gin was quick to inform me that this is Texas, and I should never by surprised by what Texas weather does. Tonight a cold breeze sends brittle oak leaves and pine needles skittering down the alleys. As the last patrons are chased out of our gates, Ben waits for me while I close up the box. My pockets jangle with clinking coins. I've had a good night, but I'm still the Girl in the Box, so it's not truly a *good* night.

"Ready?" Benjamin asks. He smiles when I turn to face him, a quick secret thing that he folds back in on itself before it truly blooms. For a brief second, I don't feel the cold.

The beads on my dress catch the carnival lights in a hundred different ways as I shift my weight. "Is this a good idea?"

He runs a hand smudged with paint through his hair. "Well, considering the last time, the worst that might happen is we'd start calling you Grenadine instead of Emmaline."

Most of the acts are winding down, but a few patrons still linger in the aisles, playing one last game or getting a bag of treats to take home. Ben and I pick our way through the carnival, grabbing things as we go, per Gin's instruction. I nab some balloons that weren't sold earlier in the day. There's a small plate of fudge samples one of the vendors gives Ben when he tells her our plans for the evening. The whole time, I feel a nagging itch between my shoulder blades, as though we're being watched. But no matter how I twist and turn, regardless of if I'm sneaky or sly, I never see anything to suggest someone is paying the two of us particular attention.

Can't shake that itch, though.

When we get back to my wagon, Gin is waiting for us, sitting on the steps. She hasn't changed out of her performance costume either, so she seems brighter and sparklier than in real life. Ben should seem as dull as a newsprint photo compared to her, in his worn flannel shirt and paint-speckled jeans. Except he's not. His eyes light up behind his old man glasses when he talks, and there's a dimple that flashes every now and then. He seems too big to be in my small wagon, but there he is anyway. The sight makes me happier than it should, and I busy myself by cutting crepe paper into crooked streamers.

Ben anchors the balloons into a corner and then helps Gin string the fringe I just made back and forth under the ceiling. Finally, the HAPPY BIRTHDAY, WHISKEY banner is strung up at the far end of the wagon. In my new tiny home, already stuffed to brimming with just three people in it, I feel calm, and almost warm. The only way I could feel cozier is if my family were here with us.

Marcel barely makes it inside before the birthday girl, and Gin pulls him over to her side of the wagon quickly, tucking herself beneath his arm. Whiskey careens up the steps of the wagon and throws her arms wide, already expecting our chorus of "Surprise!" Duncan, who was in charge of bringing her over, must have spilled the secret, but she's loud and happy, and her cheeks are flushed pink. The wagon is full to bursting with people. Pia arrives late, and she and Duncan wind up sipping drinks and chatting on the steps as there just isn't enough room for everyone.

"So what do you want for your birthday, Whiskey?" Marcel asks. He's passing around a half-empty bottle of champagne. I reach for it automatically, but when my fingers *clink* against the glass, reality comes crashing down. I shake my head, and Marcel's dark eyes go wide with embarrassment over forgetting, but he covers it quickly.

Whiskey stands, her face lost in the strips of teal and yellow dangling from the roof. They flutter prettily in the breeze from the open skylight. "I," she says, pausing dramatically as she swipes the green bottle away from Marcel, "want a pony. And a racecar. And a sea otter. And something sparkly. Someone make that happen." She plops back down onto the pillows, almost knocking me into Ben.

Instead of pushing me away, Benjamin moves an arm until I'm nestled into his side, my torso in line with his. I stiffen. I don't want him to feel that my body doesn't mold to his, to have the cold that fills me seep through his clothes to touch his skin. I start to pull away.

But then, in a movement that feels natural, he moves to the side in such a way that I have to fall back against him. He's so warm. I shouldn't be able to feel it, but I swear every pulse of blood that rushes through him beats against me. I close my eyes and melt into him.

"What about Spots McGee?" Duncan asks as he sprawls backward into the wagon. Half his body is in the wagon and half is outside with Pia, who ducks her head in to see what we're talking about.

"Spots is a seventeen-hand Clydesdale, Duncan," Whiskey says. "I want one of those tiny ponies, the ones that never get big, what are they called?"

"They're just called miniature horses, aren't they?" Gin asks. She reaches across Marcel to take the bottle back, and as she does, surprising everyone in the wagon, Marcel darts out and kisses her.

Everyone is still for half a heartbeat. Duncan lets out a wolf whistle as they break apart, and I can't help but notice the dazed smile Gin's wearing and the pleased grin on Marcel.

"Oh my God," Whiskey says. *"Oh my God!"* She flops

backward and grabs a pillow to bury her face in. Her voice muffled, she screams, "I did not need to see that! Never! I could go a lifetime without seeing my sister kiss a boy! Cities could crumble! Oceans could dry up! And that would still! Not! Be long enough!"

She yanks the bottle away from Marcel. "I have a new birthday wish—therapy!"

"My birthday wish is to see more," Duncan says. He waggles his finger between the two of them. "Do it again."

After Whiskey pummels Duncan with a pillow until his hair skews to the right like a comb-over that met a hurricane, and the laughter dies down, it's a much quieter affair. Whiskey is both too sleepy and too tipsy to walk on her own, so Duncan and Pia each take an arm and help her back to her trailer. Marcel and Gin slip out, too, but head in the opposite direction, into the sea of oaks bordering our camp. Which just leaves Benjamin and me.

I slump back against the wall of pillows, hating the fact that the dropping temperatures are more pronounced now that most of the warm bodies have left. A shudder tremors through me even though I try my hardest to repress it. But Ben, ever observant, notices. This time when he draws nearer, I let him line his body up with mine.

I am in completely uncharted territory.

Never mind the fact that I've never, ever been with a boy who charms me as much as Benjamin does. Never mind the fact that I am some weird, cursed puppet girl. Never mind the fact that having him so close makes me feel ridiculously happy. I have no idea what I'm doing.

Turns out I don't have to. Ben lies back and tugs my hand till I sink down beside him. His right arm slips beneath me and curls me toward him, so that it's easy for me to line up as much of my body with his as possible. We lie there, positioned beneath the tiny skylight, watching dark-gray clouds scud across the stars. One lantern is still lit, and as it sways, it sends panels of yellow-y light across the walls. There are no other lights inside or out, and the stars above are impossibly bright.

"I lived in a small town," I say, "but there were still enough lights that I never saw the stars. I know how clichéd I'm going to sound, but there's so many more out here, and they're beautiful."

There's no response for a moment, but then Benjamin turns against me, hesitating, and lines me against his chest so that our view is the exact same out the small window. "That," he says, pointing, "is Pisces. This star"—I see one bright spot at the edge of his fingernail—"connects the tails of the two fish." His paint-flecked hands sketch out lines between more of the stars. "That's Cassiopeia, forever chained to a throne because she said she was more beautiful than the Nereids. And that is the Phoenix, the bird who dies and is reborn in fire."

His hand drifts down to rest on my arm, and I pick out the shapes he showed me again and again, to make sure I'll remember them later. The soft rustling of leaves and Ben's steady heartbeat are the only sounds in my world. "How do you know all that?"

He shifts again and pushes his glasses up his nose. "When you're never in the same place for more than a week, you need a constant. Something that doesn't change, ever. Stars are my constant."

There's something about this beautiful piece of honesty that fills me up, and I can almost pretend I'm warm.

"I think that's why I want to leave so badly," he says.

There goes that warm feeling, flying right out the door. What will this place be without Benjamin? But right on the heels of those thoughts comes the realization that nothing can be quite as bad as being transformed into this weird puppet girl. I'll miss him—*terribly*—but I'd make it. And not only that, but I find that I *want* Ben to be happy.

"What do you want to do when you leave?" I ask. "Where do you want to go?"

For a brief second, the simple question has Ben silenced, making me wonder if this is the first time he's ever been asked. The quiet stretches out around us, and he's practically thinking so hard I can feel it. But finally he says, "I want to live on the coast."

I laugh and give him a little jab with my elbow. "There's a lot of coast in this country, you know. East or west?"

"West," he says. The answer is quick, decisive, and I know he means it.

"Okay, West Coast." I think for a moment, trying to imagine Ben without a tool kit in hand, driving to do something mundane like pick up groceries. "Well, you can't go to California—"

"Why can't I go to California?"

I roll to face him, careful to keep his arm around me. "I'm going to hazard a guess based off your relationship with the Moretti brothers and say that Cali is going to have a little too much 'dude-bro' culture for you to handle." I squint at him, at the wool cap jammed on his head and the paint-smudged Henley stretching over his chest. "You're more Washington state, or Oregon maybe."

His arms curl around me as his gaze goes thoughtful. "Hmm. That could be nice."

"Nice? You were pretty much made for the Pacific Northwest. You could wear flannel and build your own log cabin and paint window signs for all the hipster coffee shops."

"Sounds like you've got it all planned out. You going to come visit me in my log cabin?"

"Only if you have wifi."

He laughs, the deep rumble of it vibrating through his chest. I love that *I* made him laugh like that. I want to do it as many times as he'll let me. This night is a shining jewel in a box that I want to keep forever. But it still has to end.

So Ben gathers up the trash, and it seems like he doesn't know what to do with it as he tries to climb down the steps of the wagon. I laugh a little before taking it from him, crouching to be closer to eye level before handing the torn streamers and empty bottles to him once he's on the ground. His fingers linger over mine as he takes the crumpled paper back.

If it weren't for the curse and this stranger's body, I'd kiss him. I'd close the last few inches that separate us and shut my eyes and press my mouth to his. I'd run my fingers through his hair, to see if it was fine or coarse, relish in the way it shifts through many shades of gold in the light. Let his breath mingle with mine in a dizzy swirl between us. Find out what he tastes like. If it weren't for the curse and Sidney, it would be my first kiss, and it would be a wonderful one.

But I don't, because why kiss him, if I can't feel it? If he'd just be pressing his soft mouth against my unyielding one? And somehow, my kiss feels more dangerous now, like it's a trigger. Ben should be safe, if I kiss him, but even so, I don't trust myself, trust my traitor lips. Slowly, reluctantly, we pull apart. I sit down on the edge of the wagon so I can watch him go, and, even more reluctantly than when we pulled apart, Ben turns to leave.

It's then we notice his mother has been watching us from across the alley.

CHAPTER FOURTEEN

Benjamin

Fury is a terrible, red-winged thing in the shape of my mother.

She caught me with Emma. And not only did she catch me with the girl she wanted me to stay away from, she caught me making moon eyes at said girl as I thought about kissing her. God. To make matters worse, I had to ditch Emma with no explanation. Though I bet Mom's glare spoke volumes.

Mom's silent as we walk through the rows of trailers. It's like everyone could sense the coming rage and bunkered down in their homes. Not a word is said as she holds open the door of the Airstream for me. Then there is an abundance of noise. Cabinets bang shut. Doors open only to be immediately slammed. She's a whirlwind of futile activity.

I sit down on the booth of the dinette. She's pacing across the five short steps from where I sit to the door of her bedroom when I make the mistake of speaking. "I don't get why you're so upset."

"Oh, oh no. Don't you— That's not…" Her words dissolve into an angry sort of growl.

"Mom, if you want to be pissed, fine, be pissed. But you have to tell me why."

She sits on the opposite side of the booth, and I turn to face her. Her knees knock into mine.

"You want to know why this is a big deal?" she asks. She cradles her head in her hands and it's a long time before she speaks again. When she does, she talks to the table and not me. "Tell me the story of why I joined the carnival."

Is she trying to distract me? "I know why you joined the carnival, Mom."

She raises her head to look at me. "You only know part of it. Do it. Tell me."

I push my glasses up my nose and stare at her, but she's not backing down. It's in the hard, straight line her eyebrows make, in the way her mouth is pressed together.

"Seriously?" I flatten my palms on the tabletop. "You were eighteen and your uptight parents didn't like that you wanted to work outside instead of in the secretarial pool. So you ran away. Leslie's dad let you join the carnival and eventually you became master carpenter."

Mom mirrors my stance; her palms press against the table until her fingernails seem bloodless. It's like this is the Singer fighting stance.

"That's mostly true. I was a girl, in a time when women were supposed to be housewives and happy about it, who left home because my parents disagreed with my career choice. It wasn't unheard of for a woman to work in a field that required manual labor, though. And I'm sorry if I've vilified your grandparents all this time, Benjamin, but that's not the whole story."

The curtains shift in the breeze, and they catch her gaze. She stares at the milky moonlight as she continues. "Like most stories where a girl runs away from home, there was a boy involved."

At first I almost don't believe her. It's too weird to acknowledge there was anyone besides Dad in her life. But I'm not naive enough to think that there wasn't.

"He was so handsome. Curly hair like you wouldn't believe and a smile that would make an angel think about sinning. But his family had upset my family, and they didn't want us talking to each other. We thought we were our generation's Romeo and Juliet."

Her expression darkens, her eyebrows furrowing together. "He convinced me to run away. He suggested the carnival. He got us jobs here. Or rather, I became the carpenter's apprentice while he bounced around trying to find a job he actually could do. One month. We were here *one month* when the stress of being on our own together got to him, and instead of trying to work things out..." Her voice breaks and wobbles. "He got drunk and kissed the Girl in the Box.

"It was Sidney, Ben. I ran away for Sidney."

Sidney? Imagining Mom being with smart-ass Sidney instead of Dad is like trying to jam a square peg into a round hole. And if she'd stayed with him? I wouldn't even exist.

"The curse took the thing that I valued so much that I was willing to leave everything behind. I stuck around for thirty years. Thirty years of watching him half-heartedly trying to get a replacement, of him coming up with crackpot schemes to get out of the box instead of just passing the damned curse along like everyone had before him. I left my parents, my friends, my *everything* only to have the life I was building ruined a month later. And then, when I couldn't take seeing him trapped in that box any longer, I left again. I abandoned the carnival and found your father, who made me so happy that I forgot about this place. I had you. And then, because the real world is harsh and painful and isn't protected by a charm like this stupid carnival, your father died in that car crash and you almost died, too. So *that* is why this is a big deal. *That* is why I want you to stay away from her."

She takes in a big, gulping breath of air. Tears line her eyes and make her blue irises glow. "The curse doesn't get to take you, too."

I stand so quickly that the tabletop rattles, making my mother press against the back of the booth. "Are you telling me that the whole reason you can't trust me around Emma is because *Sidney* couldn't keep it in his pants?"

The flinch shifts her expression from shocked to angry, but I can't stop. Not when she's just dropped this bombshell on me.

"You mean to tell me that you don't trust *me* because Sidney's a jackass? Because you made a mistake by falling for the wrong person and think I will, too? That is *not* how things work in the real world, Mom. You have to let me be my own person. And you should *trust Emma.* She's not going to do to me what Sidney did to you."

At least, I don't think she would.

Anger roils in my belly the moment the idea forms in my head. Emma would *never* betray me like that. And I hate the fact that I thought it for even a second.

Words trip and stumble and die on my mother's mouth but she doesn't say anything. Doesn't tell me I'm wrong. Doesn't try to defend her actions. So I grab my coat from a cubby near the door, jam my arms into it, and leave.

My feet carry me among trailers and tents, through the small grassy area separating the yard from the carnival proper. Anxious prickles run up and down my spine, as over and over, my mother's words ring through my head.

A twig snaps behind me, and I whirl around, ready for round two with my mother. But no one's there. I turn again, looking all around me for the source of the noise I know I heard. Nothing.

Shame, cold and slick like an egg yolk, slides into my belly and settles there. What does it say about me that my first thought was my mother had followed me to continue our fight? I'm not saying she's right to be pissed, but isn't this just another aspect of her overprotective-mom shtick? Was I too harsh? And what the *hell* had Sidney been thinking?

Not ready to apologize, not sure where else to go, I cross the grounds until I get to Lars's Ferris wheel. I'm sure Emma would let me sleep in her wagon, but something tells me Mom expects me to run straight to Emma, and I, stupid though it may be, can't stand for her to be right.

The wooden struts groan in the wind like an old woman who can't settle for the night. I climb into the car parked by the platform and curl up against the walls. If I crane my neck just so, I can pick out the constellations I showed Emma not even an hour ago. Sleep comes as I'm tracing their lines in the sky.

CHAPTER FIFTEEN

Emma

A carnival is a sad and desolate place on a weekday morning. No matter how brightly painted the stalls and booths are, no matter how loud the music (because apparently Whiskey and Duncan have convinced the carousel operator to let them ride, and their whooping has a kind of Doppler effect as they turn around and around), it's still an empty carnival. It's veins without blood. It's lungs with no air.

Either Ben or his mom is hammering away at something fiercely, like whatever it is will escape if they don't nail it down. A horse whickers. The sun shines like a spotlight in the drab gray sky. A red-and-white striped popcorn bag drifts down the lane.

"Hey," Sidney says, nudging my arm with his elbow, "lookit." Between two pinched fingers, I see a single, shimmering strand of hair. "My first gray!" He brings the strand so close to his face his eyes cross as he stares at it. "Shit. Am I going to have to color my hair now? Am

I that vain? I think I am."

He's still babbling about whether or not he'll have his hair professionally done or get Mrs. Potter to do it as we round the corner of Gin and Whiskey's tent when we see Ben. And Ben looks pissed.

A happy bubble of delight fills my chest near to bursting. Then I find myself quickly trying to puzzle out why he's angry. Did I do something? I couldn't have done anything. Unless his mom was mad at him last night? She'd seemed pretty pissed for some reason, and he'd taken off in a hurry.

Sidney pushes me away with the tips of his fingers. "Better stay back, Em. I've been waiting a long time for Audrey Jr. to get pissed at me."

He drops his arms to his sides, slightly spread out in welcome, an almost beatific expression on his face. Benjamin barrels toward him, and I figure out his intentions about a second too late. Benjamin draws his fist back, and with the momentum of his harried walk still with him, he punches Sidney in the jaw. Sidney goes sprawling into the dust.

Benjamin stands over him but doesn't make a move to hit him again. "That," he says, his voice uneven as if he ran over here, "was for my mom." He turns abruptly and walks away, the dust kicked up by his heel drifting into Sidney's face.

I run over to Sidney. A bright pink patch and smudge of blood mark the place where Benjamin hit him. It's going to be a terrible bruise. He touches the corner of his mouth tenderly, wincing as he makes contact. As he examines the blood on his fingertip, he says, "It's okay. That was about fifty years coming."

"What are you talking about?"

Sidney looks at Benjamin's retreating form. "Why don't you go ask him?"

I must hesitate, because he waves his hand at me like he's got it under control. I chase after Benjamin.

He's pissed.

"Hey," I say.

He doesn't answer.

"Hey!"

Now he stops. I walk around him until we're facing each other.

"What was that about?" I ask.

He pushes his hand up under his glasses to press against his eyelids. "*That* was stupid. I shouldn't have. But I found out something Sidney did a long time ago, and—"

"Oh no," I say, interrupting him. "Sidney's an ass. I don't know what he did, but I have no trouble believing that he deserved it." Ben gives me a small smile that makes me disproportionately happy. "What I want to know is why you shook me off. What did I do wrong?"

The smile vanishes. "Nothing. I let her get in my head and I don't know why she'd even— It's like she thinks I'm a moron or something—I'm sorry."

He starts walking again, headed vaguely to the backyard.

"Will you tell me what's going on?"

"Apparently," he says, talking slowly like he's having trouble corralling his thoughts, "Sidney and my mom had a thing. Before I was born, and before he was trapped in the curse. In fact"—he laughs a bitter laugh—"kissing the Girl in the Box was him cheating on my mom."

We've stopped in front of the carousel, where Pia has joined her brother and Whiskey. The girl chases the spinning platform and jumps on.

"Do it, Whiskey!" Pia yells.

On the next rotation, Whiskey climbs onto the back of her slowly rising and falling carousel horse she's riding.

A breeze ruffles Benjamin's hair just as the sun's coming out, making it glint in the light. His eyelashes are golden with it. "I guess if it weren't for him being an idiot, I wouldn't have been born, but that doesn't make it any better. Damn."

It isn't hard to put together the rest. Audrey doesn't want what happened to Sidney to happen to Ben. Which makes me the lecherous villain in this story, preying on her precious son. Suddenly I feel guilty, even though I wanted nothing more than to be around her son. Last night's almost kiss flashes through my brain, momentarily leaving me giddy. Maybe I want to do more than just be around her son.

Time is one frozen moment as my mind works out what I'm thinking. Kissing Benjamin. I so, so want to. I've imagined it. I wish he'd been my first kiss and not Sidney. I wish I'd found him at a different time in my life. I wish a thousand things that all culminate in his lips on mine. When I look at him, his eyes are the clearest, prettiest aquamarine I've ever seen.

I watch Whiskey balance on one foot on top of a prancing scarlet horse with a gilded mane. Her limbs are graceful and steady as she balances out and strikes her pose, triumphant.

I have to look at her, because I can't look at Benjamin.

If I look at Benjamin I'm going to do that weird shaky shuddery thing that is what crying is in this new alien body.

The twins shout a chorus of incomprehensible gibberish at Whiskey, and the only word that jumps out is "handstand."

"I want you to know, I would never trap you in the curse, I'd never kiss you, I mean—" If my cheeks could still turn red, they'd be visible from fifty feet away. "Not that I wouldn't ever *want to*—it's just that...*damn it*." I prop my arms against the metal fencing surrounding the carousel and try to ignore the dull *thud* it makes when I do.

"I get it," Ben says.

Dry, golden tufts of dead grass sway around my feet, and I concentrate on them instead of looking at Benjamin. "Sidney was my first kiss."

Benjamin stills beside me, and I turn in time to witness the play of emotions running across his face. The way his eyes widen in shock then his mouth goes firm and thin in anger. Before he can get too worked up, I say, "It sucks, but I'm over it. Well, I'll *be* over it. Although now I'm wishing I'd just gone ahead and kissed Jack Macklin at the homecoming dance last year. *But...*" But what? *But I'd really like to kiss you, Ben, if you'd let me?* I can't say that, even if the words are practically hanging off the tip of my tongue.

That moment where my heart and intentions sit between us stretches longer and longer. God. I don't think it's humanly possible to feel more awkward than I do right now.

Benjamin seems nearer when he speaks, but that could

be me hoping, wishing. "Will you do it? Kiss someone and trick him into taking your place?" A frown furrows in between his eyebrows. "Maybe even break someone's heart, like my mom?"

His blue eyes are darker, the color shifting from cloudless sky to angry ocean. He's seeing me as a weapon for the first time, and oh God, but I hate it. "That's all I *can* do, isn't it?"

I want so desperately for him to understand. But he shifts his gaze away from mine, and I do the same, unable to watch the play of emotions on his face.

Whiskey is standing on both hands the next time the carousel loops around, and the twins are whooping excitedly. Her legs arc backward until her pointed toes almost touch the back of her head. She slowly lifts one hand from the horse until five fingers and one palm are all that's keeping her upright.

"No," he says, staring intently at me. "I don't think that's all you can do. Everyone assumes that you have to pass on the curse, but what if you didn't? What if, instead, you broke it?"

I open my mouth to respond, but the words aren't there. Even in my short time with the carnival, the curse seems as immutable as the color of the sky. Surely if the curse could be broken, someone else would have tried by now. And even if it *were* possible, what about the consequences?

"I don't know. No one told me how to break it, just how to pass it on. And Leslie said it isn't just that the carnival has a charm *and* a curse upon it, but that the two things are dependent. If I break the curse, it'll probably ruin the charm. I just don't know what to do."

"Screw the charm," he says deliberately. "If the people who benefit from the curse want it so badly, they'd bear the burden of it themselves. So don't worry about them. And as for the rest, whatever it is that has to be done, you wouldn't have to do it alone."

The grin stretches out my cheeks until I'm surprised my face hasn't cracked. "You'd help me?"

In answer, he folds me up in his arms. I fit neatly against his chest, and he rests his chin on the top of my head. It's strange and weird and I have no precedent for this kind of thing, and I'm just so damned *happy* I swear I'd almost forgotten what happiness felt like.

But all of that is lost in his warmth and the steady beating of his heart under my ear. For a brief moment I pretend I have a heartbeat, too, one that can thump in time with his.

Whiskey's shriek snaps me out of it.

I turn in time to see her hit the wooden boards of the carousel floor. Ben and I run for the gate as Pia jumps off and stumbles to the control booth.

Ben jumps on the carousel before it stills, dodging around the horses and lions and tigers. When the machine's revolutions slow a little more, I clumsily follow.

The wooden animals are still rising and falling slowly, creepily. A blue tiger with malicious jeweled eyes knocks into me with its massive paw. A giant parrot, its feathers painted a myriad of colors, each one cut with deep grooves that mark the center line and the barbs, dips in my way. As I twist around a giant bear, I find Duncan and Ben huddled around Whiskey.

A hand grips onto mine, and it's Pia, her cheeks

streaked with tears. Benjamin barks directions at Duncan. The latter has taken off his T-shirt and he's cutting off strips with a pocketknife. I can't see Whiskey around their bodies. A trickle of blood fills the grooves between planks of wood, reaching for my shoes.

Duncan lifts Whiskey in his arms. I never thought of her as small, but seeing her cradled there, her arms less than half as big around as his, her whole body neatly tucked in his arms, "fragile" is the only word that comes to mind. Ben is moving with them, winding the fabric Duncan provided him around to her head.

It's already soaked through with red.

CHAPTER SIXTEEN

Benjamin

Racing toward Happy the Clown's trailer is a blur of yelling and too many bodies clustered too close together. Happy takes one look at the bunch of us and pushes Duncan, who still holds Whiskey in his arms, inside. He slams the door shut behind him. Moments later Duncan is back outside with us, wild-eyed and sputtering for words.

There isn't enough air in the world to fill my lungs. I take in a big breath, and then another, until my heart begins to slow.

"Pia," Emma says, startling the both of us. "Go find Mr. and Mrs. Connelly." Pia nods, her eyes saucer-wide. "Duncan, go find Gin. Ben and I will wait for news."

The twins take off, and it's not until their backs are turned that I feel like I can slump down against the trailer. Never in my life have I seen so much blood. You never know how you feel about something until its existence is threatened. You hold something in your hands, never realizing that the glass sphere is actually a soap bubble, fragile and precious.

"Are you okay?"

"Whiskey doesn't fall," I say. I know it doesn't answer her question, but it's the only thought left in my head.

Emma's perfectly shaped brows arch prettily. "I know she's good, Ben, but everyone falls."

I shake my head. "In the entire time I've been at the carnival," I say, "I've never been hurt." Even as I say it, I feel the lie. I got the cut on my hand just a few weeks ago and I saw the freakish way that red lantern had fallen to the ground on Emma's first night here. But a cut and some broken glass aren't the same things as a dog breaking its neck or Whiskey hitting her head. Are they? "When I started working as my mom's apprentice, I never once cut myself on a blade or hit my own fingers with a hammer. None of the stupid but inevitable stuff that happens when you're working as a laborer ever happened to me. The Morettis should have broken their necks a hundred times over by now. And Gin and Whiskey…

"The girls are—always—flawless. I've seen Whiskey pull that same stunt a hundred times on the back of a living, breathing, unpredictable horse. To do the same on a carousel horse that's slowly bobbing up and down was something she could have done in her sleep."

I've heard it said a thousand times—we're held together by a charm and a curse. The curse appears to be firmly in place. Emma's skin is still petrified, her movements still jerky. So what is going on with the charm?

"I think the charm is wearing off and—" I pause, having a hard time even forming the words, wanting to hope but knowing it's too much of a dream come true.

"And do you think, *maybe*, the curse might be wearing off, too?"

I hold my breath, the way you do while contemplating the wish to be made as you blow out birthday candles. The air burns in my chest, still and stagnant, while I wait for Emma to answer. Her eyes are wide with horror and pity and anger all mixed together, and when she ducks her head away, shifting her gaze to the weeds at our feet, my breath explodes out of me as if she punched me.

"No, Benjamin," she finally says, a fine tremor in her voice. "I am still just as screwed today as I was yesterday. You might have gotten a splinter, but me?" She slams her arm into the corner of Happy's trailer, a move that would have shattered the bone inside if she weren't cursed. But there isn't even a smudge of dirt marking the impact on her arm.

"You're right," I say, reaching for her hands. They're cold, and when I twine my fingers through hers, they dig into my flesh and bump against my bones. But I hold on. "I'm sorry. It was wishful thinking on my part."

Emma doesn't say anything after that, but she does squeeze her stiff fingers around mine, gently. I busy myself by tracing my thumb over the flat plane of her palm, hoping that Happy remembers some of his old medical training. Despite having a medical degree, Happy came here to be a clown after having seen too much blood and horror out in the field. A clown is all I've ever known him to be, and I hope he knows what the hell he's doing.

I stare at the backs of my fingers, at Whiskey's blood caked into the grooves. My fingerprints show through the rusty grime in pale relief. My mind refuses to process what just happened. Seeing Whiskey's blood pulse out from the gash on her head. Seeing her limp and helpless, like a puppet with the strings cut.

Gin, followed closely by Marcel and Duncan, storms up the steps into the trailer. There's a commotion inside — Gin's muffled squeak, many footsteps, Happy's soothing voice — and then they're all outside again. They couldn't have been in there for more than thirty seconds.

She's a silvery flurry of motion when she's back outside again, pacing so fast that her blond hair can't keep up. It floats in streamers behind her. When she sees us, really sees us, she stops. There's an intensity in her gray eyes like I've never seen before. They match the storm clouds gathering above us.

"What the hell happened?" Her hair swirls around her in the breeze, giving her a wild look, like the elements are just as angry as she is. "Duncan said she fell, but we don't fall, we *don't.*"

"She fell, Gin," I said. "She just…fell."

It's clear she doesn't believe me, but I wouldn't believe me, either, if I were her. The heavy wrongness of the situation smothers us all.

After a while, Happy opens the door to the trailer and beckons Gin inside, and, as Pia has just shown up with the girls' worried parents, them, too. Once the door closes behind them, Happy turns his attention to us.

"Nasty cut. Did what I could, but it'll probably scar. Definite concussion." He still holds the rag he'd been drying his hands on. Traces of Whiskey's blood speckle it. "She should be fine, though."

Happy gives permission for short visits, and by then more people have arrived. I can't bring myself to see her just yet, and I let the others go in ahead of me. They

filter in and out of the avocado-colored trailer in pairs—
Leslie and Lars, Pia and Duncan, Mrs. Potter and one of
her terriers—and I watch them go. The only constant is
Emma.

She stands by my side as the parade of well-wishers
continues. The back of her hand brushes against the
back of mine. I find myself slumping against her, though
I hadn't intended to, and she holds me up.

I get ready to go in and see Whiskey, but as Mrs. Potter
is leaving, Happy decides Whiskey is done with visitors
for the day. I want to protest, but I can't seem to find my
voice.

"Sir?" Emma says, firm but polite. But no one here has
ever been called "sir," so she has to try again. "Happy?
Ben needs to see her."

Happy looks at me like I haven't been standing
there the whole time, but he doesn't waver. Yesterday's
greasepaint is still caked into the fine lines of his face.
"Girl needs to rest."

I'm prepared to let that go, though tension balls up
even tighter inside me. I didn't realize how much I needed
to see that she's okay. It's like I won't know it's the truth
until I can see her with my own eyes. The blood may as
well still be gushing from her head.

"That's her blood on his hands, Happy," Emma says.
"Let him have a second; let him see that she's all right."

I can practically hear his teeth grind, but he holds the
door open for me. "Wash your hands first, kid."

Emma holds back. But she deserves to make sure that
Whiskey is all right just as much as I do. That, and we need
answers about what happened, about the charm. Answers
I'm hoping Whiskey can give me. So I grip tightly onto

Emma's hand and lead her into the trailer.

The interior is dark with all the little curtains closed. A light is on at one end of the trailer, but not over the couch where Whiskey rests. Everything is drab, the complete antithesis of the way Happy presents himself out in the carnival. The air is stale, like no one besides him is ever in here.

Whiskey is propped up on the narrow couch that runs along the back end of the trailer. A crochet blanket that's more hole than blanket drapes over her knees, and a huge swath of gauze is wrapped around her head. Her father, a tall man who gave Gin his lean muscles and pale hair, and mother, like Whiskey in looks and temperament, are crammed into the area around her.

"Okay, now pay attention," Whiskey tells me as I wash up in the tiny sink. "I've got this down to a science. Yes, I fell. No, I don't know why. Yes, feel free to fawn all over me and possibly even consider bringing me fudge because I love fudge. Fawning may commence whenever you're ready."

"But—"

She cuts me off. "I fell, Benjamin. The end." She turns to her parents. "You know what I would *love* right about now? My own pillow. One that doesn't smell of cigarettes and sardines. Could you please, please, please ask Haps when I can go home?"

Mr. and Mrs. Connolly exchange a quick glance, but it's clear to see that Mrs. Connolly wants to get Whiskey home, too. So they edge past Emma and me to go talk to Happy. The second the door slams shut, Whiskey is off and running.

"What the hell, you guys?" A slim thread of panic

runs through her voice. Her pupils are inky-black spots floating in the whites of her eyes. "I don't fall. I have never fallen. Never. So something must have happened. Did either of you see?"

"Whiskey," Emma starts, "I don't think—"

"No," Whiskey says fiercely. Her eyes are so wide that the whites ring all around the brown irises. "No. *I don't fall.*"

"She's right," I say, and they both turn to face me. Whiskey looks at me like I'm the only voice of reason for miles around. "Something's wrong with the charm, and we're going to figure out what."

CHAPTER SEVENTEEN

Emma

Benjamin is on a warpath. Seeing Whiskey laid up seemed to ignite something in him, and as soon as we leave Happy's trailer, he takes off.

The fortune-tellers' tent is closed, but Ben pushes past the flaps anyway. Candles glow within red-glass lanterns, and the lights pulse against canvas walls moving gently in the wind. It's like being inside a ruby heart. Duncan and Pia sit at the small round table, heads in hands. A bowl of dark liquid stands in the middle of the table. When they both look up at the same time, it's more than a little unnerving.

"You guys okay?" Duncan asks.

"We'll be fine," Ben says. "What's this?" He gestures toward the bowl. Lines of salt trace complicated patterns on the table around it.

Pia seems a little embarrassed but speaks up anyway. "We were scrying to see if we could find the event that triggered Whiskey's fall." Pia sweeps her curls out of her eyes and shoots me down in an unusually somber voice. "We didn't get anything. But why are y'all here?"

"We have a question," Ben says. He gnaws at his lower lip.

"Do you know the charm and the curse are codependent?" I ask.

"Uh, yeah," Duncan says, as though this was written on a placard at the front entrance to the carnival.

I thought all the shock had been driven out of me the night I found out I was a cursed puppet girl, but apparently not. "You *knew*? Leslie made it sound like not everyone understands how it all works."

Pia waggles her finger between herself and her twin. "Umm, hello? Descendants of people who *placed* the damn things on the carnival in the first place. But Leslie is kinda right. Most people don't know the two go hand in hand. You know the old game Telephone? Where I tell you something and you tell someone else, who tells someone else and by the end, whatever I said in the first place is all jumbled up? Curse lore is kind of like that."

"Oh," I say. "Well, what can you tell us about it?"

The twins share the same expression, eyebrows arched high. "What do you want to know?" Pia asks.

"Anything you can tell us. I know about it, but in a really vague way. We want to know everything."

The siblings exchange a glance. "*Why* do you want to know now?" Duncan asks. "You've been with us for weeks." His hands slide across the table until they clasp Pia's.

Something is off, and I can't place it. Then I realize— I'm not twitching. The tent actually feels warm. I hold up my hand and see that my fingers are perfectly still. The inside of the tent must be sweltering. When I glance over at Ben, he's flushed, pink filling up his cheeks and neck. I check the twins, though, and they seem normal. Except for the way they're staring.

Both of them are gazing directly at me, and their eyes have gone pitch black.

I move to stand next to Ben again, their gazes following me. "Benjamin," I whisper.

"I see it."

The twins' chests rise and fall in perfect synchronicity. The only other movement they make is to blink, and even that they do completely in time.

"Why are you bothering my grandchildren?" The voice comes from their mouths in perfect unison, two voices layering to make up the one I'm hearing. The voice is neither male nor female, and there's a tremor in it that suggests extreme age.

Two heads cock to the side, and I realize the voice wants an answer. Oh God this is freaky. "I wasn't trying to bother them," I say.

"Then *why* are you here?"

"We were hoping to talk to them about the curse and the charm holding this place together," I say.

The dark liquid in the bowl ripples, like some invisible stone dropped to the bottom. When the voice speaks, it's discomfited, and two sets of eyebrows are furrowed at me. "Did they not tell you?"

"No," I say quickly, not wanting to anger the voice. "They told me. It's just that I feel like I might be missing something. People are getting hurt."

Understanding spreads from brother to sister in a wave. Their faces almost seem...relaxed. "Ah. I see. The charm and the curse are, ah, *symbiotic*, to put it lightly. There is much more I'd like to talk to you about, my dear. Where is the carnival now?"

"Texas," Ben says. "Due to head out toward Arizona."

Two heads snap toward Ben. They appraise him, and it's my turn to give his hand a squeeze. I can feel his pulse thudding madly where our wrists press together. "What's your name, dear?"

"Benjamin," he says.

"Hmm. Well, Arizona is no good, Benjamin," the voice says. The twins shake their heads in dissent. "Who's in charge of the carnival now? Is it still Franklin?"

"No," Ben says. "Leslie, his daughter, is in charge now."

"I remember Leslie. Sweet girl. Tell her to head for New Orleans, the quicker the better." The voice is fainter now.

"Wait," I say, not entirely sure if I want the voice to come back. "What's in New Orleans?"

The corners of both twins' mouths pick up, and the expression is all the more creepy because I've seen a milder version of the same smile on Duncan's face before. Their heads are loose on their necks, like heavy blooms on weak stems. "Me, deary. I am in New Orleans."

CHAPTER EIGHTEEN

Emma

Benjamin and I lie on the great big pile of pillows in my wagon, out of sight of anyone who might report us back to his mom. Above us, through the skylight, the heavy oak branches sway, and light shines through the browning leaves in shades of ocher and caramel.

"Would Leslie do it?" I ask, burrowing farther into his side, his warmth. Some new instinct that's grown between the two of us has him curling his arm around me to pull me in tighter. "Help us break the curse and figure out what's going on with the charm?" I can't believe the thought never crossed my mind. If the curse is broken, then no one ever has to go through this again. And if I'm not beholden to the carnival, then I can leave, I can find Juliet and my parents and brothers and tell them how sorry I am for all this. With that sitting in the distance like a pot of gold, it's easy to think this could work.

Ben pushes his glasses onto his forehead and rubs his eyes. "I think so? We'd have to discuss the possibility that the charm is weakening, though I don't know if we should tell her about breaking the curse just yet. And she needs to know about the creepy twin puppet show back there…but there are too many people here who don't have a problem with the curse or the charm. It keeps them healthy and happy.

"I never really gave much thought about it all, you know? It was just always the way things had been. But now, knowing what happened with my mom and seeing how you're affected… It's not right. And I don't feel bad about wanting to end things. The problem is there's no telling what that might mean. I know she doesn't look it, but my mom is almost seventy. Leslie looks thirty, but she's in her eighties, I think. What happens to them? Does their aging catch up to them? I mean, I know that Leslie's dad got cancer after he left—does ending the curse start a timer on anyone who has some disease festering inside them? Are they going to drop dead? I just don't know what to do."

If what Ben was saying was true, there could be dozens, hundreds of people affected by breaking the curse. They'd be living their lives, happy and content, only to have illness or age rushing up to meet them when they thought they were safe. And they wouldn't all be faceless victims, either—what about Lars? Would his cancer come back, too?

That heavy thought hangs between us, and I know it's one neither of us wants to think about, because we're both content to lie there in silence. For a long time, I just keep my hand on his chest, mesmerized by the steady rise and fall with each breath, with the persistent beat of his heart. It's only because of the angle I'm lying in that I'm able to see through the cracked door and spot someone who's not going to make his day any better walking our way.

"Hey," I say, "Sidney's coming. Don't punch him again, okay?" I get up and walk over to intercept Sidney. "Now's not a good time."

The splotchy-pink patch near Sidney's mouth is starting to blush darker. He reaches up to gingerly touch it, but instead of being pissed, he actually smiles. "Not here about that." He peers around me to look at Benjamin. "Your mom's on the prowl. I thought you wouldn't want her to find you here, so..."

Ben stands and brushes imaginary lint from his jeans. His hand lingers at the small of my back as he walks past, but otherwise he leaves without a word.

"Look at you," Sidney says once Ben's out of earshot, brow arched and grinning. "Such a bad influence. What were you two talking about?"

Oh God. How would Sidney take the news of us wanting to break the curse? Would he revel in the curse's destruction? Feel stupid for not trying it himself? So I just start to walk back toward the carnival and say, "Nothing."

"Bullshit," he drawls, keeping pace with me. "You really expect me to believe you're wasting time doing 'nothing' when you could be making out?"

I fully expect to spontaneously combust, since what he said would normally have my cheeks on fire. Instead I fix him with my best steely glare. "What does it matter to you anyway?"

"Bored," he says with a shrug. "I've got nothing to do; people still treat me like I'm the Boy in the Box, like I'm not quite one of them. Pretty much only talk to you." He pivots toward the yard and walks off through the grass, tall stalks swaying in his wake.

The admission feels like a punch to the gut. I chase after him, and as the grasses make their soft shushing sounds around us, I realize the thing I never thought could happen has—I feel pity for Sidney.

"All right," I say, lowering my voice in case anyone sneaks up on us. "We think the charm protecting the carnival is wearing off. And we think if that's the case, then maybe it's time to break the curse instead of passing it on. There might be someone in New Orleans who can help us. We just need to figure out how to get Leslie to change course."

Sidney strokes the stubble at his jaw, and though he's looking at me, it seems more like he's looking through me.

"Won't work," he says, and suddenly he's off again.

"What? Why would you assume that?" I ask, struggling to match his longer stride.

"Trust me."

I grab his arm, jerking him to a stop. "No. You don't get to say 'trust me' and brush me off. Why do you think it can't be done?"

Sidney scrubs his palms over his eyes. "Nothing. Forget it."

My stony fingers dig into his soft arm. "Sidney. Unless you want to drastically reduce the number of people who talk to you, you *will* tell me what's going on."

He draws his lip between his teeth and worries at it a bit. His eyes glaze over as he looks out at the field. Gin rides Tristam at a slow canter. The Ferris wheel rotates in the distance, stopping for long intervals as Lars cleans the cars. "I can get you to New Orleans."

We're walking between the family trailers and tents now, and have to watch for anyone who might be listening.

"I'll just tell Leslie that's where I want the carnival to drop me off," Sidney says. "That I have family there or something."

"Why?"

"What do you mean, 'why'?" He stares down at me from the corner of his eye.

"I mean you won't really leave, will you? What about you and Audrey?"

Sidney jerks to a halt and narrows his eyes at me. "What about me and Audrey?"

The wind hurtles down the alley we're in, strong enough to buffet against my body like it's a hollow reed. There's no tickle across my skin, but my body feels cooler, and I wrap my cold arms around me, as if that's going to do anything. "Come on. Ben punched you, and you let him. You and Audrey had a thing forever ago—" I hold up my hand to keep him from talking because I can already see that he has a rebuttal at the ready. "Don't bother, Ben already told me. And even if he hadn't, I've seen the way you make googly eyes at her."

His mouth flops open in indignation, like a fish gasping for air. "I do not make googly eyes at Audrey."

"Of course you don't," I say in the faux-condescending way that says I completely think he does.

"Fine. I make googly eyes at Audrey. But I think this will get Leslie to turn the carnival around. So come on," Sidney says as he continues on toward Leslie's trailer, snagging a soda from a cart passing in the opposite direction.

I think about what Ben said, and the way the twins

looked as they channeled their spooky grandmother. I think about getting rid of the curse and feeling alive again. I think about being able to kiss Ben. I think about Whiskey and how small she looked as Duncan carried her away.

I hurry to catch up.

"Liar," Leslie says as she drops down into the booth of her kitchenette. It's so quiet I can hear Sidney swallow.

"Excuse me?" Sidney asks.

"You heard me," Leslie says. "I called you a liar." She reaches behind her and finds an orange. Sidney snatches it from her, forcing Leslie to grab another for herself. "What do you really want?"

"To go home," Sidney says stubbornly. "I have family there. During summer vacation, I'd visit them, and spend whole days walking along the river, eating beignets. There was this one time that I was almost mugged—"

"Shut it, Sidney." Leslie places her half-peeled orange on the table and stands on the seat of the booth to reach a compartment over her head. From it, she takes a rust-colored leather-bound book.

The pages are old and yellowed, the edges crumbling. The handwriting is small and cramped at first, then sloping and curly, and finally blocky and precise. Leslie flips back through the sloping handwriting until she finds the page she's looking for. She runs her finger down the columns and stops.

"Sidney Parker," she says, glancing up at him. Sidney winces, and something gnawing at my brain tells me that our hastily put together plan is going to die on the pages of that book. "Born, 1949 in Portland, Oregon. Joined as a laborer in June, 1968. Recipient of the curse, July 1968, passed on from Katherine Carlisle." From over Leslie's shoulder, I can see that the printing has changed, and now it's the blockier handwriting from later in the book. "Parents, Nellie and Charles Parker, deceased, 1983. No next of kin."

Sidney stares at the dingy tile of the trailer. When he glances up at Leslie he's like a wounded, cornered animal. And damn it all to hell but I actually feel sorry for the bastard. *Again.*

Leslie's voice goes softer, as does the look in her eyes. I get the feeling she wouldn't have taken the same approach if it had been me sitting across from her, spinning a yarn about New Orleans. She understands her employees — no, her people — and that means knowing Sidney needs a firm hand. "We keep a record of everyone who joins our carnival, a fact I'm guessing you either forgot or were never made aware of. So, Sidney, do you *really* want to go to New Orleans?"

This is what we had prepared for on our walk over, and I want to feel as though I'm on surer footing, but the vision Leslie painted of Sidney's broken family tree is too bright in my head. As much as I hate what he did to me, he was tricked once, too, and had to leave a family behind just like I did. I hate the idea of him all alone in the world.

"I want to go to New Orleans," Sidney says with cool precision. "There's not much more for me to show Emma anyway, and what is left I can take care of before we hit Louisiana."

"Bullshit," Leslie says, slamming the book closed. "The two of you are going to tell me what you're planning, or Sidney, so help me, I will drag your ass around this whole carnival until we find Audrey and I make *her* tell us what's going on. Because do you know how I know you're lying? Audrey. If we dropped you off in New Orleans, Audrey will still be with this carnival, and I would lay it all down, every last game and ride and trailer—any piece of this carnival that's mine to bet—that until the day you die, you will always be found within five hundred feet of Audrey Singer. You think I don't know that you were biding your time in that box?"

All the blood has drained out of Sidney's face.

"You put on a good show, Sidney." Leslie's cheeks are pink with anger; her hair is a halo of curls. Valkyries have nothing on her. "But I know people and I know why you stuck around all those years. Even when Audrey was gone and you were too depressed to even get in the booth and *try* to pass on the curse, you stayed, hoping, *knowing* she'd come back. So do not belittle my intelligence and expect me to believe that you are going to leave Audrey behind. If you expect me to change course at the drop of a hat you will give me a good, *truthful* reason or it's not happening."

Leslie and Sidney have a staring showdown and if I hadn't just seen Leslie be such a badass, I'd have said Sidney would win. He'd spent years in the box, pretending to be a happy-go-lucky carnie not pitiful curse victim. But Leslie is seriously pissed. Finally, Sidney looks over at me.

"Tell her," he says, his voice barely more than a whisper. He stands so abruptly he almost knocks the tabletop off the metal pole it stands on. As the screen door slams, Leslie speaks.

"Yes, Emma," she says, folding her delicate hands neatly as she turns to face me. "Tell me."

CHAPTER NINETEEN

Benjamin

I'm cutting through the yard, taking a shortcut between two trailers, when Lorenzo Moretti moves into the gap in front of me. Shit. Where there's one Moretti, there are two more in hiding. Lorenzo is the middle brother, the one who always seems to be five minutes away from taking a good nap. But the eyes staring at me now are sharp and clear, shining with a dark intensity. I start to back up and hear a low laugh.

"You cause too much trouble," Fabrizio says.

I whirl around to see that he and Antonio have snuck up behind me, penning me into the narrow space between trailers. Malice crackles between them like lightning jumping from cloud to cloud, and I know that I'm in for it.

"Yeah, well, maybe if you guys weren't always harassing the newbies…" I say. I edge toward the wall of one of the trailers, but the moment I move, the brothers do, too. I need to get out of here. Fast.

"Heard you decided to have a little chat with Leslie,

roustabout," Fabrizio says. I haven't taken my gaze off him, and he stares back without blinking. "Then I was thinking. You clearly have a problem with us. We have a problem with your mom. Maybe we can kill two birds with one stone."

There's movement all around me, vultures tightening the spiral toward their prey. The air around me feels colder, the day a little darker.

"I thought, what does that bitch Audrey Singer love more than anything in the world? What would she go the extra mile to protect? And who would I like to teach a lesson about ratting out my brother?" Fabrizio grins, a flash of white teeth that feels like danger.

The first punch is quick and fast and dirty.

Fabrizio lands a kick square to my knee. My shoulder hits the packed dirt with a *thud*. A boot crashes into my ribs, the impact resonating throughout my body, followed quickly by a tingly numbness.

The brothers take turns kicking and punching at my legs, my gut, my chest. Fireworks of pain bloom from each point of impact, each layering over the other, until I'm in one hazy fugue of hurt. Already I'm trying to think of ways to cover up the inevitable cuts and bruises, because though I never would have thought them to be smart enough, this plan of theirs has a high chance of succeeding.

And as fast as it all began, it's over. Dust settles around me, coating my bare arms, the inside of my mouth.

Antonio kneels on the ground beside me. More of that fine, dry dirt flurries around when he does, stinging my eyes. My glasses sit on my nose at an odd angle, and he carefully reaches to straighten them for me. "Get out," he says.

He rises, and he and his brothers run through the gap between trailers.

I roll onto my back and stare up at the sliver of sky above me. Thready streamers of clouds fill the space, with streaks of bright blue peeking through. I watch them speed across the sky while my breathing—slowly, achingly—returns to normal. Nothing feels broken, only bruised, like I was pummeled with a meat tenderizer. After several long moments, I stand and instantly regret it.

Jesus, that was an even more horrible brand of asshole than I'm used to from those three. But I can't waste any more time worrying about them, not when Mom's looking for me. When I think that I can walk without wincing, I knock the dirt off my clothes and go to find her.

In front of the Airstream there's a scattering of boxes—boxes filled with tools, with scrap wood, with anything Mom and I can call ours—littering the ground. One of the boxes props open the door, and as I approach, Mom steps out among them.

At first she doesn't see me. Instead, she flits from box to box, mashing the lids down to secure them with packing tape.

"Mom," I say. She doesn't hear. "Mom!"

She straightens and pushes her hair back. Her eyes shine with harried impatience. "Get your things. Anything not in the Airstream already. We're leaving."

I cross the few short feet between us, palms out in surrender, hoping she doesn't notice how slowly I'm walking. The last thing I need is for her to find out about the beating I just got. "Whoa. Mom. Why are we leaving?"

She glances around, like she's afraid that someone will overhear us. I kind of hope someone does, that someone else will come over and help me talk some sense into her. "Whiskey. She fell."

I nod. "Yeah, so?"

"That," she says, going back to taping up the box at her feet, "is enough. I came back because of the charm. I came here to keep you protected. But if that charm isn't working anymore, then there's nothing to keep us here. If the carnival can't ensure your safety then there's no reason to stick around."

I swallow. Leaving was the thing I thought I wanted. But that's not what I want anymore. At some point over the last several weeks, my wants changed, and I don't know a way of explaining it that doesn't involve Emma.

Lately, I've felt more comfortable spending the evenings in her tiny wagon. When I'm there, with her, I feel calm. Sated. Home. And I don't think I realized that until this very second.

Mom takes my silence for compliance and hands me the keys to the truck. "Bring the Chevy around and we'll hitch up. I'll explain things to Leslie."

The keys sit in my palm, the heavy pewter keychain in the shape of Arkansas glinting dully in the light. I breathe in deep and that sets off a twinge of pain, but I do my best to ignore it. "No, Mom."

Immediately I see her mouth open to argue and I backtrack. "I mean, let's talk. Yes, the world out there is dangerous. And so is the carnival. The charm *does* keep us safe, and it has for years. But I got this"—I lift up the hem of my shirt to show her the slick white scar I still have from the car accident that killed Dad—"out there, not here. Whiskey was hurt. But that doesn't mean I'll be hurt, too."

Her eyes are pinched at the corners, and I know she's not convinced.

"All I'm saying is that we have to play the odds. And it seems to me that the odds are better in here rather than out there. Right?"

She slowly sinks down onto the box she just closed up and drops the roll of packing tape to the ground. Some intangible thing inside her is broken, or at the very least shaken.

"Mom, I'm not some fragile little thing, okay? I don't know what it's like to look at someone you love lying in a hospital bed, but that's in the past." I kneel down in front of her. The ground is cool and the chill seeps through my jeans immediately, centering me. Suddenly I feel everything is going to be all right; Mom will stay, I'll help Emma break the curse, and everything will work out one way or another. It has to.

It has to.

CHAPTER TWENTY

Emma

Leslie presses her fingers to her forehead, smoothing the furrows creasing her brow. "So Katarina possessed the twins and told you she can help? And you believe it? Believe it enough to completely change our course?"

Leslie stares at me, last night's stage makeup still sitting in the fine lines around her eyes, and she looks so weary. I glance down at the flat, anonymous backs of my hands. They have the same vague shape my hands did before, but they're so pale and almost…generic. Like this is what hands should look like, not necessarily what *my* hands should look like. Never would I have thought that one day I'd find myself missing the lines, cracks, and creases that make my hands *mine*.

"I believe her."

Leslie sighs and her gaze darts around the camper, lingering on the poster for the carnival with a painting of Sidney in the box. After a long stretch of silence, she pulls a stack of maps out of the same cupboard that had held the giant leather-bound book. Some are decades old, some only days, it seems like. One of them has trails traced out in faded strands of embroidery floss, marking into the paper the paths the carnival made each year. Many paths of thread are so old that the colors start to all look like they're the same creamy beige. Finally, she finds a giant one of Texas and another of Louisiana.

She lines them up on her small table, folded over to show just the half of Texas that we're in and the part of Louisiana we want to be in. My heart sinks when I see the inches marking the hundreds of miles standing between Round Rock and New Orleans. Why couldn't the twins' magic grandmother live a few inches closer?

"The plan," Leslie says, "had been to take the I-35 down to I-10, and then drive west. New Mexico, Arizona, all those places would have been warmer for you, at least during the day. But now—" She hovers in close over the map, picking out much, much smaller highways and farm roads. "Now we'll head the opposite direction. We'll still have to make stops—performing means money, and money keeps this carnival moving—but we'll get there."

She has me bring over the coffee tin full of markers and pens and highlighters, and she begins to plot out a path, turning miles of highway bright pink.

"We'll cut down to Houston and follow I-10 in the other direction. We'll stop here." She marks a small dot on the messy sprawl that is Houston. "And here—" Another town, the much smaller Orange, Texas, another mark. "Before we cross into Louisiana. And that's *if* we can get the permits we'll need. Saundra usually does that for me and she's already headed toward Arizona. I'll have to call her back." After marking out our stops along the freeway, she drops the highlighter into the tin with a clatter and pushes her platinum curls off her face. She stares down at the maps as she talks. "It'll take weeks, Emma. At least. And that's with no snags."

I look at the line marked out in drying ink. When you factor in all the stops we have to make—one day for set up, a minimum of three days in a town, another day for tear down—we are at least a month away. But then I look past the top of the map of Texas, up in the vague place where my hometown would be, where my dad and brothers and Juliet are. I look at my hands and the way they twitch. And I think about how I want to kiss Benjamin with lips that are mine, with a mouth that will mold into a new shape with his. A shape that's only ours.

"Yes," I say.

She glances down at the maps again. Her eyes flit from here to there, and I wouldn't be surprised if Leslie knew every gas station and pit stop and road marker along the way. "I'll tell Saundra, let her know about the change of plans. I doubt that anyone besides you and me and Sidney will figure out what's going on."

"And Benjamin," I say.

"And Benjamin." Her gaze is hard and steady, and the urge to look away from her unwavering stare is beaten into submission by wanting to know what she's thinking. She begins to fold up the maps in silence, the soft shushing of paper on paper the only noise.

"Are you okay with this?" I say.

"With changing course?" she asks. "We follow the warmth largely for the person in the box, since the cold is so much worse for you than for us. There's benefit for us, too. People are more likely to come out to the carnival in warm weather. We owe everything to you, and to the people who came before you. It's the least we can do to make you a little more comfortable."

I let that sink in and think about the hundred or so people attached to this carnival who follow the bidding of someone who wants to make me comfortable. It's a weird thought.

"No," I say, "not that. It's more…how do you feel about us breaking the curse? About what that might mean for the carnival?"

She stares up at me and slots her slim fingers together on top of her neatly stacked maps. She's so tiny and petite that it's easy to dismiss her. But Leslie is not someone to dismiss. "Sidney might have spent nearly fifty years in the box, but he was the only one to take that long. Before him, we had a new person in the box every year or two."

As she speaks, her blue eyes grow colder, not with contempt but with something like a hard, unyielding despair. "I watched them, shy loners and teenagers younger than you, as they were duped into the curse. I helped carry their broken, rag-doll bodies back to my trailer so I could tell them that they were stuck. I stood idly by as their hearts hardened every night they went out and worked the booth. And I did nothing as they became the thing they hated, a person willing to trick someone into taking their place at the center of this carnival.

"It took something from me, every single time. I let it keep happening, over and over, never trying to stop the cycle, enjoying the perks. And you'd think that there'd be nothing left of my soul to crush after all these years, but then Pia came barreling up to the big tent where I was about to introduce the Morettis for their final show of the night and told me Sidney had taken a bottle of wine and had a girl on his arm."

A rush of cold shudders down my spine despite the heat in the trailer. Me. The girl was me. Leslie's gaze doesn't waver. No tears sit in her lashes, there's no tremble in her voice. Leslie will tell me how she was a cog in the curse's mechanics without theatrics or drama.

"I gave the Morettis the worst intro imaginable and ran out of that tent. Pia and I saw the Ferris wheel as it stopped. Saw you and Sidney struggle. Saw you fall. And as I walked up to where you lay on the ground, I knew the cycle was starting again. The reprieve was over. And I don't think I can do this again."

It's only here, at the end of her story, that she breaks my gaze. The two maps with our new path stay on the table, but she tucks away the papers and dog-eared key maps. She falters as she lifts the old journals to put them back in their cupboard, and, almost as if on impulse, she hands them to me. "Maybe there's something in there that'll help."

As we step outside, Leslie surveys all that she can see from the top step of her trailer. While it seems people are gossiping with more ferocity than usual, life is going on as it would ordinarily. Down the lane, Marcel and his father are practicing, the taller man standing behind my friend in order to correct his form. Two of the women who run the confectionary booth, both of them with bottle-red hair teased into beehives, walk by, waving cheerfully at their boss. Lars gives us a small nod as he passes in the opposite direction. Leslie continues to watch him, and I wonder if she's thinking about his cancer miraculously disappearing.

"This carnival is my life," Leslie says absently. "My father ran it, and his mother before him. They had a few good years after they retired, but they're both gone now. All the illnesses the charm held at bay caught up to them.

"The carnival is all I've ever known. I'd do anything to keep it alive. But everything ends, Emma." She turns her bright-blue eyes to me, and tears sparkle at the edges. "Everything."

CHAPTER TWENTY-ONE

Benjamin

I'm standing in the open door of the Airstream, watching the other trucks and trailers idle on the field, waiting to pull out. The ground is trampled, used and sad. Where there had been a field of green, green grass, we're leaving behind mud and holes where stakes had been planted and, even though we're vigilant to pick up all litter, random bits of trash that escaped our cleanup crew. At Leslie's signal, the first vehicle trundles toward the road, trucks hitched to trailers following. It's like hundreds of boats launching, like a carnival armada.

Sidney told Mom he wanted to talk, and I've snuck Emma on board the Airstream. Right now, she's tucked in the bathroom, in case my mom pops back to make one last check. Never have I been so ready to get on the road.

Finally the Chevy gives a deep rumble and we're off. I stay in the doorframe awhile longer, letting the wind ruffle my hair. I catch the scent of crushed grass under so many wheels, of gasoline and exhaust. Finally, I close and lock the door and give Emma the all clear.

She flashes me a sheepish grin as she steps out of the bathroom, like she, too, feels like a stereotypical teenager sneaking around. "Do you have them?" she asks.

I turn and maneuver to the dinette booth and pull two books from the box beneath it. One is a large leather-bound journal Emma got from Leslie, records of everyone who ever worked for the carnival. The other is newer, but only because the old one had to be transcribed. This journal details the history of the curse, up until about ten years ago. The twins hadn't updated it, as Sidney hadn't had any successes or failures worth noting in that time.

I drop down into the booth and crack open the big book. I feel like I should have on those white gloves that people use to handle priceless books from the dawn of time. "I haven't really—"

"Is this you?" Emma's in front of the panel that hides our water heater, which Mom has covered in family photos. The picture she's pointing to is me at about three or four, chubby-cheeked and towheaded and even then I had to wear glasses. My cheeks and neck flush with heat. But luckily Emma has moved on from that one and has bent over to look at another taped a little lower.

In that one, I'm just a toddler, and it's one of those pictures where I'm supposed to be sitting happily with a mall Santa Claus. Naturally, I'm screaming my head off. The only reason I can see for keeping it is that my dad is in the photo, crouched near Santa, as if his proximity would make being seated next to the strange dude in an acrylic beard any better.

"That your dad?"

The photo has started to yellow around the corners,

casting Dad in a strange golden glow. "Yeah. That was about two years before the car accident."

The playful smile picking up the corners of her mouth falls in a flash, replaced with something more thoughtful, more serious. "You look like him," she says. "In that picture, he even had a furrow right—" She reaches out and touches between my eyebrows, just over the bridge of my glasses. "Here, like you do sometimes." Her fingers skim the line of my brow and down my cheek until she's cupping my jaw in her hand. Even though I know it wouldn't be the same as kissing a normal girl, all I can think about is what it would be like to pull her in close and press my lips to hers.

The trailer hits a pothole, and when Emma stumbles backward, it's like instinct to reach out and wrap an arm around her waist, tuck her body close to mine. She looks up at me, so close I can see each delicate eyelash, and my breath catches in my chest because at the same moment that I think *she's going to kiss me* another thought runs parallel in my head. *Her kiss could curse me.*

The thought shatters the bubble I'm in, not because it holds anything close to the truth—Emma told me how complicated it is to transfer the curse—but because it's so hard to shake the myth I've grown up with. She must see something in my eyes, because she pulls away, carefully disentangling from my hold.

I cough and peer at the photographs, stuck dubiously in place by strips of cheap tape, looking for something to back up her earlier assessment. In many of the photos Dad's smiling, but here and there Mom caught him lost in thought, more serious moments that are now forever trapped between me photographed in various points of parental pride. If I squint and give him glasses and imagine his hair is blonder, Emma's right. This thought makes me happier than I ever imagined it would. It's with this extra sort of buoyancy that I begin to flip through Leslie's massive journal as Emma goes through the one we got from the twins.

But soon enough, the hypnotic thrum of the road and the small, tight handwriting take their toll. I think I've read the same page three times in a row. Then Emma slides her hand over until it lines up with mine just so, and suddenly I am awake. Her twitching is particularly bad today, and I feel terrible that the heater in the Airstream isn't enough to keep it at bay. I try to ignore her twitches the way you would ignore the fact that someone has a terrible scar. It's not the scar that defines the person, just like her twitching doesn't define her. In fact, the gentle, irregular tapping becomes kind of a peaceful background noise, like a substitute for her breathing or something.

I find that I'm staring at the way her dark hair curves over and behind her ear. The line where her jaw curves down into her throat. When she turns, her lips are like red, red rubies. Even now, reduced to the simplest lines that make her *her,* I find Emma beautiful. I don't know if my brain will be able to process her when she's herself again.

That's when we hear the *bangs.*

They're in quick succession, two loud and close and three at distances farther out. The Airstream swerves sharply to the right, and it's only a quick grab onto the table that saves me from falling to the floor. Emma is thrown into me, and I wrap an arm around her, drawing her close. The ground beneath us becomes bumpy, and then we slow to a halt. It takes a second to figure it out, but I quickly realize that it's the sound of tires being blown. Enough of the cars and trailers must have had a blowout to necessitate the entire caravan stopping.

"Stay hidden," I say, and I hop out of the trailer to look around for myself. Sure enough, the truck behind us has a flat at the front driver's side wheel. I walk around to the Chevy to talk to Mom and find that the car in front of us has a flat tire, too, same wheel.

When Mom cranks down the window, there's a thin veneer of confusion over her already frustrated features. Her talk with Sidney must not be going well.

"I've never seen a flat on the line, ever," she says.

I lean on the door. "It's the one behind us, too." Her brow creases. "And I think I heard more blowouts." It's almost like I know what she's thinking before she thinks it. "I'm sure it's nothing—a construction crew dropped nails and some of the cars picked them up."

My theory is flimsy, and her expression confirms it. Before she can argue, though, I tell her, "I'll go check it out. It's nails, I'm sure." Anything to keep her from doubting the carnival's charm.

I kneel by the wheel of the truck behind us and look at the tire. The black rubber looks like the skin of some rotten fruit that's burst. Wires and tread flay out to expose the inner covering that hugs the metal wheel. I don't like the look of it. What's left of each tire wraps around the wheel in tattered strips of rubber. I check out the car in front of us and its tires are identical. It's not nails. It's way too coincidental that the flats are all the front driver's side wheels and all went at the same time. Four vehicles, all at different points in the procession, and each with a blown front tire. It's too weird.

But that's not what I tell Mom.

"Nails," I say. I'm not sure if she buys it, but I know for a fact that Sidney doesn't. Not even when I pull several mangled nails out to show them. I'm just hoping the brand is generic enough that Mom believes I found them on the side of the road and not in my pocket, where they'd been for ages. She twirls one bent shape between her fingers.

"Nails," she says. In that moment, I know she doesn't believe but wants to, same as I know I'm right that this was more than an accident, but I don't want it to be.

CHAPTER TWENTY-TWO

Emma

When Ben climbs back into the Airstream almost an hour later, I can tell he's upset. He rumples the hair that hangs in his face back and then smooths it out, again and again. It isn't until his mom's truck rumbles to life ahead of us that he sits down.

"What was it?" I ask.

"A few blown tires." He stares at the other end of the trailer, as though he could see through the flimsy walls and metal right into the back of his mother's head. In fact, I realize that he must have been talking to her the whole time, keeping her busy to prevent her from finding me in here.

I'm not entirely sure how that makes me feel.

But thinking like that means I have to think about things like What Ben and I Are, and Will His Mom Still Hate Me Once I'm Human Again or Does She Just Hate Me Because My Kiss is Evil. But I don't have to think on that for long, because he begins to flip through the pages of Leslie's journal.

"Okay," Ben says, "I figure that if we can go back far enough, there might be a record of the first person to have been cursed." But he doesn't move, just stares at the cramped handwriting on the pages.

"Well," I say, hoping to jog him out of whatever funk he's in, "this one is some sort of, I don't know, retelling of the carnival's history? The person who wrote it seems to really love a tangent. The handwriting is small, and the pages are thin, a little too thin for me to really be able to handle well, so I think I need you to go through this one. That okay?"

Benjamin nods, and then folds his arms on the table and rests his head on them. His hair curls a little where it's short at the back of his neck. I give him a minute to see if he'll tell me what's wrong, and, sure enough, he does. "I think…" He pauses as if to corral his thoughts again. "From what I've read, neither the charm nor the curse will break on its own, but the charm isn't working like it should. There's never been record of this happening before, so it must be some new factor. And whatever's weakening the charm, it's getting worse. We're running out of time."

I run my too-smooth fingertips over the tabletop. When they catch on the bigger flaws and cracks that mar the surface, they make a scraping sound, the rasp of one slightly textured surface running over a smooth one. If my fingers were skin and bone, they wouldn't be making a sound at all, and at that thought, I stop. I just want to be able to touch something again, to touch it and *feel* it.

I'm not sure what to say. My instinct is to assure him we're going to fix it, but we're not, not really. What Ben and I have in store will do the opposite of fixing the charm. So all that I manage is an ineffectual, "It'll be okay."

"I don't think it will be. People are going to be confused, and I know for a fact that if we succeed…" He turns to fix me with those water-blue eyes of his. "If we succeed then there are going to be a shit-ton of people mad at us, and that doesn't count the people who might wind up sick or worse. But before that, if there's no charm protecting the carnival, my mom is going to leave. Hell, she wants to leave now. And I'm still a minor. She'll get the cops involved if it means keeping me with her. I told her some stupid lie about the tires being blown because of nails scattered on the road, but what if next time I can't come up with a convenient lie? What if she takes me away before we can set you free?"

He plays with the pages of the journal, picking them up with his fingertips and letting them flutter back down, over and over. "We have to break this thing." His mouth opens as though he wants to say something more, but the words never come. Instead, he nudges closer to me and drapes one arm on the back of the booth, his hand dangling beside my arm. Idly, almost as though he doesn't even realize he's doing it, his thumb traces long, looping ovals on my shoulder.

He flips to the front of the journal and starts reading. And as I watch him set to work, even though the Airstream is cold and I'm too close to the drafty window, I feel warm inside.

CHAPTER TWENTY-THREE

Benjamin

The pages of the journal are dry and brittle, like the tissue-thin leaves of a long-dead plant. In many places, the once-black ink has faded to a muddy brown, blending in with the yellowed paper. At first it seems as though the page is covered in a made-up language only the author was meant to understand. But once I start to see the patterns in the handwriting—the quirky way the author draws out the lines that slash across the letter *T*, the flourish in her *M*s that make it look like there's an extra hump—it becomes easier to read.

After about an hour, I find the entry we've been looking for.

• • •

Tonight Rebecca cursed her one true love, and there was nothing we could do to stop her. Mother believes in giving someone every possible chance to make the right choice.

Even if it sometimes means waiting too long. To that end, Mother insisted I watch over Rebecca, but from the scrying bowl, too far away to interfere. I love Mother dearly, but I hope she knows that her belief that Rebecca would do the right thing is what brought this calamity on all of us.

We poured a bowl of wine and laid down the lines of salt. At first nothing but candlelight shone on the liquid surface. Then fine tendrils of gray billowed up from the bottom of the bowl, long pale arms of mist creeping across the still liquid. Tree trunks, the same as those at the edge of the forest, grew from the billowing clouds, and from them, my sister emerged. Rebecca wound her shawl around her hunched shoulders. The lights of camp glowed across the flat meadow, but they were tiny with distance.

The grass rustled nearby, and she pulled the square of creased parchment from her pocket. Mother guided us through the vision, trees blurring as she spun the bowl and shifted our line of sight, so we could read the note. *Meet me at the edge of the woods at midnight. I'll mark the tree.* The sloping, scrawling script was Jasper's, as was the red silk handkerchief tied to one of the lower boughs of the sprawling oak at the edge of the tree line.

Rebecca ran the raw silk between her fingers, and she pressed the square of crimson to her nose.

A dark shadow, lumpy, tangled, approached her in the dark. Tall grass rippled out as the figure neared her hiding spot. Rebecca twitched forward as if to go meet the new arrival, and her cheeks flushed dark with excitement.

Rebecca took a step forward, out of the safety of the shadows, when a laugh broke the silence of the evening. It was the light, crystalline laughter of a girl. The approaching shape disentangled to reveal not just one person but two—

the tall, lanky form of Jasper and the shorter, lithe shape of Susan, the aerialist.

Rebecca froze. The aerialist had been appearing in her visions more and more of late, though she had not been able to puzzle out why. And now she knew.

Jealousy had gnawed at Rebecca the moment the aerialist had joined our troupe. Susan, with her pale skin and sleek blond curls, was the very opposite of Rebecca, and her appearance in that field did not bode well for my sister.

Jasper had his arm draped around Susan's shoulder, his hand playing with the jet beads that hung from her sleeve. The moment Susan saw my sister, the laugh died on her lips and she came to a halt, Jasper stopping alongside her.

"Rebecca," he said coolly. Hard lines set across Rebecca's brow as she realized that Jasper *wanted* her to find him with this other woman. He had played her like one of the unsuspecting townies to whom he peddled his wares.

Rebecca twisted the handkerchief into a cord, the thin fabric collapsing in on itself until the silk began to strain. "Jasper, I thought we were leaving."

Susan tried to free herself from Jasper's side, but he grasped her tighter, his fingers digging into her shoulder.

"You still can, Rebecca," he said. "We won't stop you. I know you tire of the carnival. Susan and I came to see you off."

Tears welled up in Rebecca's eyes, and my heart ached for her. "But we were starting over. Together."

Jasper pulled away from Susan but kept her hand firmly locked in his. He wanted her there, as though the other woman would remind Rebecca she had fallen out of his favor. He placed his free hand on Rebecca's shawl-wrapped shoulder. "Rebecca. Bex. I have been trying to tell you for quite a while now."

Rebecca shook her head, as if that would keep the words away. The silk kerchief around her fingers could not possibly be wound tighter, but still she twisted. "You were never—"

"I *was.*" He removed his hand from her shoulder and gripped onto Susan's hand hard enough to make the girl wince. His gaze was cold and unyielding. "I think you should go."

The wind rustled the dead leaves clinging to the branches above them, threw the tall grasses around until they made a susurrus I could hear inside the wagon. Rebecca was terribly still. "You were never supposed—"

"Rebecca," he said, his words like iron, "you're embarrassing yourself now."

A twisted fork of lightning struck the oak tree behind Rebecca. The dry wood caught fire, flames licking at the night sky. Rebecca stood in a pocket of wavering air while the flames stretched toward Jasper like eager tongues ready to bring him into their gaping jaws. Jasper scrambled away. Susan was a glittering speck dashing across the field.

Darkness spread across Rebecca's eyes; a scarlet glow from the flaming tree threw her face into shadow. The handkerchief was twisted so tight it split her skin. Blood seeped through the silk and ran down between her fingers to drip upon her skirt.

"You were never supposed to con *me.*"

Power from the earth, from the spell she had been silently weaving, from the blood that ran swiftly from her wound filled her up until she radiated with it. For the briefest of moments, her eyes locked with the point in the distance that was me, in this wagon, and it felt as though she stood before me. I was thrown out of my chair into the wall of our wagon. Mother dashed the bowl of wine we had been scrying out onto the ground and knelt over me. Somewhere outside I heard my baby daughter yowling.

"Did she do it?" Mother asked. Every line on her face was softened by the candlelight, but her eyes were hard. Now, far too late, she had resolved to interfere. I only wish she could have come to this resolution before anything had actually happened.

Something tickled at the back of my head and when I pulled my fingers away they were covered in blood, a red that was bright in the candlelight. I nodded. "She cursed him."

Her lips pressed together. "Then you and I have work to do."

And so we did.

It was far too late for us to stop Rebecca's curse—blood magic is the strongest and most vile kind of work—but we could lessen its effect. Rebecca wanted Jasper dead. Mother wanted to bring him back to life. But in that moment, having seen what I had, I wanted justice. And so, as I worked with Mother to try to bring Jasper back, I hoped for him to be punished. I wanted him to be as unfeeling on the outside as he was on the inside. And so, that is how the three of us came together to create this terrible curse. Rebecca killed him. Mother saved him. And I made him what he is.

The following morning, when I realized what I had done, the guilt was nearly too much to bear. And so I spun a charm around the carnival, a protection, so they would guard and help him until he learned the error of his ways and repented.

· · ·

Blank pages follow that first story, a buffer for the horrible origin of the curse. Then pages and pages of the victims followed. Boys and girls who were crushed and trampled and stabbed, making their bodies ready for the curse. It's too much. I close the book, fiddling with the foxed corners as I gather my thoughts.

"So, some ass named Jasper was the original recipient of the curse." Emma immediately begins to hunt for his name among records of the many former employees. "He screwed over the twins' great-aunt, I think, and that's where this all started."

Emma runs a pale finger below his name. Jasper Clarke had one of the shortest tenures in the box. It took him a single month to find someone to take his place. The writings are fuzzy here—literally. The ink has faded out to a faint sepia, and it's hard to read. A few words are legible here and there: "wine," "pain," "heart," but that's it.

Emma then flips to find the entry for Rebecca, the jilted woman at the start of it all. Her fingers flick through the pages clumsily. It takes longer this time, but then her palms splay over the pages, thumbs and forefingers framing the entry. And then, so quietly I can barely hear her over the sounds of the road rushing beneath us, Emma says, "Oh God."

Emma's slender fingers ruffle her hair as she skims over the words again and again. "Rebecca Marx was a fortune-teller, we knew that. She stayed on after she cursed Jasper. And then," Emma's voice cracks, "the night Jasper passed on the curse, she rode to the top of the Ferris wheel and threw herself from it. She um…she didn't make it."

A frown tugs at the simple lines of Emma's ruby mouth as she stares out the window. It is the impotent stare of the furious; it has to be, because there's nothing but Texas fields, fallow and boring, out the window. There's nothing I can say that will help, I know that much, so I put my hand on hers and wait.

"That...*asshole*! I can't believe he... I could never do that... I just...I hate this. And she *killed* herself. She made this horrible curse and now I feel sorry for her? Somehow? And I'm still so mad at her I could punch her old lady ass. If, you know, she were an old lady. God. Now I feel like a jerk for wanting to punch a hypothetical old lady."

I want to help but don't know what to say, so instead, I just rub my fingers over her palm and the back of her hand, thinking I'll warm it, but realizing at about the same time that there's far too much of her to try to keep warm. But as soon as I'm about to stop, she leans against me.

Neither of us says anything about the seemingly insurmountable task in front of us. At the same time, now that I know with certainty there's something other than the cycle of passing along the curse, now that the person in the box means something to me, I *have* to help. But it all comes back to New Orleans. All our answers are there.

The sun washes against us through the curtained windows, the tall, thin shadows of telephone poles flashing over us. The light goes from a bright sunshiny yellow to the deep gold of the late afternoon.

I don't want the moment to end. Somehow, without my realizing it, she has become my constant. The steady thrum of the tires on the asphalt is soothing to the point where I drift off into sleep with my head on her shoulder.

Just my luck that I've always been a heavy sleeper.

Emma shakes my shoulder, a steady stream of frantic whispers in my ear. Too late, I realize that I can't hear the road rushing beneath us or feel the steady rattle of the Airstream in motion. I scramble out of the booth, pulling Emma with me. But when the door swings open and my mother steps in the trailer, there's nowhere to go.

My hand is still tangled up with Emma's when my mother sees us.

CHAPTER TWENTY-FOUR

Emma

Hell hath no fury like an angry Audrey Singer.

I have always passed the parent test with flying colors. Jules's parents love me. Every one of my friends' parents I've ever been introduced to likes quiet, well-mannered Emmaline King. I am respectful, polite, and nonthreateningly funny.

Audrey doesn't even give me a chance.

"Get out." On the surface, she's calm. But anger simmers below it all, a mother bear with claws at the ready. If I had a pulse, it would be racing.

To her, I am only the Girl in the Box, the girl whose kisses and lies can trap someone in the curse, and I'm charming her only son, the child who is the only reason she came back to a job haunted by her former lover. I guess I can see why she doesn't like me.

It only takes three long strides for Audrey to cross the Airstream. Her hands grip around my arm—so hot they feel like fire made solid—and she drags me away from Ben. I topple to the ground, my limbs *clacking* and *thumping* against every solid surface on the way.

"Get out, get out, *get out!*" Her voice goes from the angry yell of the righteous to a banshee scream. Hair flies from her neat braid, a halo of gold to frame her fury. And I won't forget the icy gleam of hate in those blue eyes for the rest of my life.

"Mom!" Benjamin yells, scrambling to get between us.

Audrey's hands—big hands calloused and lined from years of working toward making this carnival what it is—tighten around my upper arms as she shoves me toward the door. I've barely got my feet beneath me, and my legs are trembling as I back away, but she gets in another push, this one sending me crashing into the counter. Another hard thrust, and I'm almost to the door.

"I never want to see you in this home again," Audrey says. Her palms strike me square in the chest, and the last shove sends me flying out the door of the Airstream. I hit the ground so hard that for a split second, I worry this cursed body of mine might crack. Audrey jumps to the ground, looming over me. Ben tumbles out of the trailer behind her, grasping her shoulders to pull her away, but Audrey isn't going anywhere. "No one's come looking for you, not your parents, not your friends. No one wants you, and no one loves you. How could anyone love a girl stupid enough to be tricked into the curse in the first place? Find a rube, pass on the curse, and get far away from here."

"*Mother!*" Benjamin snaps, finally managing to pull her back.

Shame wells furiously within me. It starts up the shaking, hiccupping thing this body does when my human body would have been driven to tears.

Benjamin drags Audrey into the Airstream. The door slams with a metallic *clang*, and almost immediately I can hear mother and son yelling at each other.

"So she's on a rampage."

It's then that I notice Sidney leaning against the pale aqua truck the Airstream is attached to. When I finally manage to drag this twitchy body off the ground and join him, I pretend to ignore the tears dripping off his chin. His red-rimmed eyes stare at the plump white clouds that scud across a sky so pale it seems colorless.

Another shudder runs through my chest. Another sob. Stupid as it sounds, I wish I could cry, because it would at least be *some* kind of release for all this self-loathing bubbling inside me.

He chuckles darkly, brushing tears off his cheeks. He lowers his gaze to the ground—hard brown stuff scattered with weeds in shades of yellow and a sickly green. "It's not you, you know. I screwed her over something fierce.

"I don't know why I did it, honestly," he continues. The ground has become less interesting, and he's moved his gaze to the scurrying laborers who have begun to open up the cook shack for the night. "We'd had a fight. Thinking back, I'm sure it was that the two of us were nervous. We'd just run away from home. When we got here, we told Nick—Leslie's dad—that we were a couple, so that's how they treated us. They found a trailer we could share, and it's hard living in close quarters, especially when you're still learning each other."

He sighs at the memory. "A fight was inevitable, and when it came, it was a big one. I hadn't met everyone in the carnival yet, and so when the girl came over to console me, I just thought she was being nice, maybe wanted to fool around. Maybe I wanted to fool around. It wasn't that she was prettier than Audrey, just that she wasn't angry at me like Audrey. I hadn't been trusted with the knowledge of the charm and the curse yet, so I had no idea she was the Girl in the Box." His hazel eyes are dotted with the small golden lights of the cook shack. Benjamin's and Audrey's yelling still filters over to us. "It was a moment of weakness. She was pretty and I was young and stupid. It didn't take long. And when Audrey found out…

"Look. I know that you're not after Benjamin like that. And I would talk to her, but she doesn't want me talking to her at all anymore. I just"—he gazes out across the field where the sun has begun its slow descent—"I only hope that even if she doesn't want me anymore, that I can do something to get her to forgive me, at some point."

We both watch in silence as preparations are being made for the carnival to spend the night. Gin walks by, leading her horse in some exercise, followed shortly by a heavily bandaged Whiskey with her horse. Lars barks out instructions, making sure all trailers are parked safely and giving directions to the nearest town to those who want to explore. People stroll around chatting, hopefully about happier topics than ours.

His voice wavers when he speaks again, and I catch a glimpse of unshed tears glittering in his eyes before he turns away. "I just wish I could fix things."

"I think," I say as I try to repress more twitching, "that she has to want things to be fixed first."

CHAPTER TWENTY-FIVE

Benjamin

I didn't even wait until the door was closed before I began yelling.

"What the *hell* is wrong with you?" I ask.

"What's wrong with me? What's wrong with *you*, Benjamin?" My mother's voice fills the trailer until it feels like I'm standing in the eye of Hurricane Audrey.

"It's not like that," I say. "I know you're afraid that she'll try to trick me into taking the curse, but Emma isn't going to do that, okay? She *needs* a *friend*."

"She's only after one thing, and it is getting out of that box any way possible. And all she has to do *is kiss you.*"

The angry pounding of my heart reaches into my temples and the tips of my fingers. "It takes more than a kiss! And even so, Emma wouldn't do that to me."

She slams her hand down on the small counter, knocking the tiny vase on the windowsill into the sink, where it shatters. "It *is* that easy, Benjamin! In seconds you can lose your life, lose your freedom. *Stay away from that girl, Benjamin Singer.*"

I take a deep breath in through my nose and force the yell building inside me to a more reasonable tone. "I am an adult, and I can decide for myself who I will or won't spend my time with."

"You are not an adult for another three weeks, and so long as you live with me, you will do as I say."

I stare at the shards of pottery in the sink before turning back to her. "I don't know why you insist on treating Emma like she's any other Girl in the Box!"

"Of course she's like the other Girls in the Box!" My mother's teeth are bared like fangs. "Don't be such a rube, Sidney."

There it is.

I give her a minute to see if she realizes what she's said, but she doesn't. Her breathing is heavy and her gaze doesn't waver. When I do talk, I am slow, quiet, and careful. "I am *not* Sidney."

We let that heavy statement sit between the two of us, growing silently. Part of me is insulted that this is what it comes down to. That all her talk of wanting to keep me safe is less about me and more about her not wanting a repeat of what he did to her years ago. I keep waiting, hoping she'll change course, hoping she'll prove me wrong.

She doesn't.

So I push past her and have my hand on the door when she says, "I *forbid* you to leave."

I open the door and step into the cooling night air.

Emma and Sidney watch as I approach. It looks as though my mother has gone after every person she's been in contact with today, considering Sidney's tearstained face. I'd feel bad for him, if it wasn't his assholery that got me into this situation to begin with.

"I need to crash with you more permanently, if that's okay," I tell Emma.

She extends one pale hand toward me, and as soon as our fingers twine together I know I made the right choice. "Of course," she says.

I don't know who grips whose hand tighter.

CHAPTER TWENTY-SIX

Benjamin

"Hey, man, I'm driving with Gin."

Damn.

I thwack my head on the doorframe as I stand and turn to face Marcel. "You've driven with Gin the last three times. Besides, I can't ride with Mom."

"You bloody well can!" He crosses his arms as though making a barricade against any sense I might talk into him.

"No, Marcel, I can't!" Farther down the field, Gin and Emma wind through the parked cars and trucks, obviously headed this way. I lean in close to keep the girls from overhearing. "Mom thinks Emma's going to trick me into taking on the curse, and I got mad and left."

Marcel's face drops like I've taken all his Christmas presents and thrown them in a fire. "Shit, man, I had no idea. Sure. Of course you should ride with us."

I punch Marcel in the shoulder. "Thanks, man."

Gin laughs at something Emma says, the happy,

boisterous noise temporarily covering the sounds of the other carnies shouting orders and directions. A small smile cracks Marcel's face, and if I had to hazard a guess, I'd say I'm wearing a matching one.

Marcel, Emma, and I watch the slow, steady crawl across Texas from the windows of the Gran Torino. At the last minute, Whiskey begged Gin to ride in the family's SUV, because Whiskey was trying to convince their parents to let her keep a cat in the trailer and she thought Gin could help her case. I have a feeling that conversation will not go the way Whiskey thinks it will.

An axle on the truck that carries Lars's Ferris wheel breaks in two and the alternator gives out on Mom's truck. Those kinds of things, we have come to expect over the last few days. But not what happens to the Gran Torino.

We're flying down the highway after a stop for gas when something heavy *thumps* from underneath the hood of the car. Marcel and I look at each other. I'm willing to write it off as a rock or clump of dirt that must have been kicked up from the road. Marcel and Emma continue to play some sort of game they've made up involving movie quotes, and I grip onto the wheel a little bit tighter, more mindful of the road in front of me.

Fifteen miles fly beneath the tires before the dial marking the car's heat begins to rapidly crawl upward.

"Shit." I steer toward the shoulder. We'd been pulling up the rear of the long line of trucks and trailers and cars, and not a one of them has noticed our trouble. As the caravan speeds down the highway, I throw a nervous glance to Emma sitting next to me in the passenger seat. I know what happens once the curse victim gets too far from the heart of the carnival, and I can't bear to see that happen to her. But Marcel and I have managed to fix a hundred minor problems with this car before, so I push the horrible thought aside as we get out to see what's wrong.

Steam billows from under the open hood. After a minute of poking around, I find the problem. The fan belt has snapped cleanly in two. As Marcel hangs over the side of the car, checking the coolant levels, I hold the belt up and peer at it from over my glasses.

This was not a natural break. Someone cut this. I run some mental calculations and figure that without the belt running the alternator and with the radio and air-conditioning on and draining the battery, then, yeah, we probably would have made it just this far before the car gave out.

Receipts for car parts and fast food spill out of the glove compartment as I rummage through for the pre-paid cell phone we keep for emergencies like this. I press my thumb to the power button, but it won't turn on. I try again. Again. *Shit.* I fling the cheap plastic thing onto the side of the road. No one knows we broke down, and—more importantly—no one is going to stop.

"What the actual hell!" Marcel says.

"Marcel," I say.

"It wasn't a great phone, I'll admit, but—"

"Marcel!" I say quietly. "We've got a bigger problem at the moment." His eyes grow wider and wider as I explain what will happen to Emma if she's separated from the carnival for too long.

"How long have we got?" He's frowning, and I can tell he's already compiling a list of what we'll need—a new belt, a battery because ours is now dead and there seem to be no passersby on this desolate stretch of road, some coolant—and just how far away from one we might be. Before I can answer him, Emma steps out of the car and into the blazing Texas sunshine.

"What's going on, guys?" Her fingers grip at the edge of the door, and the rubber seal squeaks in protest.

"Hurry," I say to Marcel. I don't say please, but then, I'm sure he knows. Our next stop is a little town called Bryan, and Marcel jogs down the tree-lined highway in that direction.

Fear has already bloomed in Emma's eyes. "What's wrong with the car?"

I still have the broken belt clenched tight in my fist, and I hold it out to her. "Someone sabotaged the car."

She nods, most likely going over the list of potential perpetrators, just like I am. I had told her about the Morettis and the beating they gave me, hoping to get me to leave. Even now, I can see them laughing it up in their trailer as they think of us stranded, grease still caked in the creases of their fingers. But that is a problem for later.

The carnival caravan has long disappeared over the horizon, and Marcel's sky-blue T-shirt is a smudge bobbing along the side of the road. How long has Emma been separated from the carnival? Ten minutes? Twenty? And how long will it take for the effects of the curse to sink into her bones, to paralyze and trap her within her own body?

"I don't get how one little piece of rubber can keep the whole car running," Emma says.

"Well." I bring the two ends of the belt together, making them whole again. "There's more than one piece of machinery affected. This one belt—"

I hold the belt up to show Emma, but something doesn't seem right. Just as I'm about to ask her if she's okay, she screams in pain. The noise is primal and raw, and it startles all the birds from their nearby roosts. It's as though an electric shock jolts through Emma's entire body, arms snapping to her sides, knees locking straight. She tilts to the side, unable to balance. I dart forward to catch her and she collides into my chest with a *thud*, all dead weight and rock-hard limbs.

"Ben! Benjamin, I can't move my arms! I can't—" Another scream tears from her throat and I wish I knew what to do. I brace my legs and hold her tight, determined to keep her from falling. And then, just as suddenly, she goes rigid.

I put one arm under her knees and my other behind her back and scoop her up. I run for the tree line a few feet away from the road, where I can lay her down in the shade. The grass is cool but prickly beneath my arms as I help her lie down, and a constant stream of chatter spills out of her.

"I thought I had more time, and it *hurts*, bastard didn't say it would hurt so much, and don't leave, Ben, please, *please* don't leave me."

Again, she screams. Her spine goes taut, like a thread about to snap. And all I can do is kneel in the grass beside her and watch. I didn't keep count of how long the last spasm held her paralyzed, but this one seems longer. When she finally goes slack once again, I barely manage to count to thirty before another seizure runs through her.

I breathe, telling myself that on the next exhale, she'll stop hurting.

On the next one.

On the next.

She never does. There's no sound but the dry chatter of the late-season cicadas and blood rushing in my ears. A few cars slow when they see the Gran Torino with its hood up, but with no stranded driver standing by its side, they pass on quickly. I'm glad they don't stop to help. How the hell would I explain Emma? How would I tell some Good Samaritan that no, I don't want to take the paralyzed and seemingly comatose girl on the ground to the hospital and I swear I wasn't the one to do this to her?

The sun has slipped closer to the earth and my legs are cramped from crouching by Emma's side by the time I hear Marcel yell, "Oi!"

I grip Emma's hand even as I turn in the direction I'd last seen my friend in. His shirt is drenched in sweat and he holds two straining plastic bags in his hands, but he's back, and we're going to fix this.

He jogs over, muttering a litany of "Shit! Shit! Shit!" when he sees Emma frozen on the ground.

"Can you handle it all yourself?" I ask. "It *might* go faster if I help, but I can't leave Emma. Not when she asked me to stay."

Marcel's gaze darts down to where I've awkwardly twisted my hand to fit into Emma's frozen fingers and says, "Yeah, no worries."

In the back of my head, I register the sounds of Marcel working—metal *plinking* on the concrete as he trades out one tool for another, the occasional curse, the rustle of plastic as he pulls the new parts from their bags—but I tune it out and focus on Emma. "It's going to be okay, Em. Marcel will have the car running in just a couple of minutes, okay?" Both of these things could be lies, but I say them anyway. "I'm here, okay?" It's the only thing I know for a fact.

Finally Marcel runs toward us. "We're good. Let's go."

We carry Emma to the car and lay her down in the backseat as carefully as possible. The seat belts are useless, just one more thing to fix that we hadn't gotten to yet. So I cram myself into the footwell, ready to keep her steady the whole ride to the next site.

Marcel tears down the highway, but we're quickly ensnarled in afternoon traffic when we enter the town. He speeds through every yellow light and swears loudly at every red. Rocks and clods of dirt *ping* against the floor of the car and I know we're on the track leading to the carnival grounds. Marcel taps out a staccato rhythm on the horn, yelling for people to get out of the way.

When he throws the car into park, Emma rocks forward, but I catch her. "We're here," I say, more for my benefit than hers. How long will it take for her to come back to us? Where's the heart of the carnival if the carnival hasn't even been set up yet?

Marcel and I lift her dead weight out of the car and lay her down on the trampled grass. I twist one of her hands in my own and place my other on her cheek. I just want to see her move. To blink. Something. The murmurs of the gathering crowd draw closer, but my gaze never leaves Emma. I hear a litany of, "Please, please, please," and it takes a moment to realize that desperate prayer is coming from me.

My heart hammers out a panicked beat against my

chest. Then her body gives a shake and a shudder, and she lets out a trembling cry. Marcel and I help her to sit on the ground beside the car, and I kneel next to her, unwilling and unable to let her out of my reach. Her hands twist into the fabric of my shirt, tugging me close, and I wind my arms around her. Neither of us can hold the other tight enough to feel safe.

Performers and roustabouts alike gather around us to see what all the commotion is. A few people—Mrs. Potter, Gin and Whiskey and their parents—seem genuinely worried, panic etched into their brows and frowns pulling down at the corners of their mouths. Others have on the wide eyes and dropped jaws of the shocked. Far too many of them wear the stone masks of the apathetic. The Morettis are nowhere to be seen, and their absence only solidifies their guilt. As these people look down at us, all I can wonder is: *what will the Morettis do next?*

CHAPTER TWENTY-SEVEN

Benjamin

The following night, we open the gates to College Station, Texas. The tiny college town is a noisy throng of students decked in maroon. Some of the college kids are so obnoxious that Emma makes a growing list of frat boys who she wouldn't mind cursing, were it not for the fact that she'd actually have to touch them. Even through her bravado, it's easy to see she's still shaken by our breakdown between towns, and the noise and hustle of our unruly patrons does nothing to put her back at ease.

The money flows fast and easy here, but we've got to keep going, so the carnival packs up after a week. When it's time to move on, Emma rides with Gin and Whiskey in their family's SUV, which is a newer and far more reliable vehicle, at my insistence. Even though the curse is giving everyone car trouble, the odds are better this way. And though Marcel and I had traveled many miles without her, the car feels emptier without her riding shotgun.

In Houston we set up in the parking lot of a dying shopping mall, the downtown skyline a bright complement to the lights of the carnival. Sitting in the crux of several highways means that gasoline and exhaust are perpetual companions to the normal scents of the carnival. We run through a quick two-week engagement, and it's easy to tell that the other performers want to stay longer. Houston's a big town, one that could easily support us for a month, but Leslie is insistent, and we're out of there before the weeds have time to twine their stems around the feet of our machinery.

We are currently camped outside of Orange, Texas. Louisiana is so close that it makes me feel anxious, antsy. I'm lying on the floor of Marcel's family's trailer as he gets ready for his show, shaping his hair into its trademark peak.

"So will you or won't you?"

I prop myself up on my elbows to see him better. "Huh?"

He turns away from the mirror and stares down at me. "About when did you zone out on me?"

I take off my glasses and wipe the smudges away with the hem of my shirt. "Maybe ten minutes ago? Sorry."

He waves an impatient hand and goes back to fiddling around with the buttons on his shirt, trying to decide how many should stay buttoned and how many shouldn't. "I was *saying* that you should try to have some fun tonight. Enjoy the carnival. Act like a normal human being."

I grunt noncommittally.

"This is a 'yes' or 'no' situation, man." He straps a belt studded with knives around his waist. "No hiding out in Emma's wagon all night. Stop acting like a sad-sack, morose bastard. Besides. After all that bullshit with the car, you need to relax. You and Emma both."

"Are you going to give me shit if I don't?"

"You had better believe it."

I sigh and pull myself up. "Fine. And button that last button. You look like the bastard child of a Vegas lounge act and a grocery store romance novel cover."

The night is crisp, the kind of cold that stings at the inside of your nose and burns your lungs. Immediately my thoughts go to Emma and how cold she must be, how hard it'll be for her to hide the twitching. How all I want right now is to be with her. How that's all I ever want, really. And then I know what I want to do.

I race through the crowds, fast enough that the lights of the rides and booths blur into gold and pink streaks. The ringing that accompanies prizes being won and the happy shrieks of laughter from children loud in my ears as I run to my destination.

The tumblers, Lorenzo atop Antonio's shoulders atop Fabrizio's, walk down the crowded alley near the twins' tent. The column of brothers sways side to side as Fabrizo takes his careful steps. Antonio's hands clasp onto Lorenzo's ankles firmly, and Lorenzo tosses flyers for their show onto the crowd below. Would it have killed them to just walk through the crowds like normal people?

Fabrizio stops in front of a string of golden bulbs crossing from one cotton candy tent to the hot dog tent across the way. Instead of simply climbing down, Lorenzo flings his remaining flyers into the night and propels himself from his brother's shoulders, tucking into a neat ball as he clears the lights and landing lightly on his feet. Not to be outdone, Antonio reaches down and grabs onto Fabrizio's shoulders with his hands. Bending his arms at the elbows, he shoves off and flies over the lights as well, touching down on the ground and straightening with a flourish of his arms. Applause covers up all the other carnival noises, and a couple nearby murmurs about making sure to see the tumblers' next performance. I restrain myself from rolling my eyes.

Emma's mind is nowhere near the box. It doesn't take a rocket scientist to tell, so this carpenter's apprentice has an easy time of it. It's in the way she's got her chin propped against her hand, and her eyes follow a loud group of girls as they walk past without giving her booth a second glance. It's in the way her rounded shoulders scream dejection, and her mouth is halfway to a pout.

The golden light that fills the box makes her seem soft and hazy as an old photograph. Like she moves through a world of caramel-colored air. She sees me across the way, and her eyes go wide, as does her smile.

As though attracted to her thousand-watt smile, a young man starts rooting through his pockets for change, but Emma quickly grabs a card and drops it into the tray before he can get much farther. She shoos him away with her slender fingers even as he's plucking the card from the tray below, her eyes on me the whole time.

I'm nervous, though I don't know why. But as I reach into my pocket for the card, my fingers fumble, and I nearly drop it. I have one of her blanks, except I've written my own message on it.

As she reaches back to open the door, I shake my head at her just a tiny bit. I hold my card to the glass for her to read, and her smile blooms into a grin. I feel sure of her answer, but still, I worry as she reads the eight words I've written there.

Emmaline King, I think I've fallen for you.

The wind tugs the card out of my tentative grip, and I have to be quick to catch it before it flies down the alley. When I look up, she's gone, the booth dark. But when I turn, there she is, waiting for me. She holds out a hand for me to take.

"Is that card a prediction, or a statement of fact?" Emma asks, her eyes alight with happiness.

I slip my hand into hers, trying to press my warmth into her as I twine our fingers together. My other hand goes to her face, cradling her neck so I can bring her forehead to mine and look into her eyes. "It is most certainly a statement of fact."

Her grin is a thing of beauty. "Good. Because I'm pretty sure I've fallen for you, too."

My heart swells at the words, and for a brief second I can't tell if my feet are planted on the ground or if they're hovering a few inches above it. I want so much to kiss her, to show her how much her confession means to me, but she doesn't move toward me, and I want to respect her wishes. So instead I just hold her a few seconds longer, memorizing the way the curve of her cheek fits neatly into the palm of my hand, and how the tip of her nose feels pressed to mine.

When I'm finally able to let her go, I decide to not just take Marcel's advice—to see the carnival for the wonder that it is—but to also show Emma all the little things that the regular tourists never see, unless they're really, really paying attention. The sky is still in that place between dusk and evening, peaches and pinks and light blues muddled with lavender and navy, and ribbons of clouds splay out from behind the setting sun like someone dragged their fingers through them.

We go to see Mrs. Potter, and I show Emma the steady stream of treats going from her hands to a little black Scottie, because that dog won't stay still for anything. Mrs. Potter only keeps him around because he's her new favorite lap dog, and the spoiled thing knows it.

Gin and a freshly cleared-for-performance Whiskey have a show every hour. There are no secrets here, just the sheer wonder of the girls and their out-and-out enthusiasm for what they do. For a while it's hard to not flinch; the memory of what happened to Whiskey is still too raw. But all too soon we're under their spell.

They do a series of tricks where they stand in the middle of their circle, watching the horses as they're led through their paces. Gin runs up a small ramp and leaps onto the back of her spotted palomino. From there, the show plays out like some kind of Who's on First act. Whiskey jumps onto the moving horse at the same moment that Gin jumps off. While she's running across the yard and up the ramp onto the other horse, Whiskey follows suit, only to jump back onto the spotted horse. They do this back and forth until they wind up on the same horse again, but this time they're balanced on just one foot.

When the applause dies down, I am already thinking about where to take Emma next, but I'm stopped by gasps from the crowd. When I look back to the ring, I see that Whiskey is doing a handstand on the back of her horse. I think I've stopped breathing. The horse loops around the yard once, twice, and on the third lap, Whiskey lifts one hand from the horse. Her toes, stained with dirt from the ring, point elegantly over her back toward her horse's head. Her tiny body sways, absorbing the shock of the horse's hooves on the hard, packed earth. It is so much worse than riding on a carousel horse.

Emma grips onto my hand so hard I'm afraid her rock-hard fingers will crush mine, but I need it, to feel grounded, that someone else understands the utter gravity of the situation. As Whiskey laps the yard again, she bends her elbow and pushes off against the horse, landing neatly on the ground.

My breath comes back to me and fills my burning lungs about the same time that noise returns to the world. The crowd has gone wild. I glance at Emma and find myself making this weird noise that's part relieved laugh, part sigh of relief.

Both girls take a bow and begin to weave through the crowd for tips. Gin's smile is strained, and before she can pass by, I grab her free hand.

"She wasn't supposed to do that, was she?" I ask.

Through gritted teeth, Gin answers, "She wasn't, but she's been trying to prove that she's fine. You can bet your ass she won't do it again anytime soon." At that she's off to the next person, trying to grab as much as she can in tips before her crowd forgets the wonder that she and her sister just acted out and move on to the next shiny thing.

Emma and I let the crowd push us back toward the midway. Lights pulse yellow and orange around us. I want to take Emma to see Marcel, as he promises he and Gin have been tweaking their act. Gin only joins him for his last show of the evening, so Emma and I cruise the midway to kill some time. As we pass a booth with ridiculously huge stuffed animals, I get it in my head I should do the stereotypical thing and win one for Emma.

While it's true that most of the people working the midway would just give me a stuffed animal if I asked, that's not the same. So when we stop in front of a booth where you have to knock wooden milk bottles off a pillar that has giant stuffed cats as its prize, I stop. One, I know that these are the nicest prizes the carnival has to offer. Two, I helped build this setup, and I know how it's rigged.

Every rube who comes through here tries to hit the bottles. But I've balanced these things so that the pyramid is sturdy, and a glancing blow isn't going to make them tumble. Instead, you have to hit the pillar, and do it so that it looks like you've hit the lowest row of bottles, so no one can accuse you of cheating.

I give Gabe my five dollars, and he rolls his eyes and gives me a bucket of softballs. I push my glasses up my nose, take a ball from the bucket, and step back. The night is alive with happy people and the alarm on the strongman game going off. A breeze whips down the alleyway. But I push all of that away, take aim, and let go.

I knock over the bottles on the first try. Again, Gabe rolls his eyes. I kind of want to roll my eyes at myself, but I'm too damn happy at the moment. Emma picks out a cat—a fluffy orange thing that she immediately names Monroe—and we head over to Marcel's tent.

Gin and Marcel greet us at the entrance to his tent, a brightly striped pink and orange canvas monstrosity. Marcel has been very secretive about his revamped act with Gin, and I have to admit that I'm excited to see it.

"I was hoping you'd come," he says. "I've got two seats saved for you at the front."

"How did you know I'd need two seats?" I ask.

"Because I'm not stupid, moron." He parts the flaps and holds it open for the two of us.

The tent is one of the largest we have. A dirt circle marked off by cinder blocks painted in shades of blue and yellow sits in the center, and three rows of bright-red folding chairs ring it. True to his word, there are two seats in the front row with hastily scrawled "reserved" signs on them, in perfect view of his throwing boards.

The place is packed and soon after we're seated, the lights shining over the chairs are dimmed, making the orangey glow of the center ring all the brighter.

Marcel steps into the circle of light, a stark, dark shape dressed in all black. Orange gilds his cheekbones and highlights the tops of his shoulders and arms. He stands straight and tall but relaxed, the very picture of competence. He extends an arm to Gin and leads her into the light. Visually, she's the polar opposite of Marcel. The light catches the beads and the sequins on her riding costume and throws off glints like sparks. She moves her long legs and arms with strength and precision, making a fluid, graceful contrast to Marcel's sharp, controlled movements.

He pulls Gin into his arms to dance, and it's so personal, so tender, I almost feel guilty for looking. They sway in place for a moment and then he spins her. Their fingers part and she follows the spin until her back is pressed against the throwing board.

The light shifts from orange to bright scarlet. A white spotlight is lit over Gin, leeching all the color from her until she's glowing silver and blond. She strikes a pose, her arms bent elegantly, and she's only still for a second before the first knife is lodged into the wood behind her.

She moves and has barely settled before another knife quivers beside her. They play at that game for a while until all of Marcel's small silver knives sit gleaming in the painted wood. The crowd applauds as Gin yanks the blades from the wood and throws them back to Marcel, who catches them neatly.

But before they move to the next part of the act, I catch Marcel shaking his arms out as if to loosen up. Gin strikes another pose, curving sinuously against the board, one arm raised up in the air. Marcel returns the smaller knives to the holster at his waist and picks up knives that are bigger, long blades with heavy, ornate wooden handles. He throws the first knife. He's so fast that I barely even see him move. The blade quivers in the board less than a centimeter from Gin's outstretched fingers. The next goes in by her wrist, splintering the wood with its impact. The blades work down the length of her arm, each one so close that if Gin were to take a big breath and exhale, she'd touch them.

In his dark pool of red light, Marcel shakes out his arm again, flexing his fingers wide. Then he lets the next blade fly.

The sound it makes as it hits Gin in the shoulder is a terrible, meaty noise. Someone quicker than me has already run outside to get the clowns to distract the patrons from the sight of the blood pulsing from Gin's wound. Someone even quicker than that has already begun to scream.

The shriek gets me out of my seat and into Gin's white circle of light. She tries to pull the knife out of her shoulder, but she knows not to scream. We all know to never let the audience know how bad the mistake is.

Taking the knife out of her seems like the logical thing—we can't help her until we get her off this board, and we can't get her off the board until we get the knife out—but I'm petrified of hurting her further. What muscles will I rip by pulling out that blade? Is it nudging up against the bone, ready to crack it? Blood, far more of it than I saw after Whiskey fell, more blood than I've ever seen before in my life, pulses out from the wound, and I know that I have to do *something*.

The clowns have come in and formed a protective circle, shielding the patrons from the worst of it. Some distant part of my mind hears Emma shouting for people to step out of the tent, shooing them from the gruesome sight. Marcel stands at Gin's other side, paralyzed with shock. He reaches out to grab Gin's hand, and somehow, underneath all the noise buzzing around us, I can hear him chanting, "I'm sorry, I'm sorry, I'm sorry."

There's nothing else to do. I take off my flannel shirt and ball it up. "Gin," I say, glad there's no tremor in my voice like there is in my heart, "I want you to look at me."

All she can do is look at the steady spurts of blood gushing from where the metal enters her skin. "It's my arm, Benjamin, I need my arm, I can't perform—" Tears she'd held back finally slip free to trail down her cheeks. She pushes at them with bloodied fingertips, leaving streaks of red on her pale skin.

"Gin!" I say. She looks at me, her wide blue-gray eyes full of panic. "I'm going to take it out on three, Gin." *Please let someone else get to us before I get to three, someone who knows what the hell they're doing.* "Ready?" I am so not ready. She nods, though. "Okay. One." I grip the handle of the blade and ignore the way drying blood has made it sticky. "Two." She seems like she's about to look away, but I raise my eyebrows at her, and she holds my gaze. "Three!"

Gin screams. As the blade slips free, another gush of blood pours out of the opening, hot over my fingers, before I can press the fabric of my shirt to the wound. I help her to the ground, where she brings her knees to her chest, curling up around her pain.

I press on the wound and gently prod the back of her shoulder. A roll of nausea hits me when I find the exit wound. I wrap some of the shirt to the cut back there and try to position myself behind her, so that I can elevate her up onto my knees. Does it even matter trying to get the wound higher than her heart when it's so close to her heart to begin with?

Everything is slick and salty and there's a metallic bite to the air. There is so, so much blood. It creeps up the fibers of my shirt, making the blue a purple so dark it seems black, and the red a deep, rich crimson.

"I can't move my arm, Benjamin." There's a tremor in Gin's voice I've never heard before. "I can't move my arm and—" Her eyes roll back in her head and her body goes limp.

"Gin?" Marcel asks, tapping at her cheek. "Gin!"

Happy barrels into the tent, in full greasepaint and oversize shoes. The world narrows down to him and me and Gin in our circle of white-hot light. Up this close I can see that his clown makeup looks like he's just caked on tonight's face over last night's. Between his hard glare and the lights and the layers of paint he looks like a monster, and I don't know how I'm supposed to trust my friend to his care.

"She fainted," I say, the words tumbling out of me before I can register what I'm saying. "I didn't know what to do, but I had to get her down."

Happy's only response is a primitive grunt. He peels back my balled-up shirt carefully to look at the gash marring Gin's shoulder. The way the silver beads on her costume are stark, bright glints of light against the blood-soaked satin.

Without stopping his work or looking away from the wound, Happy says, "Call an ambulance. Now."

CHAPTER TWENTY-EIGHT

Emma

The entire carnival has gathered at the dining area surrounding the food booths, waiting for news of Gin. The tumblers lit a fire in one of the trash cans and they stand around it, warming their hands even though it can't be that cold out. I'm barely twitching, so it really feels like this is a show on their part to let Leslie know how put out they are by this kind of, sort of family meeting.

Even though Ben has cleaned up and has on a new thick flannel shirt to replace the bloodied one, he can't stop staring at his fingers. I think he's checking for blood, but as I helped him wash his hands, I made sure to get every fleck out of each crease and joint of his fingers. His eyes are vacant, reliving the accident over and over. That's when I notice the small spot of dried blood high on the lens of his glasses.

I slip his glasses off and rub the lens between layers of my jacket. That seems to be the only thing that gets his attention. "You had a smudge," I tell him. He hates smudges, and he seems to buy it.

The wood of the picnic table we're seated on creaks as Lars sits down beside us.

"Did Leslie give you an update?" I ask. The carnival had been cleared out with remarkable speed. Admissions were refunded and free souvenirs and trinkets were given out to those who had witnessed the worst. Thankfully for the carnival, we were getting close to the end of the evening when the incident occurred.

Lars grunts a noncommittal response. "He okay?"

Ben runs his fingers over the backs of his hands over and over. "I'm fine," he says quietly.

Another grunt. "Well, Leslie should be back soon." He glances at all of those assembled around us in quiet, shuffling ranks. "She wouldn't have asked us to gather if she weren't."

As if on cue, a pair of headlights swoops over the grounds. Leslie clambers out of the truck, quickly followed by a dejected Marcel. Gin's family has, of course, stayed with her at the hospital. Marcel drops down into the sliver of space next to Ben on the bench and folds up on himself like a bellows with all the air let out of it.

Leslie climbs up onto the picnic table in front of us in two fluid steps. The sight of their leader, still decked out in her gray velvet ringmaster's coat and in her heavy stage makeup, makes every bit of chatter die out almost immediately.

She doesn't speak until the only sound in the night is the breeze rushing through nearby trees. "By now, most of you have heard some version of what happened to Gin earlier tonight." Leslie's voice is cool water, clear and powerful. "For those of you who do not and for those of you foolish enough to have let the story get out of hand, here are the simple facts of it. Gin was helping Marcel with his act. His aim was off, and a knife hit her shoulder instead of its mark."

Chatter sweeps over the grounds, like dead leaves over concrete. It's a well-known fact that Marcel and his family are some of the best at what they do. His error is a fluke, as rare as a blue moon, and no one here will accept the word "accident" as an answer.

Leslie lets out a piercing whistle, and the crowd goes silent. However, this time, there's anger and fear, disbelief and shock on their faces. I see Audrey hovering at the edge of the crowd, her eyes locked on her son. And I see the three tumblers behind Leslie, every last one of them staring at me, as though I'm to blame.

"That *is* the truth of what happened tonight." Leslie looks as fierce as a general before her troops, standing in the mix of gold lights and flickering flames behind her. "There is, however, something I've been keeping from you."

I look to Ben, my hand hunting for his. Is Leslie about to out us and our plans?

"Everyone knows we are held together by a charm and a curse. It's a part of our lives. Recently, someone brought to my attention that the charm might be wearing off, and that's why we are having so many accidents. Whiskey's fall. All the car trouble. Gin's accident."

Marcel gives another small shudder at that, at the way Leslie has phrased things to make it seem like he's off the hook.

"Regardless," Leslie says, "it's become too much to ignore." She gazes over all of us huddled and hoping for answers. "I think it's true."

Yelling breaks the silence of the night as half a hundred different opinions and arguments are offered up. In the storm of voices, I catch flashes of my name like lightning. Leslie lets them talk, lets them think they're getting their opinions out, and waits until something close to silence settles again. It doesn't last long.

"I don't think you're telling us everything, Leslie." It's one of the Morettis, though the night makes it hard to tell which. They've moved to stand in front of the trash can fire, all three tall, slim shadows lit from behind. For a moment the only thing we hear is the crackling of the flames behind them; no one has dared to talk. Then the brothers pull themselves into the golden ring of light shining on the picnic tables, Fabrizio, the tallest, at the front.

He moves like a snake oil salesman, like a slimy politician, too-wide smile and false good cheer. "Perhaps there is something wrong with the charm. I'm just a tumbler, what do I know? But you said it yourself. 'We are held together by a charm *and* a curse.' Same as it's always been. But"—he points a finger toward me—"that's not to say nothing is different."

Oh God. He knows we want to break the curse, and now we're going to have a revolt on our hands. Gazes swivel toward me and in response, I straighten my spine and thrust out my chin, daring him to continue.

"She," Fabrizio says, jabbing that damned finger my way again, "isn't playing her part in this game. She isn't even trying. How often do you walk by her box and see that she's bored out of her mind? How often is she even there? At least Sidney showed up and gave fortunes. Maybe the charm is only weakening because of her.

Maybe, if she would just do what she's supposed to, we wouldn't even be having this conversation."

A low rumble starts at the back of the crowd, threatening to hem me in. Benjamin tenses beside me. Fabrizio's argument has weight, it's true. But Sidney was just going through the motions for years, waiting for Audrey to return. The charm weakening for *whatever* reason has nothing to do with my being in the box. I'm certain. My clumsy fingers curl into hard fists as I try to put a lid on my anger. Then I realize I don't have to.

I stand up and can feel every set of eyes here burning into my skin. I grab onto Lars's shoulder to steady myself and climb onto the table. So many faces stare at me, some of them angry, some of them scared, but all of them expectant. And many of them seem to think that Fabrizio is right. I find my accuser in the crowd. Fabrizio wears the sad smile of one who doesn't want to be right but knows he is. The words I want to say well up my throat, spitting out like machine-gun fire, unimpeded by lack of breath or tears.

"Have you ever used that pea-brain of yours to stop and think about what I gave up for your benefit? You are asking *everything* of me. Were you taken away from your family, your best friend? Was your body shattered into pieces? I was pushed off a Ferris wheel for you and your curse. Sidney!" I search the crowd for his familiar face and finally find him hovering near the back. "What did she do to you?"

He wraps his arms around himself tightly and seems to retreat within himself. I can almost see him reliving the events of the night he was cursed as he stands there. "She took me to go see the horses in their trailer, then spooked them. They trampled me."

I turn to Leslie. "What about her? The girl who turned Sidney. How did she almost die?" Because I've realized now, that's what it is. We have to get as close to dying as possible to make the carnival work. Jasper died, and the curse resurrected him. And every time the curse is passed along, the horror of that night is relived again and again.

Leslie gives me a solemn nod. "She was thrown from the roller coaster."

I fix the now stony-faced Fabrizio with my best stare, the one that's fierce and does not mess around. "Now you tell me. What have you given up for this carnival?"

The slightly petrified look in his eyes solidifies into anger, and his hands ball into fists. He takes one swinging step toward me, violence in motion.

"Sit down, Fabrizio," Leslie says.

Admiration for her warms me from the tips of my toes to the top of my head. Until I look back to Fabrizio.

The glare he gives Leslie is frightening, all malice and tense jaw. But he sits at the next closest bench.

"Now," Leslie continues, "we are going to approach this as if the charm is breaking. Some of you might have noticed that we changed course back near Austin, and that wasn't without purpose. We need to get to New Orleans to talk to the twins' grandmother, who is probably the only person alive who can help us.

"Now, there are expenses involved in keeping the carnival running, but, in light of tonight's event, we need to make a final push. We'll drive straight on to New Orleans, about a week and a half ahead of schedule. We'll leave as soon as Gin is out of the hospital.

"From here on out, we cannot take our safety for

granted. Do not take unnecessary risks. Do not showboat. Watch out for one another. And again—*be careful.*" She looks over her makeshift family one last time, and the firelight seems too bright in her eyes, as though tears lurk there. "Now get some sleep, folks. Good night."

There's grumbling as everyone leaves, which I expected, but some people—like Mrs. Potter and Marcel's parents—come over. Mrs. Potter peppers my cheeks with rosy pink kisses, and Marcel's mom hugs me tighter than I imagined her thin arms could. But the night has been long and Benjamin's smile seems more forced by the second. I put my arm around his waist and pull him toward the edge of the crowd. Lars seems to sense my plan to get Ben away from everyone, and he blocks us from view, giving me the chance to escape to my wagon. Our wagon.

Ben falls into a deep sleep the moment he's buried under every blanket I own. I lie beside him, unable to sleep thanks to the curse, but also unable to find the quiet place I usually fill my nights with. As the candle I keep in a hanging lantern sputters out and Ben's breathing slips into a steady rhythm, I try to calm the strange feeling of discomfort in my chest. I watch the constellations Ben pointed out to me move across my tiny skylight, still haunted by the look Fabrizio gave me when I fought back.

CHAPTER TWENTY-NINE

Benjamin

Emma sits beside me in the front seat of the Gran Torino, mesmerized by the long bridges and Cypress trees with exposed roots standing naked in algae-coated water. Marcel is asleep in the backseat. Every spare part imaginable rattles around in the trunk, and one of the other roustabouts—an engineer who burned out on his high-paying job and came on as a machinist—gave the Gran Torino a thorough check before we left, so I feel comfortable having Emma in the car again.

As we drive through the flats of Texas into Louisiana, I pretend everything is okay. That I'm headed home after a road trip with my best friend and the girl who's slowly stealing more and more of my heart. That Gin is just fine. That our lives aren't hinged on this carnival.

On one of those long bridges, an older truck throws one of the bolts keeping the starter in place. The engine of the Gran Torino ticks as it cools while we wait for word on how we'll proceed. None of us say anything. Marcel hasn't said a word since the accident; guilt has swept away all his charm and audacity, leaving him unsure and quiet. And Emma simply stares out the window, her fingers clumsily laced with mine on the seat between us, unable or unwilling to find anything to talk about. After a few moments, Lars bangs on the window.

"Leslie insists that we press on and send a tow for our stranded truck," he says. "Get ready to move out." I start the car and it rumbles to life immediately. Emma opens her mouth as though to say something, but closes it before a word can slip through. But I feel as though I know what she wants to say. Another downed vehicle. Another "accident." The stranded truck sits in my rearview as we drive away, a bleak reminder of how time is running out.

We have to make camp at a rest stop while we secure permits and a location. Everyone mills about, aimless with no tents to pitch or acts to practice. While some people seemed to be supportive after Emma's talk last night, things are different in the light of day. I don't know if people have had time to let things sink in or if the Moretti brothers have been running their mouths, but it feels like there are more suspicious glances thrown our way, more barely audible mutterings.

If Emma notices, she doesn't let it show that it bothers her. She simply gives me a peck on the cheek—a ghost of a touch—before perching on the steps of her wagon with one of Mrs. Potter's true-crime paperbacks. I run off to tend to a few things—getting Marcel back to his trailer, checking in with Sidney to see if Mom is at least talking to him (she's not). When I'm done, I find Emma still sitting on the steps, paperback abandoned, her eyes closed and chin tipped up to let the breeze skip over her face. It's hard to ignore the enormity of what we're doing, and I take a moment to watch her.

I don't know what this muggy, damp air feels like to her. For me, the night air clings to me heavily, like a wet towel draped across my shoulders. It wants me to know it's there, to acknowledge it. But I know that whatever I'm feeling, she's only feeling a fraction of it. The thought spurs me on.

"Ready?" I ask.

She opens her eyes slowly, languidly. "Ready."

"The first sign that we're getting too far away, we'll turn back, okay?" If there is one thing I hope to never again see in my life, it's Emma paralyzed by the curse.

She doesn't seem to share my fear. "Let's go."

According to the map we have, the twins' grandmother lives just down the road, barely more than a quarter of a mile away. Considering the carnival sometimes spreads out over an area that big, we should be okay. I'm still leery.

I've opened the passenger door for her—the handle sticks and it has to be done just so—and am about to get in on the driver's side when Pia and Duncan clamber into the backseat. "Let's go break this curse!" Duncan yells.

I freeze. The twins weren't supposed to know that we mean to break the curse. And while I don't think they'd try to stop us, I still don't know how anyone feels about losing the protection of the carnival. So as I sit behind the wheel, I turn to face them. "Um, I guess one of you had a vision about us?"

Pia raises her hand. Her smile is part guilty, part gleeful, as though she can't believe she had the vision herself.

"This going to be a problem?" Emma asks.

"Come on," Duncan says with a magnificent specimen of eye roll. "Do you really think we'd be here if we weren't okay with your plan? Besides. If you pull this off we'll have time with Grandmama to learn the family business. So I'm coming with."

"Me, too," Pia says. Her round cheeks are flushed and her eyes glimmer from beneath her perfect brows.

I glance at Emma, who just smiles a small smile and shrugs.

"I hope Grandmama baked sandies," Duncan says.

"I would eat gum scraped off the underside of the picnic tables for one of her sandies," Pia says. In the rearview, her eyes have closed and a soft, dreamy smile spreads her lips.

"I'd muck Spots McGee's stall for a month," Duncan says.

"I'd clean the fat traps."

"I'd kiss a Moretti."

"Gross," Pia says. "You win."

"You two are insane!" Emma says. The wind from the open windows makes her hair flutter around her face like a dark halo, and laughter lights up her eyes. She's stunning, and I have to force my eyes back to the road.

As we get closer, Duncan leans in between the front seats to direct me. A quick turn off the main road nearly hidden by overgrown brush, and there the house sits at the end of a one-lane road, a white beacon shining between columns of massive oaks dripping with Spanish moss. All the windows glow golden on the first floor and are black fathomless holes on the second. The house is intimidating, but as soon as the car stops, the twins are pushing my seat forward to clamber out of the car.

Emma and I follow a few paces behind. Without even knocking, Duncan opens the door and yells into the house. "Grandmama, we're here!" He disappears into the first room off the entryway, Pia right behind him. The entryway alone is amazing. It's open to the second floor and a polished staircase swoops off to the side right in front of us. A chandelier with more than a few cobwebs draped among the glistening crystals gives the room a dusky glow. Oil paintings of soft, round-cheeked women who bear more than a passing resemblance to Pia sit in gilt frames that catch the light. The kitchen must be nearby, because the scents of cloves and apples are heavy. There's a mirror off to the side, and I see Emma and myself standing around awkwardly, like children waiting to be reprimanded by a teacher. I tug Emma into the room the twins entered and find them talking the ear off an older lady who must be their grandmother.

I can't quite tell her age. She wears a slip, yoga pants, and an old maroon smoking jacket. A collection of beaded necklaces in jet and jade and a deep yellow stone hang from her thin neck. I'm not sure if her crazy clothing choices make her seem slightly mad or very charming. Her hair is white and wispy, like strands of colorless cotton candy, and it floats long and loose down her back. Her light brown skin seems papery but is unlined except for a few creases at the corners of her eyes and mouth. Her eyes are the palest shade of gray I've ever seen.

"How are things, darlings? Was the carnival able to find grounds?" she asks, ignoring us again in favor of her grandchildren.

"No," Pia says, delivering the bad news in a cheerful voice. I'm hoping that the happiness is just because she's there with her grandmother and not because of the poor luck we're having. "We had to park in some camping grounds down the road. Leslie is pissed."

The old woman pushes Pia's curls out of her eyes in a sweetly doting kind of way.

"Well you tell Leslie that she can set up on my land here. There will be fewer permits to worry about. And I think I feel like performing. Let her know she can circulate that old poster of me, the one where I look like Eartha Kitt." At that, she turns to where Emma and I stand in the doorway.

"So nice to meet you in person, darling." Her voice is clearly the voice I heard coming from Duncan's and Pia's mouths back in the tent, and it's more than a little unnerving. She gestures to the space between Emma and me. "You don't have to be nervous, dearies. Come and have a seat now, won't you?"

I glance down to see what she's gesturing toward and notice that Emma and I are gripping each other's hands. I didn't even realize that we'd done that, and, more than that, I couldn't tell you who is holding on to whom. We sit on the old fainting couch by a fireplace filled with unlit candles.

"My name is Katarina, darlings," she says grandly. Her eyes are clear and her delicate brows are set in an inquisitive arch. She leans forward, her necklaces clacking as they shift, and takes our clasped hands in hers. I can't help but notice how warm, how fiercely alive her hands are.

Her eyes flit from Emma to me and back again. "Tell me everything."

And so Emma relives her story, starting with the way

Sidney duped her and going over all the accidents and the work we've been doing to try to find a way to break the curse.

Katarina gives us a sly smile that just barely picks up the corners of her mouth. The few spidery lines at the corners of her eyes multiply with genuine happiness. "And you," she says to me, "you've been helping her?"

I don't know why I find this woman so unnerving, but I do. I push up my glasses with my free hand and nod.

"And you're going to continue to help her, yes?"

I frown. "Of course."

"And I'm going to hazard a guess and say the closer you've become the more frequent the accidents, am I right?"

Everything—my breath, my heart, the words on the edge of my lips—stutters as I think on what she just asked. Is it true? The night I cleaned up the wagon for Emma, I cut my hand. And when Emma told me she wanted to kiss me, Whiskey fell off the merry-go-round horse. Gin was hit with a knife the night Emma and I went on our date. Katarina's gaze locks onto mine the moment the truth of her question comes into focus in my mind.

"Yes," I say.

She makes a contented noise and leans back in her seat, surrounded by plump velvet cushions. "My grandchildren"—she points to each in turn—"don't fully understand their duties. Or they have grossly misunderstood them."

"Hey!" Duncan yells.

"You don't, darling," Katarina says. "It is what it is. I think that for the most part, the curse has been misunderstood for quite a long time. The mechanics of it—there's nothing misunderstood there. But a loophole has been exploited for a very long time, with little regard for the actual intent."

Emma and I share a glance. "What do you mean?" she asks.

Katarina leans forward until strands of her long hair brush against our hands. "The curse was never meant to perpetuate the way it has, deary. It was meant to be broken from the start. And the charm...well, consider the charm a sort of barometer for the curse. The curse is ready to be broken, and so, the charm is weakening, warning everyone of what's coming."

When she says it, it sounds so simple. But everyone here has lived with the tradition of the curse being transferred from person to person. Katarina snaps her fingers and shatters the silence. "Pia, be a good girl and bring me that photograph by the door."

Pia scampers across the room and returns with a heavy wooden frame. In it there is an old, old photo of three women. One is obviously Katarina. Though the hair is dark and the face completely unlined, nothing else has changed. Behind her is a woman who must be her mother. They share a nose, a mouth, and a devilish smile. Next to Katarina is another woman, much younger, with a curl to her hair that suggests a wildness. Her eyes seem to spark out of the sepia photo.

"My sister never had the best judgment," Katarina says, running a long fingernail around the face in the photo. "She gave her heart to a man who didn't know how to cherish such a gift. She was impetuous, and did not like being constrained to the carnival. We lived a freer life than most, especially considering the time and the color of our skin, but we were still following someone else's whims, someone else's plans, and she resented that."

"Great-Aunt Rebecca sounds like a loose cannon," Duncan says.

Katarina glances at him over her shoulder. "There's a touch of her in you, darling. I wouldn't be so quick to judge." Pia dissolves into a fit of giggles, but her grandmother ignores her. "I'm assuming you're here because you've found my journal?"

"We did," I say. Suddenly I'm having a hard time visualizing the old, crumbling paper of the journal being new and used by a much younger Katarina.

"Then you know what happened." Her voice breaks here, betrays her age in a way her appearance does not. "I wish my intent had been as true as Mother's. Who knows? Maybe if I could have kept the anger out of my heart, the curse would never have been born. Maybe Jasper would have gone on living his life without blemish, and you two wouldn't sit before me right now.

"But that's not what happened. Mother and I worked and worked to find a way for him to break the curse. We reconstructed the events of that night, the reason Jasper had become what he was. We made a potion and disguised it as wine. Once we had it all figured out, we explained it to Jasper. He would need to do what he could not do with Rebecca, and give his heart away, and that person would need to give theirs in return. The love between them would need to be strong enough to bridge life and death. Together, their pain, their actions would break the curse. But he found a loophole. He took our words and warped them, found the first woman he could trick and when he had passed off the curse to her, he left town and never looked back."

She says those last words like they're dirty things, like he sullied everything he was near or touched. The candles in the fireplace burn brightly, rivulets of wax already dripping down to pool in the grate, though I could have sworn they weren't lit before. Katarina's gaze has gone fierce, her skin lit by the points of flame dancing wildly on the candles in the fireplace.

"Jasper Clarke," she says, her words edged with anger, "never understood that the curse was based on something real. He never dealt within the realm of reality, only the realm of what he created and what he could sell. The curse can be passed on, yes, with lies and falsehoods and charm." She looks at me then, not at Emma. Her gray eyes are sharp enough to cut. "But the curse *can* be broken with love—*true* love, the bond of soul mates— honesty, and, above all, sacrifice."

CHAPTER THIRTY

Emma

"No. *No*. Hell no," I say. But Ben is still looking at me with these huge puppy-dog eyes from underneath his flop of golden hair. I feel like I might break. "Benjamin, you can't. Just…no."

We stand on Katarina's porch, in a golden circle of light doing its best to keep the star-filled night away. An ocean of sound comes from the swishing leaves and the sway of heavy oak branches and the tall grasses, all of them hiding in the darkness. I want him to agree with me, to say that this is crazy. Instead he stands there with his fists tucked into his pockets. "Tell me why not. In words that have more than one syllable." His wry little smile does nothing to lessen my panic.

I wonder if comfort would come if I could feel my heart pounding or my breathing becoming rapid or any of those normal signals of distress. I don't think I ever knew how much I relied on those things. As if somehow my body's reactions to outside forces made things easier to handle. As if trying to slow down the ragged beating of a nervous heart makes it seem like progress is being made toward solving the problem at hand. But all I've got is my twitching and a rising swell of panic that won't let me stand still.

"Just because that crazy loon—"

"That crazy loon can probably hear you, you know," Benjamin says.

"I don't care. That *crazy loon* wants you to almost die, Benjamin. That's what it takes. To voluntarily break your body. I can't let you do that. What if she's wrong? What if it doesn't work?" What I don't say is, *what if you don't really love me? What if those horrible things your mother thinks about me are true?* And, possibly worse than either of those things, *how can we be soul mates when we barely know each other?*

"She had a hand in making the curse. Of course she knows how to break it."

I shake my head, wanting desperately for him to understand. "We don't know that. It's not worth the risk. And it's not just the risk, it's... I'm scared of losing *you.*"

After a moment, he walks toward me and takes my hand, pressing my fingers to the side of his throat. As we stand in our circle of light I find myself soaking up the warmth of him, hungry for more.

His gaze doesn't waver, not a bit. "Can you feel my pulse, Emma?"

I can, just barely. It's a living, beating, breathing, dancing thing. It's a bird under glass. It almost seems to sing *alive, alive, alive* with every steady beat. Heat comes off him in waves, and my jealous hand wants to press closer to steal it. And somewhere, somewhere vague and fuzzy, I remember what it felt like to be that warm.

His breath is a brush of warmth on my face. "I want you to have that again, Emma. Plain and simple."

Slow enough that I can feel each finger lift from his neck, the heat disappearing with him, he moves away. He believes Katarina. He believes in me. As he walks back into the house, I can't find it in me to agree with his plan.

And I'm selfish enough that I can't find it in me to disagree, either.

CHAPTER THIRTY-ONE

Emma

The carnival blooms on Katarina's back acres like mushrooms after rain. More time and care goes into the setup than I've seen before. Leslie is careful to make sure we're far enough away that Katarina won't be bothered before she performs, and that her house won't be disturbed. However, there's only one gravel road leading to the property. Every night there will be a line of headlights waiting to get in, and a dense line of taillights crawling out again when we close.

Katarina's old posters were plastered about town as instructed, and Leslie is expecting more of a draw than usual. Apparently, the woman is something of a local celebrity. She did readings at her home after she left the carnival, but even that grew taxing in her retirement, so she quit. But the locals remember her, and will flock to the carnival to get a reading.

Ben and I don't talk about Katarina's proclamation. Now that he's spending his evenings and free time in my wagon, I see the stress eating away at him. He never says anything, but it's there, all the same. There's a permanent deep groove between his brows that had only made occasional appearances before, and I don't know if the source is Audrey or breaking the curse or maybe even something *I've* done. Every time I gather the courage to ask, it slips away at the last minute, leaving me with all my unasked questions. He sleeps fitfully beside me as my anxiety gnaws away at my mind.

I feel twisted up in knots. Does he really love me? And if he does, does he love me *enough*? How can he be willing to almost die? What if it doesn't work? Is what we're doing now—sharing this small space and filling it up with all our worries and fears—going to put a wedge between us like it did Audrey and Sidney?

I glance over at him. He's curled under a twist of blankets, his head on the pillow we share. The moon shines through the small skylight, making his hair a dull silver gray. My fingers slip through it like air. But something stirs inside me. I know what's been left unsaid by his decision. Those three all-important words were never spoken aloud, but I know he's not dumb enough to try to break the curse without being sure of how he feels.

About me.

The thought leaves me buoyant and ridiculously happy in between the waves of pure terror that hit me when I think about what it would take for him to uphold his promise—an act of almost dying. But as I watch his even breathing fill his chest, I don't think that I can let him go through with it. He's so vibrant, so alive. How can he exist any other way?

My options are now this—either dupe some poor

sucker into taking my place by nearly killing him or her, or become exactly the monster Audrey assumed I was and have Benjamin take the fall for me, nearly killing *him*. I really wish there was a way out of this that didn't involve nearly killing anyone.

And all the while, the charm is weakening.

His hand stretches out from underneath the blanket, and without even thinking about it, I reach for it. I run my hardened fingers over the ridges of his knuckles, the knob of bone at the side of his wrist. Already I know his hands better than my own.

I love him.

And I can't let him do it.

Before he can try to break the curse, I'm going to pass it on to someone else.

The first night we're open in New Orleans, it's everything Leslie expected. The crowds are denser, louder, rowdier. Everyone here has a loud drawl; each woman and man and child crowding and pushing their way down the alleys is full of life. Crushed beer cans and soda cups litter the pathways, and the trash cans overflow; our maintenance crews can't keep up with this boisterous crowd.

And trouble is on the wind.

I change into my costume while Benjamin's still working, and slip out of the wagon before he gets back. I don't want to run into him on my way to the box. I don't want him to talk me out of it. I don't want him to *die*.

I roll my shoulders in as if making myself smaller

will make me less noticeable, but it's hard to be less noticeable when you're wearing a sparkling flapper dress and a bright-red velvet coat. My mouth is a ruby, and my cheeks glow a gentle pink as if lit from within. I am the jewel in the jewel box, the bait in the trap.

I *will* find someone to take my place. Tonight.

The night whittles away in groups of passersby. The families with younger children give way to families with teenagers, and then teenagers and solo adults after that. This is when I turn up the charm. I am Sidney, trickster who conned me into trading my life for his. I am Jules, Flirting Queen of the World. I am Emma, protector of the boy she loves.

It's late, though I'm not sure exactly how late. The moon has moved to a place I can't see from my vantage point inside the box, and the crowds are thinning when a quarter makes its way down the gleaming copper chute. I glance up at my mark coyly.

He's maybe a year or two younger than me. A scattering of pimples dots his cheeks. His youth disarms me, as does the guilt that comes from the thought of separating him from his family. I don't know if I can do it.

But I have to.

I play out the events the same way Sidney did. A cryptic card. A thousand-watt smile. Using a distraction to draw the curtains that line the booth and slip out the back. When he sees that I'm actually standing behind him his smile is so big and so real that I want to back out. How can I keep this *boy* away from his family? From his mother and father and his best friend? But then I remember that Sidney did it to me, and someone else did it to him, and someone else did it to her. I hate myself for it, but I'd hate it more if I didn't have Benjamin in my life. I tell myself that it's the lesser of two evils, but even I can't believe the lie.

"I'm due for a break," I say, trying hard to not stumble over my words. "Care to entertain me?"

He's so gawky. His hands are too big for his body, like he's a puppy not yet done growing. If I could, I think I would be sick right about now.

He rumples his hair back, out of his eyes, and when I hear his voice—a voice that must have only just stopped cracking—my doubts come rushing back. "That'd be awesome."

I take him on a roundabout walk through the carnival so I can glean more information off him. He's here with friends, but they got separated a while ago and his cell phone is dead, so he's just hoping to run into them again at some point. He doesn't seem concerned by this or worried about how he's going to get home, so I take this as a good sign. When he tells me he's lived in a revolving succession of foster homes, I can't believe my luck.

He's the one.

In a few seconds, we're at the back end of the fortune-tellers' tent. The flap is only partially laced, like it always is for exactly this purpose. I reach in. The bottles are cool to the touch and I wrap my fingers around one carefully, to keep this boy from hearing the *clink* of my hard fingers on the glass. When he sees my prize, his brown eyes go wide.

I stare at the green and gold glass, at the giant magnolia flowers etched in a swirling pattern around the base. I can reclaim my life with what's in this bottle. I'll wreck his. He's trying his hardest to act nonchalant, like he's shared a bottle of booze with a girl a dozen times before.

I tug at the sleeve of his hoodie, careful to keep my stony fingers from touching him, and pull him into the shadows where this tent butts up to the next. The ground is cold beneath my legs and getting up again is going to be a pain, but hopefully when it's time to stand again, he'll be so tipsy he won't notice. The cork releases from the bottle with a soft *pop*. I hold my fist high on the neck so when I bring it to my lips, the boy can't tell I'm just pressing the bottle to my closed mouth. "Here," I say, passing the wine into his hands, "have some."

I am a horrible, terrible person.

The boy—Alexander Pritchard, he tells me—is a sophomore and cocaptain of the local swim team. Briefly I wonder how much of a stir it'll cause when he goes missing, but that will be Leslie's problem, not mine. "But," he says as he downs the last of the wine, "my foster dad was driving me crazy and I had to get out of the house."

The words sting. My family and Juliet are like a hole in my chest I can't close. But, soon, I can go back. If I do this.

"Have you been on the roller coaster?" I ask. There's a slight tremble in my voice, one that I hope the boy can't hear.

"You want to go for a ride, sweetness?" It's pretty clear he's drunk all the wine; no one sober would call a girl they don't really know "sweetness."

If Ben's safety didn't hang in the balance, I'd ditch this guy. But it does, so I plaster a grin on my face and stand, beckoning the boy to follow me. He's wobbly on his legs, and I can pinpoint the exact moment he realizes he's drunk. The knowledge doesn't seem to deter him, though—in fact, it adds only more swagger to his step, to the point where he's not so much walking as zigzagging through the rapidly emptying carnival. The whole time he keeps up a relentless chatter, about his friends who ditched him, the essay he has to write this weekend, and would I like to go to the all-night diner after this?

The roller coaster is impressive for something that is an impermanent fixture. The first drop isn't terribly high, but it's steep, propelling the cars through several twists and turns. I lead the boy to the lowest dip, where the track is barely two feet off the ground.

I could push him. Wait till the cars come swerving down the track and knock him right into them. The ride operator is chatting with someone, but when he sees the boy and me he stops, elbowing his companion, who turns to look. It's Lorenzo Moretti. The carnival is mostly empty and no one is in line for the roller coaster, but the ride operator pulls a lever and the empty cars climb up the track to the highest peak and pause there. Lorenzo gives me a nod.

The boy can barely stand straight. He clearly thinks I'm about to kiss him, and I could do it, press my lips to his when he leans in, then push him onto the track. It'll be easy. Quick.

He looks *so* young.

My resolve cracks.

"Go," I say, my voice barely more than a whisper.

Puzzlement runs down his face, starting with furrowed brows and ending with a petulant frown. "What did I do?" Now his voice *does* crack.

Like throwing stones at a dog to get it to run, I throw my insults at this boy to save him. "Go home, Junior

League. I just got a good look at your face, and what are you, twelve?" I raise my hand a few inches above his head. "You must be this tall to ride this ride."

He stares at me for a second, to make sure I'm not screwing with him. With a dejected "Bitch," he shoves his hands into his jacket pockets and huffs off.

Even from where I stand more than a dozen feet away I can still hear Lorenzo say, "What the hell?" He grips the guardrail of the ride platform and swings over, landing gracefully in the dirt. I don't want to deal with him, hear him berate me for screwing up when I had my prey exactly where I wanted him.

So I run.

The carnival is a blur as I race back to my wagon. The door is ajar, a line of pale light outlining its curve in the dark shadow that is the wagon.

When I climb inside, Benjamin is there, propped up against the pile of pillows and reading a book. He takes one long look at me, from the shaking that rocks me from head to toe to the empty bottle of wine that's still clutched in my hand. His eyes linger there for a good long while, and a tentative smile creeps across his mouth.

"You changed your mind?" He's good at hiding it, but there's a glimmer of hope peeking out of that question.

I hadn't thought of what it would be like to tell him that I wanted to pass off the curse instead of break it. And I definitely hadn't thought of what I'd say if I failed. Will he think I'm weak? A coward? A horrible person? All those things?

"There was this boy." I pause, unsure how to phrase the horrible part, the part that comes next. Turns out, I don't have to. He looks at me and my shaking and the bottle and understanding clicks on his face.

We have no words for each other. Ben slides off the pillow he'd been sitting on and quietly moves past me to slip out the door, the budding smile trampled into a frown. I want to—no, *need to*—say something, but there's nothing in me that isn't a lie.

But there is anger.

"Don't run away from this argument like you do with your mother!" I yell as I follow him into the night air. Ben stops, still within the circle of the light spilling from my wagon. The muscles of his back and arms ripple as he clenches and unclenches his hands into fists. I expect him to keep going, though I hope he won't. Finally, he turns.

"Why shouldn't I when you seem to trust me about as much as she does?"

He turns away again as I sink to sit on the steps. He heads not for camp but for the smudge of trees in the distance. I watch him until he's a dark shadow indistinguishable from the others crowding the night.

Fuck.

CHAPTER THIRTY-TWO

Benjamin

I sit near the white slatted fence bordering the edge of Katarina's property, cypress trees dripping in Spanish moss just beyond. The cool, damp ground is trying its hardest to make me the same temperature. The carnival is far behind me, the lights gone out a long time ago.

So when I hear clumsy steps behind me, I'm a little surprised.

"I know what's bumming *me* out," Sidney says, "but what about you?" His voice has the slippery slur of one drink before complete drunkenness and one after good sense. When he drops down onto the grass beside me, I can smell the warm yeasty scent of his beer before I see the bottle glinting in the sparse light.

I don't answer. I've learned that if you leave space in a conversation, people like Sidney, people who love the sound of their own voice and their self-important stories, will fill it for you.

"Not feeling particularly chatty this evening?" he asks.

"That's fine. Let me take a stab at it." He tips his head back to take a swig from his bottle. "We're here on Katarina Marx's property, and that, my not-quite-friend, isn't a coincidence. I know Emma wants to break the curse, and I know Katarina knows how."

My head whips toward him. He has to see my bewilderment because I've had no time to hide it. Sidney is not supposed to be this knowing or this astute.

"That's right, Audrey Jr." He points at me with one hand still wrapped around the bottle. It's like he has that thing surgically attached. "Now. I know what you're thinking. How does good old Sidney—"

"I was using different adjectives in front of *Sidney*," I interject. He's drunk enough to go on without me, sober enough to start talking louder in case I decide to be a smart-ass again.

"*How does good old Sidney* know that Katarina is the key to breaking the curse?"

He is the last person I want to be playing this game with. I start to stand up, and that hurries him along. His voice has lost the singsongy quality, and many of the unnecessary *S*'s that slide in between words disappear.

"I tried to break it, too, that's how I know." He stares off at the moving clouds, at the glimpses of white moon that filter through them. "After your mother grew tired of watching me fail night after night after *night* and left, I didn't care. I went through the motions but didn't really try. Leslie pitied me. She convinced me to come here, to see what Katarina might know."

"And when she told me what had to happen, that—" He pauses here and holds his beer bottle up to the moonlight like it's a cherished thing, like a lover. "That it had to be my *one true love* willing to make the sacrifice…" He laughs, a mean, coarse noise so unlike anything I've ever heard from him that it's startling. "I've never, ever loved anyone like I loved Audrey—hope this isn't creeping you out, hearing me talk about your mom like this, because I'm doing it anyway—and I knew, *I knew* that she would come back."

He gestures grandly toward the empty field. "And lo, she came back, widowed and with you in tow. Shit, but that hurt. You were a cute kid, don't get me wrong, but that was not how I saw things happening. *But.* Her coming back only confirmed to my stupid, hopeful self that I was right, that the curse could be broken and that Audrey and I would be the ones to do it.

"So I waited. I was respectful, downright gentlemanly. It took about a year and a half for her to talk to me again. She was guarded, but that was to be expected. And I just kept waiting. Because she was supposed to be my soul mate; it was meant to be. So every day I looked for a sign that she was willing. And that sign never came.

"For a while, I thought it was because of you. That she didn't want to risk almost dying while she had a child who still had trouble tying his own shoes. But you got older and she still didn't want to do it. Finally, I approached her, I don't know, five months ago. You're grown, you could take her place as carpenter for this damned carnival if she wanted you to, and *she still turned me down.* She still said no."

My insides go cold as I begin to see the shape of his argument like a distant island off a dark shore.

He turns toward me then, so close I can almost taste the beer he's been drinking. "That's when I figured it out. Audrey might have been my soul mate, but I was never hers. So I ask you, Benjamin, how the hell is anyone supposed to break this curse when Audrey and I couldn't?" Unshed tears line the lower lids of his eyes, trembling. "I waited for years. For her. Only for her. And she refused to even think for one tiny second I could be right about breaking the curse."

I clear my throat, trying to rid myself of the doubt that's built up there. "Emma and I are different—"

"You think I didn't think that about Audrey and me?" He stands with more grace than I would have thought he'd be capable of at the moment. He is a stark, still shape against the clouds that tumble over one another.

"So I found the first girl with low self-esteem who wouldn't be missed and I transferred the curse. *And it worked.* That is what sealed the deal for me, *that* is what convinced me that breaking the curse is impossible— when I put myself to the task, when I *tried* to pass the curse along, it happened. I have loved your mother for so long it's all I know how to do. So I ask you—" His voice breaks here, and for a moment I'm not sure if he has it in him to keep going, but he does. "If she and I can't break this damned curse, who the hell can?"

CHAPTER THIRTY-THREE

Benjamin

The next night, I stand among the townies in line to have the great Katarina Marx read my fortune. They jostle in a good-natured way, like being at a carnival has made them revert to their kindergarten selves. The air is humid enough to make their closeness uncomfortable but not enough to make me want to give up.

I could pull rank and jump the line, citing that I need to fix something in the tent or that I'm there on carnival business, but I don't. I want to steel myself, to make sure that this is really what I want to do.

Sidney rattled the hell out of me. But it's not the same with Emma and me. A little voice nags at me—*but they knew each other longer. They had time to get to know each other. They had a relationship before the curse.* A hundred doubts are having a rave in the empty warehouse of my brain.

The line moves faster than I expected. Most patrons leave the tent much happier than when they went in. A few do not. I don't even know what I want to ask Katarina, but something is pushing me insistently, telling me I have to see her. Suddenly I'm standing before the painted entrance to the tent, with nothing separating me from her except some brightly colored canvas. Then, after a couple who look like they're on the brink of an argument rush out, all tense angles and tight mouths, I go in.

The twins have been relegated to a small side table immediately to the left of the entrance to give their grandmother the place of pride in the center of the tent. A cat, black and sleek and with a small white triangle on its chest, has draped itself on the shelf holding all those precious bottles of wine. Incense burns, but not so much that it's obnoxious or overpowering. And then there is Katarina herself.

Fortune-telling must merit changing out of yoga pants. She wears a beaded black dress not all that different from the one Emma wears as part of her costume. The similarity is so strong that a pang hits me in the chest hard and fast. Her eyes are lined with black, her lips stained like wine. I take my seat on the little chair in front of her.

"Benjamin, darling, what a surprise." She is most definitely not surprised. "How can I help you this evening?"

"Would you read my fortune?" I have always let the twins use me as a guinea pig. Palm readings, tarot cards, tea leaves, divining—I've done it all. And while they've been right about far too many things, I never took it seriously. Until now.

Her long spindly fingers reach across the table and beckon for mine. If fingers can be taunting, hers are. Her hands are smooth, but the flesh around each knuckle clings close to the bone, and each joint is pronounced.

Rings with stones of black and red and blue glint in the reddish light of the tent. Her nails have been filed to a subtle point and are painted a red that's darker than blood but brighter than black.

I place my hand in hers.

She leans forward to examine my palm, her long hair piling up on the table underneath her. One of those dark fingernails traces some of the heavier creases; the big one running almost straight across until it suddenly veers toward my pointer finger, the one curving around the meat at the base of my thumb. There are half a dozen smaller ones that catch her attention, and even the tiny creases that gather just under my pinkie finger merit inspection.

Finally, she lays my hand down on the table and leans back in her chair. Movies and books and the few times Pia's read my palm for fun told me what should have happened—as she pointed out each divot and line and fold, there'd be an explanation to go with it, a theory, a ridiculous number of children I'd surely father somewhere down the line. Instead she just sits in that overly big chair that I now recognize from her living room, and she peers at me over steepled fingers.

"Darlings," she says, gesturing toward the twins with a beckoning wave of those tricksy fingers, "I think it's high time to further your education."

Pia gasps at the same moment the cards Duncan is shuffling go flying out of his hands.

Duncan slaps the table with his palm. "Hell yes, Grandmama! We've been practicing our scrying and—"

Whatever else the twins had been practicing, I'd never hear it, because Katarina shuts her grandson down with a wave. "You," she said, pointing to Duncan, "tell everyone outside I am closed for the evening." Duncan rushes out of the tent, the flaps to the entrance billowing behind him.

"You"—she points to Pia, who looks so excited she might explode—"bring me those candles and extinguish all the others."

"And you," she says to me finally, carefully, powerfully, "stay here." Her knowing eyes seem black in the dim light, and pinpricks from the flames dance upon them. "You and I have much to talk about."

CHAPTER THIRTY-FOUR

Emma

A hint of rain falls through the air. I can't quite remember what the close, damp touch of humidity feels like, and the thought both scares and saddens me. The giant oaks sway a wicked dance just past the edges of the carnival. If there's a storm coming, none of the carnival patrons notice or care, so I head to my box. I don't want to be there, but I can't stand the thought of being in my wagon without Benjamin, who I haven't seen since last night.

I've become so used to the jostling and the crowds that it takes me a moment to realize the reason things seem weird this evening is that there are fewer people crowded around booths and games, and a good number of them are all funneling toward the center of the carnival. I slip into their stream, letting them propel me toward their goal.

Once I push away my own thoughts and concerns and start to pay attention to my surroundings, I begin to figure out what's pulling this crowd away from the kettle corn and sleights of hand. A man is shouting, his voice just this side of hysterical and more than a little drunk. Although the noise of those around me keeps me from hearing everything, I have a terrible feeling about what I'll see.

When I turn the corner, it's worse than I imagined.

Sidney is thirty feet in the air, walking across the top of the long shack that is the haunted house ride. The tall building suddenly seems taller, the construction more rickety. And up as high as he is, the wind is unhindered by the booths and rides.

"Aud-rey Sin-ger," he croons into the night. It's a wailing birdcall, repetitive and forlorn.

Some of the laborers have gathered at the base of the ride and lean against the metal railing to look up at Sidney, talking about finding a ladder or Leslie or both, but no one actually moves to do anything. Sidney treads along the edge of the roof on unsteady feet, and the sight makes me angry.

Clowns gently usher the townies down other alleys, toward the bright flashing lights that are much better than the bright flashing lights right in front of them. Vouchers are slipped into palms, free samples that are much, much bigger than normal are offered, anything to get them away from Sidney and his spectacle.

"Sidney!" My voice feels small in the wide night, eaten up by the bleating of games and the muttering onlookers and the gusting wind. He scans the crowd that's gathered but can't seem to find me, so I step into the empty space in front of the ride. "It's a fine line from 'goofing around' to 'actually suicidal,' you jackass!"

"Emma!" He leans over the brightly painted spider in front of him, and it wobbles dangerously. I hear a dozen intakes of breath, feel the crowd shift back to a safer distance. "Emmaline, darling, did I ever tell you I was sorry? And, when I say that, I mean did I tell you I was sorry and mean it? I don't think I did, so I'm going to say it now."

He hasn't said that he's sorry, but right now, I don't care. If he has to say it, I want him to say it while he's on the ground, where I can hit him for being stupid enough to be drunk and walking on top of a falling-apart shack. His dark brows furrow into worried triangles. "I am so sorry, Emma. I'm sorry that I dragged you into this, and I'm sorry that I'm too chicken to take the curse back, and I'm sorry, sorry, sorry."

"It's okay, Sidney," I yell. "I forgive you, all right? Just come down."

"You"—he points at me with a hand that's wrapped around a big green bottle—"don't get to order me around."

"Regardless, it's a damn fine suggestion, son," Lars says. Oh thank God. Lars. He is a giant by my side, a figure to be listened to, but if height makes you an authority figure, then Sidney is the boss of us all.

That is, until Audrey Singer bursts out of the crowd to my right.

Her eyes are wide, a shocked swath of white surrounding the blue. A pink flush creeps up her cheeks, and her chest heaves like she ran to get here.

"Sid! Get down here, you moron." Each word has to wait for a frantic gasp of air to be sucked in before it has its turn. Long, calloused fingers grip at the stitch in her side.

"No, no, Audrey," Sidney says. "Not when I've got your full attention for once."

Sidney begins to pace the narrow ledge between the giant spider he had been lounging against and the snarling hellhound on the opposite side.

"Do you have any idea how long I have loved you, Audrey?"

Audrey's breath marks the seconds in bright little puffs. "Can we talk about this down here? I'll talk about anything you want as long as you *come down*."

Off to the side, Leslie directs someone to ease a ladder against the haunted house, but the tension gathered in my chest only coils tighter. Something big is happening here. I can feel it in my bones. I edge toward the ride, hoping to do something, though I don't know what.

Sidney takes a swig from his bottle, never breaking eye contact with Audrey. From the rubbery way his legs almost give out beneath him and the loose way his arms swing about, I know this is not his first drink of the night. "You don't want to take a stab at it? Not even a little guess?"

Tears tremor in Audrey's eyes but don't fall. "Years. I know it was years. The same…" She takes in a big gasp of air. "The same as me. I love you, you giant idiot."

Sidney stops pacing long enough to see he's gotten Audrey well and truly upset. And if I've learned anything here at the carnival, it's that Sidney can't bear to see Audrey upset. A look passes between the two of them, and if I didn't know it before, I know it now, as does anyone else standing there—when it comes to the two of them, what Audrey Singer wants, Audrey Singer gets. And I think that finally, Audrey knows that, too. The hard line of her brow softens, and her frown has been replaced with a hopeful lift of the lips.

And even though this woman hates me, something

joyful swells in my heart. Maybe they can be okay.

Sidney smiles, slow and somehow heartbreakingly sad. "I love you, too, Boss Lady." Audrey gives a strangled half laugh when she hears the nickname. "Always will."

At that moment the roustabout Leslie sent up the ladder hefts himself on top of the haunted house, and Sidney, startled, whirls about to face him. The scuffed soles of his shoes slip on the rain-slicked surface, and before the man can reach him…

Sidney falls.

For one long second, Sidney hangs in the air, the copy of the marionette boy on the card he gave me a million years ago. There's a crunch and a squelch as his head hits the metal rail that borders the ramp to the entrance, and when he crumples on the ground, he doesn't move.

No one dares to breathe. Maybe if everyone is very, very still he will get up. But the wind howls down the alleys and a broken sob comes from somewhere to my left and Sidney doesn't get up. No. It's *Sidney*. He's a jerk and he's my friend and if there's anything he does well, it's *survive*. I have to see; I have to check.

Lars makes a grab for my coat sleeve as I dart toward Sidney, but I pull away. My fingers clench into hard fists. Why? Why isn't anyone checking on him? He's one of theirs, don't they care? He carried the curse for them, or did they forget?

Audrey pushes her way in front of me, but she freezes at the foot of the ramp. "I can't look," she says, her voice barely more than a whisper. She doesn't ask me to do this for her, but I hear the request anyway. I walk up the ramp.

Sidney's blood drips down the plywood platform, falling with a soft *pat, pat, pat* onto the trampled grass below. I realize that seconds are precious, but I can't seem to make my feet go up the ramp.

I know he's gone the moment I see his body. His blank eyes stare into the dark square entrance of the haunted house, hollow and glassy. If he were conscious, even a little part of him, those eyes would be searching for Audrey. More blood pools under his head, the lights playing across the slowly spreading surface. His dark curls are matted with it. I crouch beside him, struggling to reconcile this Sidney with the exuberant one who had been pacing above us just a moment ago. With the trickster who charmed me into taking the curse. I reach out and for once, my fingers are steady. I gently press his eyelids closed. When I raise my head to look for Audrey, I realize that she's standing beside me. For once all the hate she has for me has disappeared, replaced with something I had never seen in her eyes—desperation. I give her the smallest shake of my head.

She crumples to the ground. Sidney's blood creeps toward her, as if, even in death, he can't bear to be away from her.

CHAPTER THIRTY-FIVE

Emma

Chaos breaks out among the gathered crowd and in that chaos, I see a point of stillness. Fabrizio Moretti. He is a rock in a surging ocean of people, and he's staring right at me. With a flick of his fingers, two lines of people move against the crowd surging toward Sidney, headed right for me.

I have to run.

I don't want to leave the crumpled heap of a body that is, *was*, Sidney, but I have to get somewhere safe, where the Morettis won't touch me.

The laborers and performers who had stood idly by are now rushing toward Sidney, as if they know something, some miraculous cure that will bring him back. There is nothing to bring back. But still, they push against me.

Someone shoves me into the railing halfway down the ramp, my hip clanging hard against the metal. I don't think anything of it until a hand grips my arm. It's Antonio. His mouth curls up in a slow, sinister grin.

"We're done doing this your way," he says.

He yanks my arm, and the crowd parts before him. I see more than a few glances my way that are quickly diverted, like they, too, blame me for this mess. I search the crowd for Leslie or Lars, but Leslie is trying to calm everyone down and Lars is trapped by the rush of people trying to get to Sidney. My feet hit the dirt, and there's a small gap in the crowd. I yank my arm free and run.

I am empty and hollow inside. I have no breath to fill my lungs. No heart to beat against my chest and thump in my ears. My legs do not burn or ache from running. I have nothing in me, nothing at all. But I do have Benjamin, and I need to get to him. If the Morettis want to hurt me, they might go after him, too, and I cannot let that happen.

I dart between a child and her mother, around Happy the Clown as he runs toward the body. Right into the arms of Fabrizio Moretti.

He spins me around as I try to dodge past, his grip ten times firmer than his brother's. I slam my heel into his foot; his face twists into a grimace and his fingers tighten like a vise. His eyes skim the crowd, and when he finds his other brother, Lorenzo, he jerks his head to the side and starts to drag me between two tents.

"Help!" I scream, hoping to grab the attention of someone, anyone who might get the wrong idea and decide that Fabrizio is a boy hoping to take advantage of a girl. I see nothing but hostile eyes set in familiar faces, those of carnival workers and performers who I have been slowly getting to know over the last several weeks. Some of them, the ones who nodded eagerly during Fabrizio's speech the night Gin was hurt, look away. Some of them subtly shield me from the curious eyes of townies who have no idea of the horror lying in front of the haunted house. And some of them join the mob.

I scream, one long wordless, endless note of fear in hopes that someone will feel guilty or heroic or something and help me get away. Fabrizio jerks me down another alley so hard that I fall and am dragged for a few feet before I can get upright again. I twist, hoping to tear myself out of his grip, but fail. Fabrizio pulls me toward a tent, and one of his cronies lifts the flap to let us in. We're in a food tent, one that sells ice cream. There's a giant freezer in the back corner, and at a signal from Fabrizio, someone starts to empty the contents onto the ground.

I throw up my fist and graze Fabrizio's immovable jaw. My legs fling out, trying to catch anyone, but no one is close enough.

"Find the roustabout and get him far away from here, then take care of him," Fabrizio barks out. "The charm isn't the problem. The two of them are."

Antonio tries to grab my legs, and I kick. My shoe connects with his chin, opening up a gash on his lip. "Goddamn it!" He dabs at the blood dripping from his mouth. When he sees the red on his fingertips, he glares, and wraps an iron hand around my ankle. They drop me into the freezer, and the cold pierces me. The twitching starts in earnest, so fierce I can't hold still long enough to try to pull myself out of the freezer. My fingers claw at the walls and flakes of ice slough off before my hand jerks and I lose my grip.

As Fabrizio lowers the door, the big shiny lock swaying ominously from the hinge on the lid, he stares at me.

"Things have been going downhill ever since these two have been more concerned with making time with each other than passing on the curse. We're going to fix more than one of our problems tonight, boys." His eyes glitter. "Then we're going to show Emma what we do to trouble-makers in the carnival."

CHAPTER THIRTY-SIX

Benjamin

The world outside of Katarina's tent is an ocean of confusion. Shrieks and screams pierce the night, and they are not the terror/joy hybrid that comes from riding the roller coaster, nor the delight of seeing Mrs. Potter's dogs run through their tricks. These are the screams of very bad things happening.

The ground seems to slide out from beneath my feet as I run through the carnival, straight into the flow of people running to get away. I trip but catch myself before I face-plant and get up with only a few scrapes on my palms.

Everything hits me as I try to figure out what's wrong and where to go. The wind rattles the trees near the edge of the carnival, long trails of Spanish moss whipping around. Everything feels like *more*—the smell of popcorn and sugar, the bleeping machines, the very air that fills my lungs is heavy and sweet, sugar and pine. People rush past me and down the alley, all of them panicked.

Some roustabouts are directing townies back toward the gates, passing out vouchers to come back another night, so whatever it was must have been bad. A crowd gathers around the base of the haunted house, and an agonizing wailing from that direction hurts my heart. It's the cry of loss and it's one I've heard before. Then I see the dirt-stained canvas tarp covering a distinctly body-shaped lump on the platform, and the black lines of what has to be blood trailing out from beneath it.

My heart stops for a moment, but restarts when I realize it can't be Emma, because she wouldn't be bleeding. As I walk toward the haunted house, a gust of wind picks up a corner of the tarp and I see a familiar thatch of curls.

Sidney.

All the noise in the world comes back, louder and sharper. I turn toward the keening I heard earlier and find Mom. She's collapsed onto Lars, a shaking mess. Oh God, Sidney. I didn't like him, and I hated what he did to my mother, but he didn't deserve to die. And now Mom has to deal with another lost love. I start to cross the yard to get to her, when Lars catches my eye and shakes his head minutely. He mouths two words. *Find Emma*.

I survey the rest of the area quickly and see Marcel trying to push through the people nearby to get to me. I throw one more look at Lars, torn. I know I should go to Mom, but I also know that if Lars is telling me to find Emma, then I need to find Emma.

The ground feels unsteady beneath my feet as I run toward Marcel. I almost overshoot and crash into him.

"Are you all right?" Marcel asks as he grips my arms to keep me upright. His eyes narrow down to inspect my face, and I struggle to get it together.

I don't feel fine, but that's not important. A full bottle of Katarina's wine and blessings ride through my veins, and neither will stick around for long. If we're going to break this curse, it has to be now. "Where's Emma?"

Marcel's dark eyes harden. "I think the Morettis took her. It can't be good."

My heart thumps wildly. "Which way did they go?"

"Right behind you."

I whirl, and see Lorenzo Moretti's face a second before his fist connects with my jaw. I'm on the ground, and I don't know how I got here. My blood is on my tongue and dirt grinds between my teeth. Marcel's voice is somewhere far above me, and then it goes quiet, packed away in cotton. Everything lurches as someone grabs hold of my ankles and drags me across the uneven earth.

And then, my world goes dark.

CHAPTER THIRTY-SEVEN

Emma

The blackness is complete. The cold is so fierce it sends sharp pangs through my body. I can't stand another second in this freezer, but I do, and then another, and another.

I keep expecting to pass out, but this body doesn't need to sleep or breathe, so why would I pass out? I wonder if I would be hyperventilating. Would there still be air to breathe? Would I be dead by now?

The only advantage that I have is this stupid body, so I need to use it. If there is any luck in this universe reserved for me, then this stupid ice cream case is a billion years old and its hinges are nearly rusted through. It's the only thing I can think of. I scrabble over the ice until my feet are beneath me, and brace myself.

My back hits the lid, and the shock of all that ice makes me pull away as though I'd been burned. I swallow a scream. Outside, I hear angry voices, muffled into incoherence, but I can't tell what they're saying. I press up and back, using my legs to push with everything I have.

Shards of ice rain down. I can feel each sliver as it falls. I push harder. There's a tiny squeak, but it's enough to give me hope. Again. My legs twitch violently, and my fingers and toes feel like they're on fire, the pain is so constant. But still I push.

The case rocks to the side, and I tumble as it crashes to the ground. There's a dull screech as the canvas tent rips. I topple into an alleyway crowded with townies rushing to leave the carnival, but my limbs are twitching so fiercely I can't stand. Lights streak across my vision and everything is a gauzy haze. A blobby shape bends down and grips my arms and I try to kick but can't. Then I see my rescuer.

Marcel.

His left eye is so swollen it's almost closed and there's a streak of dirt on his cheek to go with it. His eyes are wide and a steady stream of swearing tumbles from his mouth. But then he yells one word and it's clear as a bell. "Go!"

We run.

The carnival has descended into chaos. Shouts and screams fill the night, and townies rush past us toward the exit. Every time my foot hits the ground, a sharp burning pang runs up phantom veins, but I keep going. Marcel leads me in a twisting path past tents and booths, past faces that aren't sure whether or not they should stop us, until we burst out into the clearing where all the carnies' vehicles are parked.

"They have Ben," Marcel says as he draws in great gasps of air.

The world stops spinning.

"Who does?" I yell, my fingers seeming to behave for the first time in weeks as they grip the front of Marcel's shirt, forcing him to look me in the eye. "Who has Ben?"

"The Morettis."

I am still, more full of rage than I'd ever thought a single person could be. "Take me to them."

CHAPTER THIRTY-EIGHT

Emma

Not twenty feet ahead of me, Lorenzo Moretti struggles to heave Ben's limp body into the trunk of a beat-up Impala. My fingers grip into the fender of the car Marcel and I hide behind, and I swear the metal creaks.

"Stay here," Marcel says, his voice barely a whisper. "I'll go get Lars or Duncan or someone… Hey!"

There's no time. I stride between the cars separating us, not even trying to hide my approach. Let Lorenzo see me. Let him see me and be afraid.

"Hey, jackass," I say, planting my feet wide in the dying grass.

Lorenzo turns, brow glistening with sweat furrowed in frustration. I twine my fingers toget lock my elbows, swinging my arms as hard as his stomach. It's like hitting him with a base air *whooshes* out of him, and his eyes go before he tumbles backward.

Marcel skids to a stop beside me,

Lorenzo. "Holy hell, Emma!"

I don't have time to think about what I did, about how close Lorenzo got to taking Ben outside the confines of the carnival, where I wouldn't be able to get to him. I just have to make sure Ben is safe.

"Help me get Lorenzo into this trunk," I say.

Marcel grabs Lorenzo's legs, and I take his arms, tossing him—with little regard for his comfort—into the small space. Marcel moves to lock Lorenzo away, but as we're slamming the trunk down, I hear a little groan. Ben.

"Marcel, tell Lars where Lorenzo is and then bring whoever you can here." I point toward an abandoned booth in the shadow of the Ferris wheel. "No one will think to look for us there. Okay?"

"Yeah, okay."

I don't take my eyes off Ben, but the crunch of gravel is enough to tell me that Marcel has run off to do as I asked. Kneeling beside him, I shake Ben's shoulder. "Hey. I need you to wake up."

"Don't want to," he grumbles, one hand slipping beneath his glasses to rub at his eye.

If fear weren't fizzing through me, I might find this absofuckinglutely adorable. But I don't have the luxury of thoughts like that, not till we're safe. I lean in close, until we're inches apart. "Ben! It's still dangerous. Two of the Morettis are still out here, and—"

It's like my voice has finally pierced through the fog. His eyes fly open, so blue, so bright, and he focuses in on me.

"Emma," he says, my name a gentle exaltation. "Are ou okay?" he asks, even though he is the one I found sed out and about to be abducted.

"I'm fine—" Better than fine, for the first time in a long time, but I can't think about that. "But we have to hide. *Now*."

He doesn't question, just acts. Quicker than I would have thought possible considering the state I found him in, he hops up and takes hold of my hand, his grip fierce. He lets me lead as we dart through the parked cars and trucks, headed back toward the shouting and panicked people. We only have a short distance to cover before the Ferris wheel looms above us.

It's a perfect circle of golden light set apart from all the other attractions.

"Let's go," Ben says. "We'll stop at the top, and no one will think to look for us up there."

The short stretch of matted down dirt and weeds between us and the Ferris wheel feels like it's a million miles long. There's no cover, and the whole point of hiding on the ride would be for nothing if someone saw us. I can feel his pulse pressing against my wrist where our hands are joined, can feel his shoulders heaving from the exertion of running.

The yelling and sounds of confusion behind us are the confused squeaks of small woodlands animals. Benjamin stumbles on a rock or a root or something and almost goes down, but his fingertips brush against the ground and he pushes himself back up.

Our feet make hollow pounding sounds as we run up the steps to the ride, and I throw open the door to one of the cars while Benjamin pries the cover off the control panel and roots around inside. I keep my eyes on the rows of shining booths and tents, sure that someone is going to burst out of the line and find us at any minute.

Finally Benjamin pulls out a small box and jumps into the car with me.

He wrenches an antenna up, flips a silver switch, and presses a green button. The world grows smaller as we drift up, and the whole time I find myself praying that no one sees the lights of the Ferris wheel moving in a slow circle against the blue-black of the sky.

When we're almost at the top, Benjamin punches a red button, and the wheel slows, stopping just past the apex. The car rocks gently with dying momentum. The night is breezy, but nowhere near as windy as the night I'd been up here with Sidney.

Sidney.

Unbidden, I am reminded of his bright grin, of the cocky way he had tipped back his hat to look at me under the moonlight. I hunt the grounds to find the top of the haunted house. I see the line of winding taillights of cars trying to escape the horror they'd seen, and a flicker of orange, more like a fire than the electric glow of a game. Dark shadows cluster here and there; a group around Happy's trailer, and lingering by the spot where Sidney died. A soft, dry rasp escapes my throat.

Ben slides an arm around my shoulders, rubbing small, soothing circles onto my back. "It's okay." His voice is distant, and I can tell that he's on the lookout, too. But for the moment, we seem to be safe. "Emma," he says, an odd wobble in his voice, "I need to tell you something."

His cheeks are ruddy from running, and the wind has rumpled his hair into seventy different angles. His eyes are too bright, wide like baby moons, and even after everything that's happened, he wears a lopsided sort of grin.

I have a terrible, terrible thought.

"Where were you earlier?" I ask.

"Doesn't matter." He steals another furtive glance toward the carnival and I do the same. At the edge of the tents are two figures. I freeze.

But Benjamin doesn't see them.

"Emma, I know you're nervous about breaking the curse, but—"

I whip around to face him again. It all clicks. His stumbling over nothing. The happy, sloppy smile. And the only, *only* reason he'd bring up the curse now, after all that happened.

No.

If I could still feel, his skin would be hot to the touch. If I could smell, the scent of flowers and alcohol would be all around me. If I asked him, he'd tell me his mouth feels as though it's lined with flower petals.

"You didn't."

"I did." His eyes are unflinching. "I love you, Emma."

I want him and everything he's offering. But can I watch him almost die?

I turn away, and that's when I see the two dark shadows peel away from the alley and start walking toward the Ferris wheel.

"Benjamin," I say, gripping onto his arm.

"It's going to work, I promise. We'll follow Katarina's instructions and the curse will break. I've drunk the wine. You know my true name, but just in case you need all of it, my name is Benjamin James Singer."

He moves across the small space that separates us and kisses me.

His mouth is soft and insistent, and one hand reaches

up to cradle my cheek. He's not just warm, he's a fire, and I want to bask in his glow. My eyes flutter closed, and for a brief second, everything is okay because I am with him. When he pulls away, the heat of him lingers. The night is alive with colors that hadn't been there seconds before. A thready pulse of life throbs in the center of my chest, my hands and arms trembling with it.

"Kiss me when you get down there, Em," he says, pressing something hard and cold into my hands.

And then he throws himself from the car.

"No!" I lean over the edge, dropping whatever it was Ben gave me as I grip the side of the car tight. Ben seems to fall forever, his golden hair rippling in the rush of air. I can't look. There's a terrible crunch and a scream of pain, followed by the sound of splintering wood.

Far, far below me Benjamin lies like a broken doll in the dust, his legs splayed out at an angle that's all kinds of wrong. Blood trickles from the side of his mouth, the mouth that had been kissing mine moments before.

And in the dirt beside him are the broken remnants of a remote control.

CHAPTER THIRTY-NINE

Benjamin

I am on fire.

My glasses are skewed across my face, and between that and the tears, everything is blurry. A swirl of golden lights tilts above me, and I fight the bile rising in my throat. Something hot coats my tongue, my throat. And a stabbing, searing pain marks every breath.

I'll be fine as soon as Emma gets here.

I'll be fine…

CHAPTER FORTY

Emma

I throw my leg over the edge of the car, hunting for purchase with my foot. My fingers grip into the metal edge of the door until I feel it digging into my skin. The breeze plays along my bare legs as I climb out, whipping my skirt around, threatening to tangle it between my legs. The night air is cool, and when the realization hits me, I stumble over nothing and have to struggle to keep from falling.

I can feel again.

The metal beneath my fingers cuts into my softening flesh, the line of bulbs that outline the skeleton of the ride give off a halo of warmth. Pine and sugar ride the air and fill my lungs. My heart pounds in my chest, each thumping beat a reminder of what Ben is losing. Because Ben is wrong; he's either dying down there or he's cursed.

And if either of those things is true, I'll never be able to forgive myself.

I stretch from strut to strut, picking a path down the

Ferris wheel's frame. One step down. Then another and another. That's when I hear Fabrizio yelling below me.

"That dumb asshole," Fabrizio says. Benjamin cries out in pain, and my head fills with images of Fabrizio kicking Ben, torturing him while he's dying on the ground.

The Ferris wheel lurches, and I wrap my arms around the struts to stay on. It moves slowly, putting me closer to the ground, closer to the two waiting brothers. Fabrizio watches the passing struts as though timing them, and then leaps aboard. He's much quicker than I am, climbing around toward me as I try to climb down. That's when I feel it.

At the center of my chest, where my heart has been pounding again for the last minute, something cold and heavy settles and spreads like poison. And then I know—*I know*—Ben is dying because I haven't transferred the curse.

Antonio waits at the base of the Ferris wheel, ready to grab me if Fabrizio doesn't reach me first. I don't know what they plan to do, but I can't let them catch me, because if they do, I might not get to Benjamin in time. So I hook my arm around the strut and wait for the Ferris wheel to curve closer to the ground. Then I jump.

It's too much like that first night, falling into nothing. But it's over much more abruptly. I crash into Antonio and we hit the ground hard, the tumbler bearing the brunt of my fall. We're a tangle of limbs and knees and elbows. When I stumble away, my right leg crumples beneath me, but I can limp over to Benjamin faster than the Morettis, who are still sprawled in the dirt.

Benjamin's glasses are broken. Dirt flecks the lenses, and the sight of them, normally so pristine, sends me over the edge. I don't know what I'm going to do if he doesn't make it. My fingers slip around to the back of his neck. I can feel every hair prickle my palm, the ridges on the collar of his T-shirt. The way his chest is barely rising and falling against mine. The pool of too-warm blood that's gathering around my knees. The hot trail of tears streaking down my cheeks.

I lean over and kiss him.

For a moment, all I can think about is how I can finally actually *feel* him and not some approximation of what his skin might feel like. How he feels warm and not burning hot. That this is what a kiss should feel like, soft and gentle. But...was this how it was when Sidney turned me? Hadn't I already started to lose some of these bits of my humanity? Did the transfer not work?

Fabrizio yells behind me, and I pull away. Benjamin is impossibly still. There's nothing, not even the jagged rise and fall of his chest. I grab his hand, hoping to feel the blood pulsing through it, but I can't.

I failed.

There's a buzz and the pop of shattered glass, and my head whips away from Benjamin's unmoving body, searching for the source of the noise. The bulbs on a line of lights running between booths are bursting, a shower of sparks drifting to the ground. The futile hum of generators trying to accommodate the power surge is almost drowned out by the popping of more lights around the carnival and then, as everything goes dark, the night falls silent.

"What did you do?" Fabrizio asks quietly.

I whip around and stare up at the tumbler. He must have jumped off the Ferris wheel when I wasn't looking. The moonlight curls silver into his hair, onto his shoulders. From where I sit on the cold ground, he's impossibly tall.

I hold Ben's hand tighter even though there's nothing he can do to help me now.

"Let me ask you again," Fabrizio says. He moves forward, with the menace of a shark in still waters. "What did you *do*?"

His fingers clench into fists and release over and over. There's a fluttering in my chest and my breathing threatens to trip and falter, but he can't scare me. Nothing, *nothing* is worse than what lies motionless in the dirt beside me.

"Nothing that concerns you," I say, staring into the hollows where his eyes should be. Behind Fabrizio, his brothers are closing in.

"You've ruined every good thing about this miserable carnival, so I think it does concern me," Fabrizio says. His fingers curl up again, and this time, his fist draws back.

A silver glint races between us, and he screams. One of Marcel's throwing-knives is lodged into the toe of his boot to the hilt, blood spurting up through the leather.

Katarina's voice booms like a thunder. "You will not touch her."

Katarina stands at the line of tents, Marcel beside her with a fist full of knives. Running to join them are Gin, one arm in a sling and carrying a metal post in her good hand, and Whiskey, armed with a bucket of baseballs from one of the gaming booths. In the shadows behind them are the twins, Duncan pushing his sister away from the fray.

Antonio rushes toward my friends, dodging the baseball thrown at his head but unable to avoid the throwing-knife now lodged in his thigh. He pushes onward, but I can't worry about them. Fabrizio is much closer.

He pulls the blade from his foot and swings it, the small knife whistling as it slices toward me. I throw myself to the ground and roll, springing to my feet. A hot flash of pain runs up my leg but I ignore it, and I put myself between Fabrizio and Benjamin's body. Blood squelches from Fabrizio's wounded foot every time he takes a step, and as he nears, I dart out to stomp his wounded foot underneath mine, putting all my weight on it.

Fabrizio yells, drowning out any other noise. His fingers crush my arms and he shoves me to the ground before dropping to his knees beside me. He draws a heavy fist back, but before he can throw his punch, a baseball cracks into his nose.

Spatters of his blood drip down onto me, and before I get out from under him, Gin swings at his stomach with her post, sending him flying backward. Whiskey helps me to my feet as Gin stands over Fabrizio, ready to hit him again if he makes another move.

He doesn't.

I let go of Whiskey's hand and go back to Ben. He hasn't moved. I drop down in the dirt beside him as a fresh wave of hot tears line my eyes.

After a few seconds, a swath of gauzy skirts comes into my view. Katarina joins me in the dirt, one frail arm around my shoulders, the other gently placing an old-fashioned iron lantern on the ground beside us.

She cradles Benjamin's face in her palm, and when

I see the extreme gentleness with which she handles him, I start to sob. The world blurs, and rather than be amazed that I'm actually crying and not making that stupid gasping hiccup-y noise, I just want it to stop so that I can see him while I still can.

Katarina looks at me, the lines in her face ghoulishly lit up from below by the lantern's flickering flame. That same slightly amused smirk from the night we met is back on her face, and I want to scream at her for smiling. "Didn't he tell you what he was going to do?" she asks.

After months of being a husk, I suddenly feel like the sloppiest, mushiest thing ever. I'm an armful of sopping wet towels. I push the flood of tears from my cheeks with my palms before I answer. "Not until right before he threw himself from the stupid Ferris wheel." Gin's slender, strong arms snake around me, along with a tangle of silvery hair. Whiskey wraps herself around both her sister and me and sobs quietly into my neck.

Katarina's many layers of necklaces clatter as she cranes her neck to look up at the massive Ferris wheel. It shifts with a heavy metallic groan, as though its girders can no longer support it. Farther away, there's the sound of collapsing wood and several startled shrieks. Finally, she turns that cryptic gaze back to me. "Benjamin was perhaps a bit...*overzealous*, shall we say."

Her hands hover above his body, straightening out his arm, fixing the grotesque angle of his leg. "I'm not saying that he didn't do the right thing, but—"

"What do you mean?" Marcel asks. He stands over all of us, knives at the ready, as though he expects more trouble. Wet tracks curve down his cheeks, and a fine tremor shakes his shoulders.

Katarina gives Marcel a wry smile. I want to smack her, wouldn't even mind if she cursed us all into oblivion. "He threw himself from a goddamned Ferris wheel. I don't know how bad the damage is, but it's guaranteed he broke some bones and he likely has internal bleeding. Magic can do a lot, but magic works on its own timetable, not ours."

I draw a ragged breath into my expanding lungs. Ever since my mom left, I've felt like the only thing worth fighting for was my old life. But I know I'm wrong. I don't have to go back to that. I can make a life I want, and right now, what I want includes Ben. *I want Ben.* "What are you talking about? He's *dead*, and—"

Yelling at the edge of the carnival cuts my hysterics short. "There she is!" One of the cooks steps out of the shadows. A woman who works in one of the gaming booths screams, "This is her fault!" It seems as though half the carnival has found their way to us, pouring out from among the tents and booths. Some of them are confused. Some of them bear cuts and the beginnings of bruises, as though caught in the way of the self-destructing carnival. Every single one of them is furious.

Gin and Whiskey stand. Gin pushes her tears away with the back of her hand before shifting her grip on her metal post. Marcel's gaze darts from face to face, trying to determine who is a friend and who is a foe. We are terribly outnumbered.

All around us, rides collapse into heaps of bent tubing and screaming metal, tents faint to the ground in dizzy twists of fabric as people rush to the safety of open air. There is so much screaming. "The carnival is falling apart because of her!" the guy from the cook shack yells.

Somewhere far away but edging closer, police sirens wail into the night. The mob surges forward with a roar.

A massive voice rises over the ruckus. "*Stop!*"

Lars, his flaming-orange hair visible over the heads of everyone else, draws in a big breath, as though readying himself to fight the crowd off single-handed. But in the silence following his roar, I hear the one woman capable of stopping this riot.

"Anyone who hurts my employees will answer to me." Like a flipped switch, the angry crowd goes from feral tigers to day-old kittens. They part, and Leslie walks into the clearing.

Her blond curls are frizzy from sweat, and her stage makeup is smudged. A gash runs halfway across her forehead, blood drying in dark red lines down her face. "The carnival is falling apart because we're lazy and ungrateful. But more importantly, this carnival is *mine*, and if I want to let it fall to ruin, so help me, I will. The keepers of the curse have given up more than any of you here, and I will protect them with my last breath. As it is, I will make it my mission to see the Morettis rot in jail for what they did tonight. Anyone who has a problem with anything I just said has ten minutes to get off this property."

A dejected sort of mutter runs through the crowd. The man from the cook shack and several others melt into the darkness. More than a few hostile glances are directed at me, at Leslie, at anyone who dared to help break the curse, but all my friends hold their ground.

I want to marvel at Leslie's strength. At the way the crowd obeys and begins to disperse. At the fact that Whiskey looks as though she could keep a hundred attackers at bay with a bucket of baseballs. At this family I made, when I felt like I didn't fit in with the family and friends I had.

But I don't get to do any of that.

Because right then, Benjamin's hand twitches in mine.

CHAPTER FORTY-ONE

Benjamin

The sky is a pristine blue the day we put Sidney to rest. My leg still hasn't healed all the way, and though Happy would prefer it if I used the wheelchair that looks like he got it cut-rate from a nineteenth-century insane asylum, I walk across the lawn to the ceremony, leaning heavily on Emma.

I could lean on her forever. With the curse lifted, it's like I've never really seen her before, because now she has detail. A tiny scar curves toward her cheek from her upper lip. Her irises had always seemed to be a flat brown, but now they're flecked with gold. She's the Emma I fell for, but intrinsically, wonderfully different.

She's alive again.

She wears a gauzy gray dress that swishes around her knees, and the somber color reminds me of what lies ahead and takes my smile with it. Not only is Sidney dead, but the Moretti brothers are in jail, and soon Emma and I will have to testify against the many assaults they committed. Emma straightens the tie Marcel loaned me and helps me hobble out to the field where I once listened to Sidney rant under the moon.

The ceremony is simple. Leslie speaks. Pia sings the hymn we all agreed Sidney would hate the least. And then Mom scatters his ashes, the wind swirling them toward the trees.

At the party afterward—Katarina insisted on throwing a traditional New Orleans wake, including a four-piece jazz band—Emma and I gather our friends together in the foyer to say our good-byes.

Because we can't stay. Even though Leslie intends to rebuild the carnival and there would be plenty of work for a more-than-apprentice carpenter, I have to go where Emma goes, and—among other things—Emma wants to tell her family she's okay.

"You're going to call me when you get set up, right?" Marcel asks. After all our talk of leaving, he's decided he can't abandon the carnival.

"Of course," I say. I watch Lars—a little paler and more prone to coughing fits—lift Emma up in a hug that nearly swallows her whole. "You guys are part of my future, whatever and wherever that might be."

So we get in our hugs and grab the bags we stowed beneath the plush velvet bench by the door. We're about to step onto the porch and shut the door behind us when my mother calls my name.

"Benjamin?" The lilt at the end makes it a question, like she doesn't know what I'm doing, even though we've discussed my leaving. Her eyes are constantly red-rimmed these last few days, and her limp curls are shoved into a perfunctory twist at the back of her head.

I squeeze Emma's hand before letting go and hobble toward my mother.

As I approach, the old Audrey Singer takes shape: her gaze hardens, her jaw sets like she's ready to take a punch. "I can't convince you to stay."

If she had made some gesture toward apology, reconciliation, *anything*, then maybe my answer would have been different. Maybe. But she is a master carpenter, and in the days since Sidney died, she's built up walls between us even more impassable than before.

"No, you can't." The hug catches her off guard. But after a second her arms soften and wrap gingerly around me. Her tears bleed through my shirt before I hear her shuddering intake of breath. "Just because I'm leaving doesn't mean I don't love you. Don't forget that."

Her fingers cling to mine as I step away, but eventually, she lets me go.

Emma stands beside the small table in Katarina's foyer. "I know. I know. I am so, so sorry I put all of you through this, Juliet." She's on an ancient rotary telephone next to the gilded skulls of small animals. Tears leave slick paths down her cheeks, drip off her chin. When she sees me, she smiles. "I gotta go, Jules, but I had to tell you I'm coming home. Tell my mom and dad. And tell Mom she's not allowed to fly back to Guatemala till I get there."

It seems as though Emma is finally about to hang up, when she stops and says, "Oh! By the way—I wanted to find a way to make things up to you, since, you know, I went missing on your watch. So I had one of the girls who works the midway teach me how to make a deep-fried Snickers." Even from five feet away, I can hear raucous laughter from the other end of the line. "I'll be there soon, Jules," Emma says, before hanging up. She brushes the tear tracks away, and though her eyes are puffy and red from the crying, they sparkle.

"Hey!" It's Marcel. He holds a small metal box in his hands, the keys to the Gran Torino balanced on top. "Take it."

A peek inside shows the neat rolls of cash we'd saved up over the last few months, along with some loose bills that look as though they were hastily thrown in.

"It's from all of us," Marcel says, grinning.

"But I c-can't," I say, stumbling over my words. "I can't take the car *and* the money."

"You can, and you will." Marcel presses the box to my chest until I'm forced to take it from him. "You couldn't leave without her." He tilts his head toward Emma, then toward Gin. "I can't leave without *her*."

And I get it. Of course I get it. Marcel wraps me up in a hug, and for a second I wonder if I'll be able to let go. But then I see Emma from the corner of my eye, and all my doubts melt away.

The door clicks shut behind us with a gentle finality as Emma and I step onto the creaky porch. Every hair on my arms stands at attention as a cool breeze cuts across the lawn, and it stings at the back of my throat as I breathe it in. I am more alive than I ever have been, and I'm sure Emma feels the same. It's in the giddy smile, the way her arm trembles—trembles and not twitches—against mine.

I stretch across the space that separates us and kiss her. My fingers dance in the short length of her hair, letting it slip and slide through my hands. She's so warm, and there, in the hollow behind her ear, thumps her pulse.

We break the kiss, but neither of us pulls away, not yet. Her breath is hot against my cheek. Her smile is dazed, relaxed, and content. It's the first time I've seen anything like that on her face.

"Are you absolutely sure you want to go?" she asks.

I look at the road in front of us, winding between the pine trees and waving moss. I think about how all I ever wanted was somewhere to call my home, unaware that home could be a person and not a place.

"Of course I am. You're my constant."

Her hand grips mine, and where our wrists press together, I can feel her pulse beating in time with mine.

Alive, alive, alive.

Acknowledgments

First and foremost, this novel wouldn't exist without my critique partners, who read the short story I presented them about a girl who was cursed with a kiss and demanded to know what happened to her. Thank you Tracy Jo Barnwell, Andrew Kozma, and Jeylan Yassin for insisting I write more. And to Kelly Renwick and Emma Bentley, who joined our group; I am so grateful for your wisdom and your words.

Many, many thanks to my agent, Patricia Nelson, who understood this book and what I wanted to do, and whose faith in this project never wavered. You are the best agent an author could ask for, and if I could send you a bouquet of corgis, I would.

To my editor, Stacy Abrams, and her assistant, Alexa May, for championing my book and for all their insightful words. If your enthusiasm could be bottled, you'd be billionaires. To my copy editor, Greta Gunselman, who caught all my little mistakes (I swear I will never spell "blond" with an "e" again!), and Christine Chhun, my production editor. And to everyone at Entangled and Macmillan, thank you for putting so much faith in a debut author. Many thanks also to Anna Croswell and Toni Kerr for the cover and interior artwork that made this graphic designer very happy.

I'd like to thank my family, who are the most supportive family a person could have. This is for my mom, who never said no to a Baby-Sitters Club book and my dad, who would wordlessly pull out his wallet when I brought home a book fair order form. (Extra thanks to my dad, who talked to me about cars and exactly how far one could drive with a nearly broken belt.) For Nana, who always said yes when I approached her in a store with a book in my hands, and to Grandy, who introduced me to *Anne of Green Gables* and *Little Women*. And for every other family member who indulged me with a book for a birthday or holiday, no matter how weird it seemed. You helped fuel my imagination, and I never could have even tried to write a novel without that.

A super special shout out to Stephanie Burke, Karen Lewis, Paula Leveston, Ida Yassin, Susan Crispell, Kathryn Rose, and Kelly J. Ford who were this book's first readers and its cheerleaders.

My friends and family are amazing human beings and I can't thank you enough for your excitement and your kind words. Please know that I would invite you all to my magical carnival and I wouldn't curse a single one of you.

To the Revisionists–I am so happy to be in your company. You are some of the most funny, clever, talented, and warmhearted people I've come across. To all of my fellow Electric Eighteens, thank you for all the support and the laughter.

Thank you to Violet and Harlow for inspiring me every single day. I am so proud to be your mother.

Finally, I am so grateful for my husband, Dane. You were the one who made sure this book happened. You had the unenviable job of urging me to write, even on the days I didn't want to, and you were very good at it because look! It's a book! You listen to me complain, you offer advice and the occasional foot rub, and are generally awesome. Thank you.

GRAB THE ENTANGLED TEEN RELEASES READERS ARE TALKING ABOUT!

THE NOVEMBER GIRL
BY LYDIA KANG

I'm Anda, and the lake is my mother. I am the November storms that terrify sailors, and with their deaths, I keep the island alive. Hector has come to Isle Royale to hide. My little island on Lake Superior is shut down for the winter, and there's no one here but me. And now him.

Hector is running from the violence in his life, but violence runs through my veins. I should send him away. But I'm half-human, too, and Hector makes me want to listen to my foolish, half-human heart. And if do, I can't protect him from the storms coming for us.

NEVER APART
BY ROMILY BERNARD

What if you had to relive the same five days over and over?
And what if at the end of it, your boyfriend is killed…
And you have to watch. Every time.
You don't know why you're stuck in this nightmare.
But you do know that these are the rules you now live by:
Wake Up.
Run.
Die.
Repeat.

Now, the only way to escape this loop is to attempt something crazy. Something dangerous. Something completely unexpected. This time…you're not going to run.

Combining heart-pounding romance and a thrilling mystery *Never Apart* is a stunning story you won't soon forget.

entangled teen

an imprint of Entangled Publishing LLC